AMY ROSE

For
Elizabeth
old days at UC⊃
Library from
which we have
blessedly
escaped

Noel Peattie
29 Apr 1995

AMY ROSE

A NOVEL IN
FOUR PARTS

by

NOEL PEATTIE

REGENT PRESS
1995

For two who inspired; and two who launched. You know who you are; I don't want you to *die* of embarrassment (see p. 80, and p. 91).

The quotations or paraphrases in Part II, *Amy Rose, friend of the Chinese people*, are from *I Ching, the hexagrams revealed,* by Gary G. Melyan and Wen-kuang Chu (Rutland, VT and Tokyo: Charles E. Tuttle Co., 1986, and are used by permission of the publisher.

ISBN: 0-916147-61-4

Manufactured in the United States of America

REGENT PRESS
6020A Adeline, Oakland, CA 94608

Contents

Part I

AMY'S WILL:

or,

THE LAST SENIOR

Peace, ho! the moon sleeps with Endymion,
And would not be awaked.

Merchant of Venice

Là, tout n'est qu'ordre et beauté,
Luxe, calme, et volupté.

Fleurs du Mal

Librarians are novel lovers.

Bumper sticker

Amy's Will

AMY DROVE HER old blue Subaru across the bridge which led to the island from the mainland, its small towns, and the school libraries where she worked. With relief (for this was yet another Friday of another week in which she had solved five separate crises—Monday, Tuesday, Wednesday, Thursday, Friday, at three separate schools, making fifteen crises in all for the famously unflappable Amy), she drove her car onto the island's sandy roads, stopped at the market, and then turned right-left-right on side roads, past mailboxes hidden among Douglas firs, toward home. A glance at the Sandbergs' lot proved that nobody had come by that day to round off their tour of island yard sales. A glimpse of the Sound's incoming fog warned that evening would be lulled by the five long blasts of ferries outbound to the northwestern islands. Around the blackberry hedge which she had planted to surround her private pool; into the driveway under the trembling aspen; and Amy Mary Gregory, school librarian, long the widow of Doctor George Rose—was home. Alone.

The minute Amy opened the door, Olivia the cat plopped off her perch (Amy's maternal grandfather's pedal-pumped missionary organ, survivor of the Japanese bombardment of Tientsin)— and rubbed against her legs. Amy, whose long swishy scarlet skirt was topped with a white high-collared blouse, brushed the cat hairs off the hem and quickly obeyed her nudging furry friend. Two little cans of Fancy Feast, Amy allowed her, spooning them out by halves; while Olivia (named after the famous novel of that title) lion'd up her cat food, Amy put the groceries away, and looked around the old farmhouse which she had bought the year after she had lost her husband. The Gregorys' Waterford crystal, the Sirmionis' majolica, spoke to her of her father's family; the Æblegaard silver from Copenhagen, the Wessels' sturdy Norwegian pewter, reminded her of her mother's side. Her father's photograph, as tweedy teacher of philosophy, and his great-great-grandfather's portrait in naval uniform (defeating the British on Lake Champlain in 1814) decorated the mantel of the cobblestone fireplace. But she preferred the Mary Cassatt which her mother (whose own self-portrait, and watercolors of the Aegean, decorated the sunny dining alcove) had acquired in Paris, long ago. A simple color print, it welcomed her into her bedroom: a mother giving suck to her child.

Tomorrow, Amy told herself, everything in this house would have to be scrubbed to a sparkle. Old linoleum cleaned and waxed, silver polished, Mexican rugs shaken out, and (most important) the small secret lawn in front of the small swimming pool: mown close. The library's annual report and circulation statistics: she'd have to work them in somehow, though they were due Monday. Everything, for Amy, now depended on pleasing the last and latest choice of her own personnel selection policy.

Amy Rose, slipping out of her long scarlet skirt and high collared blouse, and stepping into a plain black T-shirt and bermudas, relaxed on her Empire chaise-longue (tan, gold stripes, same decor with the pillows) and opened her mail at leisure. A notice of a new publication from the American Library Association's Young Adult Services Division (OK, but second priority). A legislative alert from ALA's Social Responsibilities Round Table's Feminist Task Force (her secret allegiance, although she couldn't attend every meeting; but still, high priority). The Mills College Alumnae *Bulletin*. The usual appeals from environmental organizations to help save small furry things (Olivia, you are one, but whales have no fur and I can do just so much for otters). As for people, she could only save Will this year, and he was coming, by her own irrevocable invitation, Sunday afternoon, after lunch. And the end of Friday was here now!

Her personnel policy! Its criteria? Review them! She poured herself a glass of French Colombard, put a small halibut steak under the broiler, and reviewed them aloud to Olivia, who ate at her feet:

"1. Over eighteen (so, no legal complications)

2. Shy, virginal, no sweetheart (so, no medical problems)

3. Soon going away: first, to a summer program (never mind what), then off to a distant college (so, no crushes, no hang-ups, on either side)

4. Free access to car/bicycle (she mistrusted boys with pick-ups, 4-wheelers, or motorcycles)

5. Above all, that certain *je ne sais quoi:* sweetness, innocence, willingness to learn."

But now, Amy told Olivia, there were two new criteria: "no. 6, that I be able to attract him; and no. 7, that I be able to let go of him." At thirty-six, widowed eight years, in a small town, forty miles from the largest city in a small state, Amy Rose, city-bred wife of a physician who loved small towns, found herself early in her library career (for she had met George, as a friend of one of his patients, in the city by the Bay), left widowed, in the limiting world of school librarianship. Years of writing to public and academic libraries, visits to ALA conferences (when they came west of the Mississippi), had brought her, at last, a job at a big research library in the Bay country. Now, at last, the game she had started (was it for comfort, or in jest?) would have to stop. Will Newcastle, her Sunday guest, would be her *last* senior.

Olivia, rubbing up against her (I know, you're half-Siamese, you're so beautiful, darling, you're so sweet, and you just set off my long raven hair! I should make you a cat-ornament, and wear you down my back, if you'd only stay there! You want some more savory salmon feast? And will you, for once, be my friendly cat and not jealous of my friend? Come on, lovely, you're so graceful, have some more. Yes, I'm right here. Try it!) reminded her of the days after which she adopted this kitten—almost eight years ago.

Eight years after the day when another surgeon, brimming with post-operating-room confidence, had told George, "I can do anything! I just operated on a heart for seven hours!" had taken him up in a light plane, and had then spun that plane into a Douglas fir in the Cascades. Amy had moved out here from the city to the country to live with her grief, deny it, face it, overcome it. At last she had learned to rediscover herself in her long mirrors (bedroom and bathroom) as tall: smiling: creamy: mysterious. Since then, Amy had taken only five lovers newly-graduated from the senior class: three girls and two boys.

For it had not always worked out. Daphne was too shy. Heather was too brisk—wanted to play volleyball—why didn't Amy have a court? John was an unwilling fundamentalist—a poor substitute for full-breasted Sue—who, however, only wanted to talk radical politics. Unpredictable, the fortunes of an older, discreet lady librarian who only wanted to teach (legally permissible) graduating students her private extension course: Love: a brief, tender introduction.

Time to start the veggies. Time to select the right wine from the coolroom (an old icebox in the cellar). Friday was pamper-yourself time for Amy: with a long bath before bedtime, and pleasure reading before that: the poems of Karla Andersdatter, Ellen Bass, Lynne Savitt, Cornelia Veenendaal, Joanie Whitebird—library literature she set aside for the office. Midway among choosing from these, the telephone rang. The wrong time exactly! She turned down the flame under the zucchini (with cheese), reduced the dial for the little steak, thrust the wine back into the fridge—and gasped as she picked up the phone. It was him: Will Newcastle, son of the late music professor at Washington State, the long brown boy who was coming Sunday, by invitation, at three in the afternoon. Now: was there a cancellation? a delay? was her heart to be broken? Scarcely: she had taught herself to be detached. (But, he *was* nice).

"Yes, it's me. By bicycle? Take you about two-and-a-half

hours to get here. Yes, your swim trunks." (She wanted him in swim trunks). "There's a pool. No, it won't be cold. The breeze out of the Pacific doesn't pick up until later, and usually there's a south wind. And, I've planted Douglas firs and canoe cedar, and there are natural brambles all around. So the water is quite warm, even in the afternoon. No, just you. This is special. This is *my* doing. Special? I'll explain later. Three exactly. Leave home no later than twelve-thirty. Can you make it? Then see you Sunday!"

This was exciting! The first good one in a long time, Amy hoped. She checked the stove, turned up the zucchini, and stepped outside for a moment to face the cool hay-scented sea air. Olivia the cat followed her, hoping for a hunting expedition. A seagull cambered on broad wings out to the fisheries to the west. Is this lad a sweet one? Amy asked herself, tilting her face to the sea air. Her dark hair lifted; she felt it flow in the ocean wind.

NEXT MORNING, AMY, in kerchief and jeans, gray sweat-shirt (bearing the University's seal: she had taken extension courses there once) spent so much effort in tubbing and scrub-bing, silver- and window-polishing, that she gave herself little time to think of the lad for whom she was doing this. Will's last name might have been Shakespeare, for all that she was thinking about him (much of the time)! Instead, Amy was thinking about her profession: how good it would be to get out of the trap of school librarianship ("once a school librarian, always a school librarian"). And how good it would be to get out of the circuit-riding of three different libraries, two high school (including Will), one elementary-secondary: story-telling here, helping with essay questions there, and battling teachers who wanted to use the library as an overflow classroom. (There was that class last year, who demanded all her floor space to make papier-maché reliefs of the western coastline of the state). Now! to have an eleven-month year, and real money! While she dreamed thus, a Dave Brubeck recording on the radio brought Will suddenly to mind: thin, brown, hard; dash of red on his cheekbones; river of hair down his open shirt.

Will's voice was low. She had observed him, over the past year, respectful to all women. She had found him, in her school library, reading Shelley and also Michael McClure, and once she had seen him in the city at a rare Jerry Mulligan concert. Good qualifications for an [undeclared, indeed: unknowing!] candidate!

Amy Mary Gregory Rose paused from doing the full-length bathroom mirror. She stared into that mirror; the skin around the green eyes was still clear, although she was a light step beyond the mid-thirties. Good for you, girl! but she bit her lip. If only the lad would be as kind as he looked.

Why, he's only a boy! she told herself. You'll turn him inside out! then let him fly free as a bird—or kick him out of the nest. A few weekends should do it: then see that he flies! Trouble with these gentle sensitive guys, all it takes is an instructive afternoon nap or two, then they want you to be their wives/mothers/concubines, when an older man would know it was time to go (well, they wouldn't necessarily know either). Anyway, there was a risk for both Amy and Will in this game, called: Two vines clinging together.

Is it indeed a game, said Amy, after working the sink with cleanser: is love a game? Well, maybe it wouldn't be if you were not a widow; but how many opportunities do you have in small towns where you are the circuit-riding school librarian? The male teachers were properly married (and most of them jerks). The female ones had never read *Olivia* (by "Olivia"). Her husband's medical friends had all been married: doctors, it seems preferred to wed (or at least bed) nurses. One school teacher, a young squirt, (meaning no harm) had teased her about the possibilities of choosing from among the young officers at the island's naval air station. Amy Rose, who did not wish to be thought of as pursuing any man, and certainly not a young naval officer, lost her cool; she hadn't been so irrationally angry in years. "I am not a camp-follower," she told him. That broke the last tenuous friendship with an unattached male at school.

Actually, Amy thought, I'm not anyone's follower. She loved George deeply and mourned him long: but being a doctor's wife had been difficult, and she was living and loving her freedom.

That was the way she'd chosen: her *own* way.

SUNDAY GAVE AMY time to think about that way. First of all, one was not supposed to do it on Sunday: but she always did. But then, whose business was it, anyway, what a young widow (an honorable state) did, discreetly, in her spare time? Her smile faded, and her anger rose, as she slipped out of bed for a quick trip to the bathroom, at the way single people, especially women, were treated in small towns: as if they were both dangerous and unreal. She remembered parties, at which she had been invited to meet strange men; and then she remembered meeting the very *strange* strange men; and then there were the parties which she only heard about after they had happened, since only the strange strange men were there: apparently the non-strange never went to those parties, and the strange had stopped inviting her. Even among the non-strange, she had gained two or three friends only. She knew she was seen by most of the school people as eccentric, accomplished, efficient, but distant: by others as simply stuck up. Well, there were the boys and girls, and she liked them, and they generally liked her (there were exceptions, as always). "And very few to love," quoted Amy to herself, and retired under the covers with her favorite magazine.

Yellow Silk, of course: "journal of erotic arts": isn't it your favorite too? She became so absorbed reading this delightful story, "The dozen kisses," that she was nearly late dressing for church. She slipped out of bed, showered, brushed her hair, tied a silver bow in it, and put on a gray shirtwaist with a pattern of silver leaves.

The nearest church on the island was Methodist. (Amy had been married in an Episcopal church, but the one here on the island was full of University people, who commuted thither from the mainland: she didn't know them and found them hard to know). This church, and its theology, were protective coloration for Amy. It wasn't that she was going to church to meet the right man, nor did she expect to; they were all married, and she made light conversation with the couples, who were (many of them) the age her parents would now have been. But when she explained that she was a doctor's widow, they clucked their sympathies, promised something vague, and invited her to their potlucks. Barbecued chicken and potato salad prevailed at these potlucks, but Mrs. Cutler prepared the most marvelous homemade dill pickles. Amy adored pickles. She felt brash and almost unladylike devouring the cool green spears.

Today's sermon concerned "Sharing." Amy was indeed prepared to share. There was no potluck today, so once she got home, she ate a light lunch (smoked salmon on toast, and chablis); washed up, and put on a two-piece swimsuit (blue, with white cloud-flecks); and, over it, a long wraparound summerdress, striped, blue and white, with large gold triangles (she fancied it had been designed after a painting by Gustav Klimt—perhaps, by Klimt himself). She poised, scarlet feather-duster in hand, at once prepared for housework and pool, checking moldings and shelves for the last cobweb. "The house must appear immaculate, and I, insouciante," Amy told herself, but finding no cobwebs on the old gold wallpaper, no dust on the oval frames of the family portraits from the turn of the century—she tossed the duster into the log carrier, in a manner truly insouciante, and settled down into the chaise-longue to pick up a title from the magazine box at random. The *Newsletter* from ALA's Office of Intellectual Freedom: she read it dutifully. True, they were solely concerned with *intellectual* freedom; but that was all to the good. A librarian's life was her own. Or ought to be. Reading absorbed her, as always. ("Amy! ['She's fallen into print again!']" was the cry of her childhood). She was reading, now, all about some library in Texas, forced by local citizens to ban *Our bodies, Our selves,* and thus became so preoccupied that she almost jumped when the little Japanese bell tinkled at the door.

"Kling-a-ling!" A real voice this time. She opened the upper half of the Dutch-style door (actually, Norwegian; it bore the lion and the axe of St. Olaf. She had secured it from an old cabin, about to be torn down, on the Peninsula across the water).

There he stood. As in her dreams: a little sweaty from the long bicycle ride over "her" bridge to the mainland; still, blue-

and-white striped shirt open to the waist; brown curls leading southward, high cheekbones, bright brown eyes: smiling. The chosen one tingled her bell.

"Good afternoon, Mrs. Rose!" said the light low voice.

Amy extended a long white arm—almost brought it to his lips. He took it lightly. "And good afternoon to you, Will Newcastle!" she said. "I'm Amy now. You've graduated. Remember? So come right on in."

AMY CAUGHT HIM looking round. His eyes were quicker than other boys' and girls'. "What's that? hanging from the wall?"

"That's a brass warming-pan," Amy answered, "they used to fill it with hot coals, in the old days, and then stick it between the sheets and blankets, and that's the way people kept warm in the winter."

"It looks new," said Will.

"I polish it," said Amy. They smiled at each other.

"And who is that?" inquiring for the history of the oil painting of a naval officer, which surmounted the cobblestone fireplace.

"That's my great-great-great-grandfather, Lieutenant Gregory," Amy informed him. "As your history course surely informed you, he's the fellow who helped Captain Thomas McDonough win the battle of Plattsburgh Bay, Lake Champlain, eleventh of September, 1814..." Will, however, had fixed his glance on the old missionary organ.

Quickly he seated himself before it, pumped it up a few times, and made it give forth a chorale prelude by Bach. "You've kept this in excellent condition," the young man informed his hostess. "I congratulate you."

"Thank you. It's almost impossible to find anyone to repair these things. I had a man out from the city and ended up paying him a vast sum of money."

"I'd say it's worth it. I expect you play."

"A little; but not much above the level of simple hymns and duets." She noticed him looking over the top of the organ toward the bedroom. She followed his glance. "Oh, you mustn't look *there,"* she told him, smiling.

"But who *is* that?"

"Now that you insist on asking," said Amy, as graciously as she could, "that's a Mary Cassatt. Just a print of a woman, giving her breast to her child. It's not in Adelyn Breeskin's *catalogue raisonnée.*" She met his glance. "No one knows it's here."

"It's lovely," said Will. "But I don't understand. It's not supposed to be here?"

Good, thought Amy. He's passed test number one: he plays along. "Nobody knows it exists. Or maybe it's somewhere marked down as lost—but I've had it checked out, very discreetly. And I'm quite sure it's an original!"

She started to give him a tour of the house—all save the bedroom. "My mother was an artist; I'm their sole daughter, so I got everything. These are the watercolors she did of Delos. And my husband collected Chelsea vegetable ware. You must be burning hot." If he was, she was. She was only half-an-inch shorter than he, but she reached up and touched his brow, with her white hand. "Let me get you some iced tea."

She swung around to the kitchen. They always liked iced tea, since they always came in the summer. She poured the tea into tall blue-ribbed smoked glasses, each with its own rattan coaster. There were little rice cakes, which Amy brought out of the refrigerator and put on Flora Danica plates. Amy placed the whole tea service on a Chinese enamel tray, Pacific blue in color—one of her favorite pieces.

Will watched her move around smoothly, quickly. "I always meant to ask you: you walk so nice. How come?"

"My mother made me take ballet lessons." She watched him smile, and loved him for it. "It's good for girls, and boys should do it too. Here, come on outside, and let's sit down."

A deck chair for him, a long chair for her. She noticed him noticing her legs. "Tell me more about yourself," said Amy. "Where did you say you were going this summer?"

"Well, before I go off to Pomona College, I'm going to be an instructor at a swimming and sailing camp. Then, in August, I'll do the same thing at a music camp."

"Then I'm afraid my tiny pool will hold less challenge for you than my organ. It's barely enough for one lone woman to dip in. You say you're going to Pomona?"

"Yes—did you go there?"

"No, I'm a Mills girl—and before that, Foxcroft, back East. I went to girls' schools. I hear Pomona is first-rate in music."

"Yes," said Will, sucking the tea greedily through a glass straw. She guessed what was coming next. "Where's..."

"Around the corner, indoors, and to your left," said Amy. "Long as you're there, put on your swim trunks."

He was in and out in a flash, and then *she* was in there, very privately. Amy's bathroom (may we peek?) was covered in orange-pink wallpaper, with little white roses all over. The ornate shell-shaped antique marble tub had once belonged (so her mother had been told by the Paris dealer) to the Empress Josephine. As long as this assertion could not be disproved, it might as well (for Amy) be true.

She came out to find him examining her library. He was back of the organ, opening the ten-volume Gyldendal edition of Ibsen's *Samlede værker*. "You read Danish?" said Amy.

"No, but then I never saw a sample of it," said Will. "Do you? I see you have a nineteen-twelve Yeats here..."

"My mother picked all this up, way back when," Amy said. "That's the first collected edition of Ibsen." She opened the lovely striped dress with great gold triangles, and stood ready, as an egret spreads its white splendor, for the pool. "Unless you prefer first editions," said Amy, "let's go for a swim!"

The weather was still warm at this time of day: another hour would have killed it with cold. "Ooh, that feels so good," Amy said as her two-piece suit took the still-sunlit-warm water. He plunged in, too. "Sorry," said Amy, "this must be a big letdown. You can't even take a lap in this. It's just a glorified tub."

AMY AND WILL splashed around in the pool. She saw him: delicious, water dripping from his niplets. She saw him: surveying her body. She preened, stroking her sides. "Can you swim under water?" she challenged.

Of course he could. They swam under water, and her long smooth arm reached out: then, with her bubbling hand, she pinched him. A toe, an ear, a tit. She had got pretty good at this, over the years: with boy, girl, boy.

Will and Amy surfaced. She drew him toward her and made him kiss. Kisses were nice and warm after cold water!

"Amy?" he said.

"I can do somersaults in the water," said Amy. "Can you?"

He could, but not as well as she could. Tiny as it was, she had a whole pool to herself, as long as the Pacific Northwest summers might last. He had to wait for somebody's class to be over, before he could get his practice in.

They were full of splash! and she poured water over his head, clean and cold, and they had a water war, and then she suddenly cried "King's X!"—staggering up out of the rock-lined pool, toward the blankets she had prepared on the grass. She had carefully placed them to be only in part-sun: for warmth, for secrecy (so the pilots from the naval air station could not possibly see what they were doing).

Amy dried herself quickly before lying down. Overhead tilted a big seagull, rising over the island from Saratoga Passage. She watched its hard black eye, saw it waiting till Will came up, when it veered away. She rubbed his chest, his arms, his hairy legs. Then he lay on his back, and she lay beside him: attending the right moment: the one in which she would tilt her own body to his.

"That feels so great," said Will. "You must have enough water pressure, you should get yourself a real big pool."

"I don't have that much pressure," said Amy, "and I don't need a big pool. A little pool is enough for a lady to cool off in." The short-clipped lawn was too brisk under the thin beach towels. Her towel said: "Catalina." His said, "San Diego."

She rolled over, flung an arm over him, and rested on his shoulder. She could feel his heart beating. This was good: he was warming up.

Will's head was turned away from her; he was obviously a little bit scared. She slipped off her swim cap and let her long black
hair spread over her shoulders and cover them both. She felt him
caress it: then lightly go on to her back and shoulders. She lifted
her halter, lay down in his arms, on his chest, and gave him a
long, penetrating, gentle kiss.

Amy and Will stayed that way for a long time. It was sweet.
Suddenly she thought of something to ask him.

"When did you say you were leaving for that water sports
camp?"

"Weekend after next," said Will.

"Then we have less time than I thought," said Amy, sitting
up. "Come along, we have lots to do." She trailed him behind her,
her hand leading his, into her bedroom.

Amy's bedroom was blue, white, and gold: the colors of heav-
en. The wide low bed was covered with a bedspread from India:
blue, starred, with rows of marching gold elephants, tail to trunk.
It wrinkled under the passage of their love.

"Here, slip off your shorts," said Amy, and the boy's limb rose
before her glance. "I'm going to cover you all over with little kisses." Quickly she touched his lips, nipples, belly, fleece and instep.
"You're trembling: don't be afraid. Here: give me that: we're both
ready. Now, quick! support yourself on your elbows." She locked
her long white legs behind his thighs. "Now gently—not too
hard—but keep it in there, until I let you go."

"Oh, but this is sweet!" said Will. "I never thought it would
be this easy!"

"Easy does it," said Amy. "Let me guide you in there."

"Ah!" they both said, as they reached the sweet peak together.
Then she clung to him more tightly, so that they could both pass
in waves, moving together, from pleasure to pleasure.

At last Amy let Will roll off her. Then Amy sat partway up:
"That's only the first part," said Amy.

"Oh, but that was heaven!" said Will.

"There's afterplay," said Amy, and took his hand in hers. She
taught him how to move over her, how to stroke undersides, how

to touch her flower with a light touch; how to be gentler than he had ever dreamed of being. "Light, like this," she said, and drew him to her love-bud, to show him just how she wanted it touched.

"I didn't know," said Will. "Is that it?"

"Yes, the underpart, here," said Amy. "Men don't usually understand. Slowly, that's right ahhh there!"

"I like doing that."

"Undersides," said Amy. "The underside of any part is more sensitive than the upper side. For example, If I kiss the top of your head"—and she did—"it's not as much fun as if I kiss you under your scrotum"—and she did. "All the difference in the world, isn't it?"

"Oh, isn't it!"

"And so with backs of things, angles," said Amy, kissing the boy's armpits, backs of his knees, every nerve-part. "It's touch, not just sex," said Amy.

At last Amy sat up. She assumed the lotus position: dark hair curling under her breasts, hands folded under her delta in the *mudra,* or ritual position, of contemplation (this was as far as she'd gotten with Buddhism)—and finally told her initiate: "The first thing you have to learn is that this doesn't happen all the time."

"No?" asked Will. "You mean we invented something new?"

"No, silly, I mean not on the first date. It's not"—she paused—"usually right, and certainly not to be expected. Nor safe! Besides, while I went to Mills, I'm sure Pomona women aren't all that different. They won't do it the first time."

"You look like a water lily," said Will, propping himself up: elbow, hand, head.

"I am one," said Amy. "But to proceed." She was going to raise her right hand in the *mudra* of instruction, but dropped it when she realized that it would be more decorous to keep it where it had been. "The girls at the camps you're teaching at are off-limits; they're too young. Also the boys!" She was smiling at him.

"I know!" said Will, sitting up on the bed. "But I'm eighteen…"

"And they are not."

"And I'm not interested in boys!"

"Mind them all, then. You're responsible. Now then: another splash, then I will show you a book. After that: home, until next time."

"Next time?" asked Will with delight in his brown eyes.

"Certainly," said Amy. "You don't expect to learn love in one afternoon, do you? Even Mozart had to practice the fiddle."

"Fiddle?"

"Go on, I'll meet you out there." She slipped into the bathroom, and came back out, clad only in the wraparound dress, the one she fancied had been designed by Gustav Klimt. They swam naked, around and around, pursuing and pursued, like the dolphins in the big round tank at the Monterey Aquarium. They stood in the shallow part of the pool and embraced. He caressed her flanks. She put her hands on his shoulders and kissed him, long, long. He was indeed gentle. He made as if to braid her hair; it was soaking wet; she had forgotten to put her swim cap back on. They dried each other off, with the towels marked "Catalina" and "San Diego," and then Amy, who had resumed the Klimt dress, brought Will his clothes from the bathroom.

"I'm going to have to get my hair dry," said Amy. "Here, dry yourself off. My music's inside the organ bench, if you want to play," knowing exactly where, among Bach's preludes and Scott Joplin's rags, she had stashed Alex Comfort's comforting books.

Amy took her time; her hair was sopping and she had to wring it out, bending naked as a Degas model over the shell-shaped tub. It was quite reasonable to expect that Will might never have encountered *The Joy of Sex*, or *More Joy of Sex*. Still more reason to expect that he would quickly find them, and most reasonable of all to expect that he would pore over them to the exclusion of all other works in the music bench. He would not leave without studying them, and certainly not while a beautiful woman was in the bathroom.

Amy's blow-drier roared and hummed; it took quite some time, and she was still damp when she came out in the wraparound dress, to find that her reasonable expectations were all fulfilled. She also found that her slender brown lover had also got dressed, shirt open, long brown fingers caressing the organ keys silently as he turned the lovely pages.

"But I never saw these books before!" he said. "Why do you keep them in a music bench? Why not on the bedside table?"

"Supposing the Duchess should stop by for a visit? She'd peep into the bedroom, and see them, and be shocked! You know how strict the Duchess is."

He caught on to the game at once. "But suppose the Duchess is a musician?"

"Then I'd have to hide them in the kitchen, with the cook-books!"

"But suppose the Duchess goes into the kitchen? Suppose she's a good cook?"

"Impossible. No Duchess is a cook. And nobody cooks in my kitchen save me." She sat down beside him, put the Comfort books aside, and propped up Haydn's *Il maestro e lo scolare.* "Come on, let's play duets."

They pumped up the organ, she took the pupil's part, he the teacher's. Bit of role reversal here, she thought: that's what you get for playing around with music students, Amy!

Amy dreamily turned the pages of *More Joy of Sex.* "Which of these pictures did you like best?" she asked, without looking up at him.

"Oh, all of them; that one, especially!" said Will. (They were on page 56-57, if you want to be bibliographically precise). "I'd like to take them home!"

"To your mother? You're not a fool," Amy reminded him. She lifted his two hands, put them around her face, and let him draw her to a kiss. "The books stay here till next time. Can you keep a secret? Can you tell one?"

"Of course, both, I mean..."

"Very well," said Amy, looking him straight in his brown eyes, "the first secret is that you've never been here. Or if you've told anyone where you were going this afternoon, you never tell what we did here." This was the usual oath, exacted with great solemnity, a deep gaze from lowered green eyes. It had never been denied, nor ever broken.

"I told no one, and I won't tell anyone, I promise."

"Very good. The next is: is it true you have a boat, and that you can sail it?" (Amy kept, in her study here at home, a card file of her possibilities; the information on them was gained through social conversation at the school library reference desk).

"I gotta confess," Will said, raising his left hand, and then changing it, confusedly, for his right, "that my father left us a J-24; that its name is *Hornpipe,* and that it's moored at the marina on the east side of this very island."

"And do you know what to do with it?" Amy demanded. "I mean, which do you haul up first, the mainsail or the jib?"

"The mainsail, of course," said Will. "And you know," he added, putting his arm around her, "I like the cut of your jib."

He stood up, drew her toward her chaise-longue, and started to unbutton her wraparound dress. "You're very saucy," she told him. She rolled away from him, buttoned herself back up: "No. No is the earliest command of love. Learn it! Now then: do we go sailing next weekend?"

"All right!" said Will.

"Then it's time for you to go," said Amy, leading him toward the Dutch door and his bicycle, which was parked on the front lawn under the aspen. "One quick kiss, and then I have some homework to do." She put her hands on his shoulders, and gave him a light kiss. "You're a darling," said Amy.

"You too," said Will. He looked bewildered, no doubt by all that he had gone through, all the surprises he had been taken by today: but he seemed happy. His brown eyes, she noted, really were kind.

"Off with you!" Amy told her lover. "Give me a call! See you next weekend." She watched him as he mounted his bicycle, turned to wave, and finally cycled away.

It had gone well, thought Amy. She closed the door, walked into the bathroom, and put on clean clothes: white cotton shirt, and black shorts—they looked very good against her fair skin. She checked herself in the mirror: there's a woman who has success-fully carried out the most important plan of her day. Now to lesser things: the annual reports. She picked up her artist's portfolio, in which she always kept her professional papers, strode into the study (clear white walls, a favorite aunt's bequeathed escritoire [French, ebony, silver trim, nineteenth century], family photographs of parents and cousins), opened the portfolio, and settled down to work.

WORK, FOR AMY, HAD LONG been a troubling experience. She did it well, for she had been brought up to do all things well, and she valued her reputation as one who could handle any crisis. Still, the role of a school librarian in a small town was confining, and she could only carry it off by suppressing parts of her personality, which nevertheless came out in other ways: wearing interesting clothes, and collecting secret dear ones. The only person she ever confided these adventures to, was her friend Joy. They'd planned to take off Tuesday, now that exams were over, to go shopping in the big city down the Sound.

Amy was buttoning herself into a pink flowered shirtwaist when Joy phoned from the island's harbor town. "Amy! Front and center! Are you ready?" demanded the little soprano voice.

"Of course," said Amy.

"I'm so excited! I haven't been into the city in months!" said Joy. "See you in fifteen minutes!" And before Amy could say good-bye, Joy hung up.

There would be no time for breakfast; Joy was quick and gave one no time—unless she herself was late. There were important things to remember about Joy, Amy reflected as she replaced the receiver. Joy de Grasse was French: her father had come from the south of France, her mother was Norman, and they met, as all French people eventually do, in Paris. They'd come to America thirty years ago, and Joy Michelle was their first child, born in California. Joy was also a school librarian, but happier in her role than Amy was in hers.

However, there were things one didn't mention with Joy: her disastrous one-year marriage, for example. Bart had promised to take his bride skiing, but it turned out that the only "snow" he knew much about was the kind smuggled in sealed tins from the Andes. He twisted her wrists when he got angry, and he had a volcanic temper; and worst of all, he didn't appreciate her cooking. All Joy could tell Amy about this last was that the Battle of the Saucepans ended in the divorce court. *Basta!*

As a consequence, Joy had a low opinion of men. Lovers were few in her life; and she liked to tease. All the world's follies were bubbles, created for the light touch of that excellent needle-woman, Joy de Grasse. As for the next world, let that be confided to the care of *le bon Dieu,* until such time, no doubt far distant, when He could call her to His side with the title and role of Permanent Consultant. Meanwhile, there was shopping to be done.

Amy heard "toot-toot!" even sooner than she expected, and out of her green VW bug stepped Joy, five-foot-three, golden-crowned, neat black dress and little gold locket. They squeezed each other. "Ready!" said Joy. "Let's go!"

There was room for the little car on the ferry taking them to the mainland. Joy and Amy watched the gulls float, now sideways, now sinking, as the ferry churned its way to shore. A white volcano hovered in the distance, improbable even though familiar, above the fog.

"Let's start at the big stores," Joy said. "I have no street suits for summer, and nothing at all for fall."

"Look how clear the mountain is," said Amy dreamily. "I'd like to get something nautical-looking." Amy was thinking of Will and his boat.

"My dear, how absurd!" said Joy. "Not a sailor suit. Not at your age. Only *little* girls wear sailor suits," she added firmly, "unless you're going to tell us that you're not *quite* fourteen."

"That will do, Joy," Amy answered. "You're seven years younger; a little respect, please!"

"But really, Amy, you never wear clothes, you always wear a costume. I mean, like the time you came to an Intellectual Freedom Committee meeting dressed in a black dress and a Spanish lace mantilla, and even a comb in your hair, and a pert young man asked why the Spanish Inquisition was being represented at an Intellectual Freedom meeting?"

"I spoke to the chair of the committee afterwards, and the young man was severely reprimanded. Burned at the stake, I believe. I just felt…well, Iberian that day, that's all."

"And then there was the time that ALA met in Dallas, and you went, and you were the only girl to bring back a Texas hat. And you didn't even like Texas."

"It wasn't a ten-gallon hat; it had a flat crown and a silver headband; it was more Indian than Texan. I don't usually wear hats."

"Finally, darling, then there was the time that you appeared in a silver pantsuit at the principal's Christmas party, and so totally distracted poor Mr. Johnson that he couldn't finish his prepared speech."

"All I did was sit meekly, about three yards away from him. Anyway, he's a fussy little man, and who wants to hear a principal speak anyway?"

They were descending the iron stairs inside the autoferry to be in the car when the doors opened. "You lay a lot out on clothes, and you make some too. It's a lot of time and money. I've always wondered why."

"Well," said Amy, "look: I've been a doctor's wife, and librarian. Those are, well, submissive roles. You're expected to be long-suffering and patient. Wear little prints and pink silk scarves—that sort of thing. And that's not me!"

"You would prefer to be Elizabeth of Austria, no doubt," Joy said, "or Cléo de Mérode. Really, *chérie*, we're coming to the end of this century; you can't go back to the end of the last one."

The ferry nudged, shuddered. "If I were taken up by a rich, handsome young count," said Amy, "I could go on the stage."

"Are you sure you wouldn't rather be the impresario?" Joy smiled at her from behind the VW's steering wheel. "You do manage people, you know."

"I contrive pleasant arrangements for them," Amy answered, thinking of Will again.

"Ah, we know about your arrangements!"

"I hope nobody does, except you."

"Of course, dear Amy, I haven't told anyone but the corre-spondents of *The Washington Post,* and *Le Monde.* But have you made any new young friends?"

"Only one," Amy said faintly; "his name is Will."

"And will he?"

"He's very good at learning."

"From an excellent teacher, I'm sure. But you know, Amy, this little program of yours—how did you get started? I'm looking in vain for a motive—unless pleasure is the only and sufficient one."

"Perhaps because I was innocent when I married, and so was he—I didn't want others to go through the same thing. As for how it got started: you remember, I invited a shy young friend, and—then things happened. I've been a widow eight years."

"How unfortunate," Joy said; "I mean the innocent part. I abandoned that when I was sixteen." The car swooped above the suburbs on broad freeways. "Amy, Amy, one of these days you're going to get caught. Some loose-tongued lad will boast. Or repent, and tell Mamma. You're playing with fire, Amy."

Amy sat silent. The car surmounted bridges and descended into the city. The fire was beginning to burn her heart. She hadn't been able to stop thinking of Will since Sunday. He was so shy and gentle. His musician's touch was *pianissimo.* How was she to get through a week without him?

IN THE DEPARTMENT STORE, Amy and Joy found them-selves in front of a Hat Bar. Amy picked up a straw boater with a pair of pink ribbons. "I thought you said you didn't wear hats," Joy said.

"No, but really—this one would blow off in the wind. How about this round blue cap with the red pompom on top?"

"That's the cap of a *matelot,* a sailor in the French Navy. They wear it with a striped jersey and a blue coat with flared light blue collar. You want to be taken for a sailor?"

"Maybe I'm taken *with* one," hinted Amy.

"Ah, we're getting some information here. I must telephone *People Magazine* as soon as I get home. Now come on and help me select some summer knits. Even when it's summer, you want something warm around here."

They sat in the store's lunchroom, which was decorated with fake awnings and Toulouse-Lautrec posters. The entrance said CAFE MENTON. "I'm not entirely pleased with what I'm finding here," said Joy; "we should go on to some other stores before we head home."

"Then we should issue a 'We Are Not Pleased' manifesto," said Amy.

"A what—oh *that* thing, it appeared in *Library Journal*. The complaint of people who struggled to get to the top, and now they don't like the top. I thought it was rather—" and she let her wrist dangle.

"That's not entirely fair. I agree with some of their complaints. You must admit, the profession is quite obsessed with all these CD-ROMs, to the exclusion of people's real concerns."

"That's true, but then writing manifestoes doesn't do much for that old image people are always talking about. Not that the public will ever see the paper, but if we modernize maybe people will take us seriously as librarians."

"I think about the image a lot of the time," said Amy. "It's a big concern of mine. You never read a story that has a librarian in it without her being a minor or even silly character. I mean, is there any place in the Sherlock Holmes stories where he says, 'It utterly defeats me, Watson, I must ask the staff of the British Museum?' Or does any romance show a muscular hero in a torn shirt embracing a beautiful librarian?"

"One in a tweed street suit?" Joy laughed. "Look, we've got a good profession, why worry what people think of it. I'm tired of those little columns—'As they see us'—in *American Libraries*."

"But you just got through saying that writing manifestoes doesn't do much for the image problem. Obviously you read those 'As they see us' pieces in *American Libraries* yourself. And what about that article in the *New York Times Book Review* that dismissed stories about 'the pallid loves of lady librarians'? Didn't that get to you?"

The small golden-haired lady looked up from her soup, at the tall raven-haired one. "I didn't see it, and I wouldn't give it a thought," said Joy. "Look, Amy love, you're in no danger of becoming the stereotype. You dress like a queen, and you have a discreet, if rather indiscreetly discreet, love life. Why should what perfect strangers think about librarians trouble your beautiful head for a minute? There are thousands of happily married, or unmarried, librarians all over the country, who don't fit the flat-chested image at all. You certainly don't, and yet you're worried about it. Why?"

"It's like this, Joy: you're divorced, I'm widowed, we're both school librarians: the lowest-paid segment of the profession. We're stuck here, way up in the northwest corner of the map. I've got another job, but unless I run for ALA Council—and fat chance I could make it—I'm just going to get older, and more and more frustrated—and then I'll *be* the stereotype. It's a real occupational hazard: call it burnout. What burnout looks like to the people outside."

"And you're saying it'll happen to me," said Joy, smiling and stirring her iced tea. "Thanks for the compliment."

"No, not you, but—"

"No, not me, because I don't take the whole charade that seriously. I have a neat job, I keep my boss on his toes. I go to a movie, I enjoy my freedom. In winter I ski: if I meet a healthy unattached man at a ski resort, maybe I take him for a lover. It's fun, but love itself is not that big a deal."

Amy looked into her empty soup bowl. "I don't want to be stuck in life. Joy, I want to rise, I want to be loved." She looked up at her friend. "I want...something more. The sense of my own life and career in my hands. Is that absurd? Joy, aren't there other women who dream of a greater role in life? Joy, don't you?"

"I enjoy the comedy of life. It's brief enough, you know. I enjoy watching you: you and your adventures. One of these days I might steal one of your laddies, just to see how much he's learned from you."

"Oh no, please don't do that!"

"No, I wouldn't really. But—you want to rise? Can you really handle it?"

"Well, you know they call me 'the unflappable.' "

A vrai dire. But then, are you really interested in rising in a bureaucracy? Can you see yourself with a ribbon that says, 'Immediate Past President of CLA'?"

Amy laughed. "How did you know they do that down there?"

"I had a friend who went to the California Library Association conference in Oakland. But don't forget: *if* you rise, the higher you rise, the less possible your 'arrangements' will become. You'll have to choose between ambition and love. And you'll have to get tough—and become the stereotype. Remember your Shakespeare? 'Ambition should be made of sterner stuff.' Lady Macbeth, I think."

"Julius Caesar, darling."

"And darling, remember what happened to him."

AMY ARRIVED HOME tired from the long drive. She put away the city dress, changed into T-shirt and jeans, and paddled barefoot around the summer kitchen while Olivia followed her.

"Look, Olivia," said Amy, "this is the most promising young lover I've ever had. He's learning—God knows, I taught him—all the special ways and places to touch me. Now, come on, it's a savory feast. It says so, right here on the can. And it costs forty-three cents a can. What's to be done with a cat who won't finish her cat food? Ohh! what's to be done with a woman who can't let go of her love?"

For she did love him. That was undeniable: her *heart* told her so! And they had only one more weekend together, before he went off to work at the first of two summer camps! By the time he came back, she would be gone, two states away, working at a different job. The sadness of the one prospect, and the excitement of the other—pressed tears from her eyes. She left the little cat, to wander into the bedroom, and to straighten herself before the mirror.

So little time! No silver yet, in the long black strands, no crow's feet at the eyes, body still trim. These things she could attribute to sunblock, wide hats in summer, cycling, a strict diet. However, even if a woman is designed by the Goddess Creatrix, clothed by William Morris and unclothed by Gustav Klimt— time claims its small victories.

She had never told any of the young people that she loved them. She would never have allowed herself to get too entangled, lest they come back, alone or with someone else—and she feel herself the loser. She had only said "I love you" to George; and it had been hard being a doctor's wife; and now she had no one to say those words to. She needed to say them to Will. Of course, it could be a mistake, she could get her heart broken; so she wasn't going to say those words to anyone. There were more tears.

She might meet someone in the big city. But big cities scared her. Olivia would have to stay in a tiny apartment, or risk being chased by dogs.

Amy remembered that fear is always inherent in early love. (It had been a long time!) He hadn't called her; was he avoiding her? Would he want her, in that way, if he came this weekend? He might decide that he just wanted to be friends; this would normally be a relief, even necessary now that she had his summer schedule; but now she wanted *him*. "I love you," said Amy Rose, to the cat, to the circumambient air, to an invisible presence in the bedroom designed in the colors of heaven.

AT LAST HE CALLED! Breathes there the lover with soul so dead who never to him/herself hath said, "At last, [s]he called?" But the date? Saturday! and the time? seven in the morning. The sun was up, but behind a summer fog.

"Hello?…My God, yes. Within the hour? My dear, you must be mad. You can't get here that soon. You know it, and please, give me a chance to shower first. Because your mother couldn't make up her mind? On which day to have a birthday party for your kid sister? Do I remember?" cautiously, "Yes." Hope he remembers it—in the right way. "Look, come over mid-morning, and we'll have lunch somewhere near the harbor. Afternoon breeze will be better anyway. Hurry, but take your time, if you know what I mean!"

She wondered whether his mother, whom she had never met, had all his phone calls monitored. Maybe she should be applying for a library job in Madagascar.

AMY DROVE THEM in the blue Subaru, to the little Dutch-flavored town on the island's east side. Stepped gables, and young lieutenants in Navy whites; then down to the summer harbor. This harbor faced south into its cove, and the only marina, adjoining the naval air station, but at right angles, actually faced west. They sat outdoors at a cafe: coffee, croissants with ham, an Italian salad.

"You've been sailing before?" asked Will.

"Yes, my husband used to charter boats. We belonged to a club, but I dropped our membership after he died. It was just too expensive. I'm afraid I've forgotten a lot."

"It'll come back," said Will, "don't worry," and at that moment along came Joy, in a green dress, swinging a handbag from one shoulder.

Since Amy's school libraries were all on the mainland, she felt positive that no one on the island would recognize Will. Joy was her island friend; but friends don't often encounter each other downtown, even when the town has only seventeen thousand people in it.

I should have thought of this, Amy told herself. She had mentioned her young friends to Joy, but had never introduced them. There was, meanwhile, no way the two friends could avoid each other; Joy was closing fast on the couple at the cafe table. "Well, hello!" said Joy.

"Hello, Joy! Joy, this is Will Newcastle; this is my friend Joy de Grasse."

"I'm very glad to meet you." Will stood up and took Joy's light hand.

Joy sat down. "I'll be only a minute. Charlotte, Emily and

Anne—you remember them, from the University, Amy?—want me to help them set up a panel on women's literature of the nineteenth century. Imagine, talking shop on your day off—they want me to dash into town and meet them. Maybe we can do a little shopping afterwards, to take the heat off. And what are your plans?" she turned to Will.

Will looked surprised. "We're going sailing!" he announced.

Amy looked down at her hands. She wished that she had never hinted anything to Joy.

"Ah, indeed!" said Joy, and with a pleasant smile, took a mental snapshot of her friend's lover. "I'm sure it will be brisk out there."

There was a pause. Amy suddenly had to find a restroom. "Will, please entertain my friend; I'll be right back."

Will sat in silence. He isn't used to keeping up conversation with older women, thought Joy.

"My father left me and my mother a boat," Will said at last. "We keep it here because there's a year-long waiting list for a marina anywhere close to the city."

"And now you're in college?" Joy knew the answer to her own question.

"Oh, no, I'm about to get there. I've been accepted to Pomona."

" 'Fair Pomona, in honor of thee.' I had a friend who went there once. What will you be doing?"

"Music. I know the piano, I want to really learn the organ."

"Meanwhile, you're a student of my friend Amy."

The experiment was successful: the boy blushed to the roots of his hair. Joy was satisfied. "She's a very good librarian. She likes young people. She…" and here came Amy: "hopes that her association with them will be always a sweet memory."

Joy rose: "Amy, your young friend is a charmer. I'm sure you'll enjoy sailing together. I envy you; but Charlotte awaits with our friends. *Chérie, je t'aime;*" and the two friends hugged and kissed.

Amy watched her friend disappear down the sidewalk. "I hope you didn't tell her about us," said Amy.

"Not a thing," said Will quickly, not looking at her.

THE HARBOR FACED SOUTH into its cove, and the only marina faced west: so they had to check the boat out, stow the jib on the foredeck, don their PFD's, and lower the outboard into the water, check hull, topsides, fuel, bilge, and rigging, before backing out to sail.

West out of the marina, southwest out of the harbor, the inner shores of the island in sight the whole time: finally they were able to raise the mainsail, and it wasn't until they were well into Saratoga Passage that they raised the jib, and honed into the land wind. *Hornpipe* bounced south through the Saratoga Passage chop.

Amy crouched in the cockpit: secure in white pants, white shirt and red cardigan sweater. Her black hair was gathered behind with a silver clasp: the one with a big turquoise in the center. "Let's tack," cried Will. "Ready about!"

"Ready!" Amy answered.

"Helm a-lee!" cried Will. Amy knocked the line off the port winch: hauled in the line on the starboard one, secured it with a winch handle, and cleated it.

Amy seated herself on the windward bench. Off to the northwest streamed the wind-shapen cloud from a remote volcano. "And so you're going to Pomona College on a scholarship?" Amy knew the answer to her own question; it was all on the card file, but she needed more details for her loving.

"No other way! My father died two years ago, followed by my elder brother," Will answered. "So I and my mother have been co-breadwinners. And my kid sister's just too young. She'll have to do her part and find a job, though, once she's eighteen. I'll have to work, too, as a student at Pomona. Fortunately they have some jobs open there."

"And that's why you're going to two summer camps, as an instructor?"

"That's what it's all about. Work, and responsibility."

"And that's why you haven't anyone close to you," said Amy. She wanted to make sure of this.

"No time!" said Will, and the red flecks on his cheekbones

deepened, till, from brow to breastbone, his skin flared deep red. His face turned windward, his brown hair ruffled. "Time to tack," said Will. "Ready about!"

"Ready!" Amy chanted.

AMY HADN'T FELT this excited about a man since her husband died. She lay on her bed, unbuttoned her red cardigan sweater and her white cotton shirt, and drew him down to her. Her bra unclasped in front. He sought her tender breasts, the great round paps, and then he kissed her shoulders, her throat; then their tongues met, pressing against each other. Amy unbuttoned Will's shirt, kissed his throat, his long brown chest, sucked his niplets; finally she opened his belt, and followed, with tender fingers, the line of black hair. Soon the mast of the skipper of *Hornpipe* rose before her—needing to be taken down. Amy rolled over, and reached into the straw basket where she kept her bedtime reading.

"Slip one of these on you," said Amy, stretching it. "You better get a supply at the local pharmacy. Women will expect you to take responsibility from now on." And then, smiling tenderly, she helped him pull it on him. Once her lover was secure, Amy slowly revealed her creamy beauty to him.

Amy watched Will's pleasure as she lowered herself onto his body. Once covering him, she let herself go. She rode him as the boat rides the waves, she surged up him as the high tide whelms the beach. She moved back and forth over him, milked him inside her.

"My darling," said Amy. "My lover. My beautiful one."

"Amy. Amy, you're so sweet, it's so wild!"

She could feel him twist and labor under her, she could feel him touch the tip of her womb; but she didn't let him go free until each had flooded the other with love. The moon swept over Endymion.

She lay on her back as his hands smoothed her hair, caressed her white flanks, gently rounded the curves of her bosom. "What are we to do?" Amy asked Will. "I love you." Now, she had said it.

"I love you, too."

"Well, but you're going away," said Amy. "And I am too. Did I tell you about the big research library job down south? This is a kind of ending for me. You're a last chance here, before I go."

"Yes, you did," said Will. He looked down at her, his brown eyes puzzled. "A last chance?"

Amy thought for a moment: the pause spoke for her, she realized, in spite of herself. "Well, a last time for both of us." She looked away from him. The blue curtains trembled; an afternoon breeze was pressing against the windows, rising from the Strait.

He arose, went to her bathroom, was back in a moment.

She saw him, when he returned to her, looking thoughtful. He lay at first on his back, hands behind his head; then, on his side, he was facing her again. He reached up and caressed her shoulder. "Amy," Will asked, "did you ever do this before?"

"Make love?" She nestled close to him. "My dear, remember, I was married."

"I mean, love someone else. Someone you had chosen."

"Whom?"

"Like, bring someone out to this house and love them. Some young one. Someone who would be going away, real soon."

None of the other boys or girls had ever asked Amy this question before: they had accepted her love as a child might accept a barley-sugar candy, without searching and probing. "Why do you ask?" asked Amy. She was not supposed to be on the defensive; that was not her intended role. "Are there rumors going around?"

"Nobody would ever spread a rumor about Mrs. Rose," answered Will. "You're thought of as gracious but aloof; maybe a little too good for a small-town environment. No, so far as I know, nobody has said anything about you."

"Gracious but aloof," said Amy, eyes half-closed. "I can live with that, if there are no rumors. But is that how *you* see me?"

"No, but Amy; I'm still wondering how come you're so sweet. It comes as a surprise. Put it this way: suppose a lady wanted to play a kind of game, she could bring someone out to her house in the country, seduce them; and then when they went away, nobody would ever know. The news would never get back to the school."

Amy glanced at her lover, quickly: "It isn't seduction; you're eighteen, at the legal age of consent."

"I'm very glad that I consented," said Will, bending down and tenderly tonguing her navel. Her left hand played with his curly hair, until he rose again. "But still, I'm eighteen, and you're…?"

"I'm thirty-six," said Amy. "Does it matter?"

He looked down at her quickly: she saw that it did. "I'm half your age," said Will. "I just graduated from high school. I can add, subtract, multiply, and divide."

You're too clever by half, thought Amy, caressing his thin nose and then drawing her finger down to slip it between his lips. What was Will after? Surely, the other boys and girls had been able to enjoy a brief intimacy and then go off to Europe or wherever, and thence to college, without wondering what it all meant.

Will took Amy's finger gently away, held it close to his flank; pursued the question: "Let's suppose that you did bring others out here—boy or girl, it doesn't matter." (How did he know *that?* Amy asked herself).

"Did they really expect to be introduced to love," Will continued, "by the school librarian?"

Amy was shocked. She sat up: naked, defenseless, her long black hair slipping down over her white shoulders. One tear rolled down her cheek. "Why did you remind me that I was a librarian?" she demanded. "How could you? Aren't librarians allowed to love, too?"

"Amy, dear Amy," Will began, but dear Amy interrupted him: "I'm only a librarian. That's what a county supervisor told the women librarians down in Oregon, when they demanded pay equity. I heard all about it at PNLA. Oh, how could you remind me of my profession, my job, at a time like this!" And another tear rolled down the other cheek.

Will touched her tenderly. He had to sit and learn to listen, as she put her face in her hands: "You can't understand what the stereotype has done to us! I'm not like that, ever! You know perfectly well, I *never* put up my hair in a bun!"

Amy raised her face to look at him, and sobering, saw that he was more at sea than if he'd left the Strait in *Hornpipe*, and was halfway across the Pacific without sextant, radio, or Loran. He needed help, surely, as much as she did. "You wouldn't know. All us librarians are seen by everybody, even on television, as fussy little old ladies. And you know I'm not like that. You know I'm not."

"Amy," said Will, trying to be helpful, "my grandmother was a librarian."

"You see! We're all *grandmothers!*" Fresh tears.

"Amy, let me finish. She met Melvil Dewey."

"So what is that, to *me!*"

"He tried to back her into a corner, at Lake Placid. She told me so, herself, before she died last year. Of course, she resisted him."

"Melvil Dewey did *that?* Why, the dreadful creature!" said Amy, not crying now, but curious. "You know, I never admired him all that much. He always seemed the patriarchal type."

"I don't know about that," said Will, "but about us, well: being loved by you isn't what I would have expected, though I've loved every minute with you. And I didn't say, 'only a librarian'. You're a real person, to me. It's just…well, as if Mr. Johnson the principal, decided he loved me. I wouldn't know what to do with it."

Amy smiled through her tears at the thought of the tubby, fussy little man to whom she reported every Monday morning. She looked up at her lover, bewildered: "Why? Is he gay?"

"Not that I know of," said Will, "But you gotta admit, anyone who wants to be a school principal is probably weird in some way. Still, if he knew about us, he'd probably say, 'Now you know, Mrs. Rose, you shouldn't be doing that.' "

Amy lay back and turned her head on the pillows, which she had specially cased in gold-threaded silk to match the bedspread. "No, you haven't quite got it right. He'd say, 'Now, you know, Mrs. Rose, that's not in your job description.' " Will laughed, but Amy could only smile.

Will took her hand and drew her finger to his lips, kissing it softly. She felt a little better now, thanks to his tenderness. Perhaps he really did love her. He was telling her, "Maybe you should be more than a librarian. Maybe there's such a thing as arch-librarian, like archbishop. Is there a Pope of the librarians? You're fit to be it."

"There isn't really," Amy said, turning to him, "ALA is just a bureaucracy. But thank you for the thought. As for my job description, what am I to do? I love you anyway!" Amy, you've done it now.

Will drew her to his chest. There was a long time of tears and caresses. The wind blew sea-sounds in from the Strait. He touched her slowly, shyly: round each breast, down her flanks, back up under her hair.

Amy said, after a long time, "Let's take that big green coverlet, and pull it over us, and take a little nap, before you have to go home." They pulled it, together, over them both.

THEY DROWSED TOGETHER for an hour, lying tilted toward each other on Amy's wide fortress bed, surrounded by gold and blue pillows. So long they slept, that Olivia the cat came back from her secret anti-stranger hiding place under the house, and curled up at Amy's feet.

Amy dreamed that she had caught a wild bird that slowly slipped out of her hand, and flew away.

THEY BOTH WOKE UP and looked into each other's eyes without speaking. Out beyond the trembling aspen at the door, came the scent of the island's crop of hay. The *shook-shook-shook* of a Steller's jay came from the Douglas firs beyond the bramble hedge. It was one of those times, the so quiet times, in which Amy convinced herself that she could hear the ebb tide rush out of Deception Pass.

AMY AND WILL HAD TOUCHED the bottom of the ocean, and were now floating, like the chambered nautilus, on the surface. They had not settled anything. Time and rest had settled it for them.

Will was fully awake now. He watched solemnly as his own beautiful special librarian pushed back the coverlet and explored his chest, abdomen, pelvis...with slow, small, kisses.

"You need to feel skin," Amy told him, "not just place. Men know place; they don't understand skin. Some Pomona woman will be glad you learned."

"It feels sweet," said Will, smiling up at her giving him kisses.

"And perhaps she will know how to do this for you, and for her," said Amy; slipping down between his legs and placing his secret part between her long breasts. She heard him draw breath, call out her name, but still she teased him until she felt him flow over her body. Then she lay back and guided his own finger, until she herself felt release.

Now they were smiling, kissing lightly, happy again. Amy, in control once more, remembered time.

"It's time," said Amy, "you learned how to bathe with a woman!"

"How about a swim instead?"

"No, too cold! Warm water and soap removes the stickies. You need to learn. No time to swim!"

The shell-shaped marble tub (and did it really belong to the Empress Josephine? Any more than that was a real Mary Cassatt on her bedroom wall? One of her games had been found out: what about the others?) was placed on a special surface of tiles (each one bore a hand-painted goldfish) fitted with a drain, while the whole space was ringed with an oval shower curtain (blue, with little white waves on it) and with a brass rail circling it for support; the faucet was fitted with an aluminum hose, long and flexible, tipped with a brass shower head. The tub itself could barely hold one creamy-white woman, head-butt-heels; but Amy and her lover could take a safe shower standing up, on the lilypad-shaped green rubber mat. Splash! and it all drained away, past the shower curtain, down over the goldfish tiles, through the drain to the island sand.

Sea air cooled them as hot water steamed. The capable Amy showed Will how to shower, soap, then rinse a woman.

"Gently there: that's my part. Now, do all of yourself. You're so big and healthy!" She dried herself and handed him the towel; before he had even started, she was gone like an arrow, fled in the terrycloth robe that bore a single blue dolphin over the left breast.

AMY THOUGHT FAST. If she was to see him again—and there was a good chance that she wouldn't, since both of them were going away, to different parts of the same state—she would have to find some way to reel him back to her, keep in contact, until they could find a time together. She could drop him a line at college, give him her new address, and wait to see if he responded. Or she could just happen to be in the area, and drop in—but there might be surprises there. He certainly knew now, how to love a woman; and there was a good chance that he might find someone at Pomona, and marry her. Of course she could find someone else herself, but then her chances were not as great.

The young man wanted to be a musician, why not a music librarian? It was her opportunity, nay, her duty, to recruit for her profession: and her only hope. The lad, thought Amy, has a touch like a hawkmoth visiting a four-o'clock, as intimate and gentle. How else, save by recruiting him to the library profession, could she contrive another meeting, without wasting her time or putting him in an embarrassing situation?

Amy emerged from her bedroom in a pressed white cotton shirt, tight tan slacks and brown espadrilles: her no-nonsense clothes. She read that signal, and his surprise, in his face. "A last tour of the house," she told Will, "and I'll race you up to the bridge."

"You have a bike?"

"You'll watch my dust. Now then: these oval portraits, this is my Norwegian pastor grandfather: he's the one who rescued the organ, the one you played so well on, out of China...say, why don't you become a music librarian, once you graduate? There are never enough of them."

"I never thought of that," said Will. "What do they do, give out scores?"

"Oh, there's a lot more than that. There's acquisitions, and cataloging, and comparing of texts—and a whole association just for them." She took him by the hand, and her glance dropped to his slim brown legs. "But then I wouldn't see you again. Unless you came to ALA conferences."

"You've already found me a career," said the boy. "Amy, I must say, you do arrange things for people!" He was smiling at her. She looked up, and she blushed—they both were blushing.

"That's what Joy says," Amy said, her arms on his shoulders. "Let's us both arrange something, then."

"Like what?"

"I'll send you a card at college, and I'll give you my address. That way we can keep in touch, and manage to meet somehow."

Will looked dubious. "But you said—well, I might meet someone at Pomona."

"Oh, you will! And please don't! I mean—you're so gentle, and I'm older and it's harder for me. It's not just being a librarian; it's being older, and widowed, and you're the first one I ever really loved since my husband died." She pressed her face against his clean white shirt. "Darling, *please* don't forget me!" He saw that her eyes were wet, and kissed the tears away. "Please think about becoming a librarian, so we can be together!"

He laughed softly. "Imagine me applying to library school. 'Dear Mr. Dean, I want to be a librarian so I can get back together with the woman I love.' Amy, love, you're such a romantic, how do you know *you* won't find someone?"

"Nobody has gentle hands like you. I don't want to think about anyone else. Please, if you receive a letter from me, you won't be offended? You'll write?"

"I promise, I'll write."

"Then that's a promise. And I promise I'll write you. We'll keep in touch."

She took his hands in hers and kissed them. He covered her face with them gently, and his hands were wet when he drew them back.

Amy straightened up and looked at him forthrightly. "Now I know we'll be together again someday. Is your bike ready? I'll race you to the bridge."

The harder she pedaled, the better she felt. Let him be younger; she would beat him to the bridge. A flame entered her heart as she whistled round the curves, just humming along the edge of the pavement, black hair flying free; reckless, without helmet or little rear-view mirror. She rejoiced to know that a man half her age was actually right behind her. But he would catch up in thirty seconds more.

HE CAUGHT UP, and they kissed. They were both astride their bicycles, so their hug was awkward. "Remember now," Amy told him, "we're to keep in touch."

"Yes, because I love you."

"And because you love me, and I love you, you'll end up a librarian."

They were both laughing: they were parting with an in-joke. "Yes, darling."

"But I do love you. So now quickly, please go! Before I cry."

"I'm going—but I love you!"

He gazed at her for a few seconds, then he turned and cycled off across the bridge. Traffic almost hid his backwards wave; she prayed for his safety while he disappeared.

THE JUNE TWILIGHTS ARE LONG up here, and low lies the light on the evergreen hills. Amy cycled homeward slowly, for all that she was hungry from sailing, loving and cycling. Amy was sad, and if (gentle reader) if you've never felt sad as Amy felt sad, then you need another story, from another librarian.

She reached home, parked the bike in the garage. Olivia met her at the door. The cat and the cat-lover began a search of the lair for food. There was a small steak, and a can of Fancy Feast in the refrigerator. "I'll feed you, darling," said Amy, tiredly; "it's part of my job description."

She opened a can for the cat, and poured half its contents in the blue dish. Over a glass of chablis she started to consider her future, when the phone rang.

"Hello!" cried Joy merrily, "how did the sailing go?"

"Oh Joy, he's so beautiful, his hands are so gentle, he says he loves me, do you think he means it?"

"That's not an excerpt from a ship's log," came the flute-like voice over the phone. "Evidently the pleasure began when you were back on shore."

"We're going to keep in touch. I told him he ought to be a music librarian. Listen, Joy, did you tell him anything special? About me?"

"No," said Joy, "but of course you're special."

"But Joy, I think he knows. He suspected that I've—brought others here."

"Which you neither confirmed nor denied."

"Of course. But now maybe he'll go off and decide I'm—wanton."

"Well, darling, you must admit that your service, as you call it, might just be a bit—redundant. Pleasant enough, but perhaps not quite appropriate, or should I say, quite necessary."

"How so?"

Joy's voice was serious, advisory. Amy dragged the telephone to the Empire chaise longue and listened: "Look, Amy, left to themselves, these darling girls and gentle boys would have deflowered each other. Don't you think so?"

"But I only selected the shy ones."

"I'm sure they're very grateful, but should the school librarian be the one to do it?"

Amy gasped, and spilled a little chablis. "Joy, Joy, what did you tell him?"

"Nothing, darling, only that you liked young people."

"Oh dear, oh dear! It's out now! He put it all together in that clever head of his. Oh, Joy, how could you?"

"Darling, look, it's time you grew up. Let's face it, this kind of activity doesn't count as professional—on any evaluation form. It's not the kind of service offered to young adults by the Young Adult Services Division." Amy giggled. "It would not be advocated by *Voice of Youth Advocates*. Nor would it be honored with an award administered by the ALA Awards Committee. It wouldn't even be a task of your blessed Feminist Task Force!"

"Stop, stop!" cried Amy, laughing.

"The Library Bill of Rights says nothing about caressing young readers. And the Freedom to *Read* Foundation…"

"Okay, okay, I get the point!"

"…is just *that.*"

Amy answered, "I admit all this, Joy, but if I've lost my lover because of you, I'll never forgive you."

"Don't forget, you've given him the knowledge that will enable him to attract another woman. You've given him away yourself, Amy. If he doesn't come back to you, maybe that'll be the real reason. And not anything I had said."

"I know he will come back," said Amy, firmly. "We've promised to keep in touch. I believe in love, Joy."

"I don't trust men, Amy."

"Love is strong!"

"Amy, *chérie*, I don't want you to get hurt. You must give him up. This whole thing sounds like one of these little moral fables they publish in *Library Journal*—what's the name of the series?— 'How Do You Manage?' Little stories about personnel problems at the 'Harborville Public Library.'"

"*Manage,*" said Amy, "is a word I never liked—it derives from the control of horses—did you know? I just—arrange matters for friends."

"You could call this story—why don't you write it up? 'Staying within your Job Description.'"

"Yes, Joy," said the older woman, feeling talked to.

"Or, 'Be good, even in your spare time.'"

Amy was feeling edgy. "Joy, look. This has been a long day, and I'm emotionally exhausted. I need a quiet dinner with Olivia by myself. I'll see you next weekend—give me a call. And please, don't say anything to anyone any more!"

"I won't. I promise. Now you promise to be good."

"Bye, Joy," said Amy firmly.

"Bye."

YES INDEED, thought Amy, starting a little salmon steak, and washing some carrots: now she would have to be *good*. She was a good school librarian, but now with a research library job in the big city, she would have to be good. Frowns rarely wrinkled Amy's nose, but this one did. Be good? Be moral? For Amy, those virtues were associated with all the wrong clothes. Good librarians wore tweedy street suits, ruffled shirts, and black boots with low heels. They cut their hair or put it up. But clothes were a language, for Amy. Some women's clothes said, "Who cares, it's warm, decent, and comfortable." Others said, "I am a busy professional lady." But Amy liked to wear clothes that said, "I am artistic, beautiful, and unapproachable. Eat your heart out." Then once a year she gave herself away most generously, to a surprised, gentle, deserving young person. Now she was going to be *good*? Oh, Will!

Amy stepped to the other long mirror, the one in the bathroom. She worked herself up into a short swivet of remorse at her past, of regret that there hadn't been more of it, of anger at some future hypothetical supervisor: "You want me to look like a *librarian!* You want me to wear little black suits, and plain white shirts? You want me to put my feet into Old Maine Trotters, and give up my lover? *Never!*" The defiant spirit of Lieutenant Gregory, the hero of Lake Champlain, flared in her nostrils. Not for nothing was the lady Irish, and the widow of an Irishman! "I'll wear espadrilles forever! I'll never wear Old Maine Trotters! I love him!" She turned from the mirror, hurried to the chaise-longue, and had a good cry.

She stopped in time to get up, butter the carrots and turn down the heat on the little salmon steak. She selected a Fontana Candida from the cellar. She would be faithful, and he would be faithful to her. But even if Will found some girl at college, there might, after all, be some delightful man in the Bay area. Surely not all of them were married or gay. And surely no real employer would ask her to give up her handmade dresses. She turned on the television, watched the evening news report, ate dinner, and having had enough TV, washed up, and finally walked out on the sandy island lanes to view the northern sundown at its latest and longest. It was a pilgrimage she always made on Midsummer Day.

FOOD AND DRINK DID WONDERS for Amy's spirits. If she were to lose her Will, she still had her will. "I am lovely," she said to herself, "thou art tender, he is my lover, we are parted, you are all free, they may someday see each other again." Yes, if her instant recruitment would have any effect on him! Probably if it did, they might still not meet for years. He'd be a stoutish married gentleman, she'd have silver hair, and they'd end up peering at each other's tags at an ALA conference. No, surely it would be sooner than that!

Olivia and Amy stepped homeward along the lane. The aspens trembled around her, but she wouldn't be here when they turned gold in October, like dancing lovelies beside their dark cedar partners. The ferries would hoot three times before going astern in the Sound fog, and she wouldn't hear them. She would be down there in a job with higher status, with more opportunities for professional activity. She would be in a better position to work with the Feminist Task Force, to fight the Forces of Evil she saw threatening Libraryland: the worship of machines, the neglect of people, the racism masquerading as neutrality, the power plays of administrators. She'd tried to introduce the Hennepin County Library list of subject headings into her school libraries' catalogs, but had been reprimanded and frustrated. Now, she would have colleagues after her own heart, and a wider field to work in.

Amy saw herself, as she sat on the front steps and let her dark hair flow in the island wind, a real librarian at last. She could get onto SRRT's Action Council; from there progress to ALA Council, and the ALA Executive Board; and indeed become, as Will had suggested, "The Pope of the librarians." There was the presidency of ALA; but why stop there? After all, you only got to play that for one year. No, what the Republic needs is a real librarian for Librarian of Congress, and a woman at that. For her confirmation hearings she would have to wear a neat black dress with a gored skirt and a silver rose brooch; the white linen suit would

do when the President of the United States administered the oath
of office: but how the myrmidons of LC would swarm around her
in astonishment when she arrived for work on her first day in a
white wool dress with silver threads in it, with a scarlet Indian
sash with a gold fringe, and a scarf of the same material! The
Subaru, of course, would long ago have gone the way of all good
things; she would have the official Lincoln Continental as a pre-
requisite. Was it black, silver, or bronze? And would they let her
choose?

Olivia shrank back against her ankles. Amy looked up; the
great gull passed overhead again, and they sized each other up: he,
the wild bird knowing neither remorse nor regret, she, the con-
science-limited, but infinitely resourceful woman.

Olivia mewed. "Come on, darling," said Amy, picking the little cat up and turning toward the door, "let's go inside. I have to
plan a campaign."

JOY STOOD IN HER SUNNY KITCHEN, wearing her morning white pantsuit, when the telephone rang.

"It's you! Down south! How is Olivia?"

"Olivia disappeared for three days. I practically *died*. It was all
I could do to drag myself to work, I was that worried. Eventually,
she came back—went exploring and got lost, I guess. But listen,
Joy, you're not going to believe this, but I called you, because I
wanted to read you some parts—just some parts—of a letter."

"Okay, so go ahead."

" 'Darling Amy,' this is from Will Newcastle, you remember
him? You didn't think I'd hear from him again, did you? 'Thank
you for your first letter. I'm looking forward to a lot of them.
Please be assured that I love you and will never forget you' and
then there's a lot more and he goes on: 'There's been a lot of
freshman activity and I have a heavy practicing schedule, so I
haven't much time for social life. You're right that Pomona women
are very cautious, but while they're very nice, they're not as interesting as you are; you have a lot more to talk about, even in your
letters. That's why I wish I was with you right now, even though

I've had some nice dates.' And he goes on; there's some questions about my new job, and so on. But mostly it's about—well, us. Isn't it wonderful?"

"Amy, I don't know! I'm positive he's going to get involved with someone down there—he has, after all, four years in which to do it—and then you'll get—not a 'Dear John' letter, but a 'Dear Amy' letter. I'm afraid you've turned a nice boy from the east shore into a rake!"

"Joy, surely not. I taught him how to be gentle."

"Then you've made a worse mistake, the seducer's biggest mistake: you've fallen in love with your victim!" Joy's laugh was tender.

"What do you mean, I've fallen in love with my *victim*? He writes *me* a sweet letter!"

"Are you going to go and visit him?"

"No, 'cause I'm scared to ask. He says he has little time for social life. And I want him to concentrate on his studies. He's going to be a music librarian—did I tell you?"

"Then you better let this passionate romance rest, for a while, and come and visit me instead. I have someone I want you to meet."

"Another man, someone for me—or for you."

"Not another *man,* dear Amy, a *woman.* I find them a lot more palatable. No bitter aftertaste."

"For your sake I hope not. But women have been disappointed in women before, don't forget."

"But don't forget my motto: never too seriously. And Laura is calm."

"'Rose-cheeked Laura, come,' remember the Campion poem? And I'm glad for you, because the lesbian thing was never as important to me—and anyway, I didn't have the bad experience you had" (avoiding a direct allusion to Bart).

"She is rose-cheeked—rounded, caring. Why don't you come and see us? I bet you miss the island, the whole Sound country."

"Yes, I do. I miss my island home just terribly. I suppose the people who bought it have installed a real pool, cut down the shrubbery, and—ugh! Could you please drive by and see what they've done to it? It'll be good to know, either way before I come up."

"I will. But when are you coming up?"

"Let's say—Thanksgiving. I can't get off any earlier."

"It'll be cold, but Laura and I will have a driftwood fire for you, and toddies. Do come!"

Amy thought about driftwood fires and special company. It had been so long since she'd shared one with George. "Listen, Joy, I just turned thirty-seven, what am I to do?"

"That's right, you share a birthday with the Virgin Mary, eighth of September. Do? You'll have to find something to do, darling. There's the opera, all those plays, sailing and hiking. Find some friends where you work and don't be too—preoccupied. Then you won't be disappointed if something doesn't—work out."

"I'll try," said Amy.

"Meanwhile, you know, as you get on, you'll be working with younger librarians. Don't get involved with *them*, now, Amy," said the younger woman; "remember, you're thirty-seven; you're supposed to be a role model to them."

"Oh! a role model! I've totally forgotten about that! You know, I've never been a role model to anybody!"

"On that, dear friend, we can certainly agree. Amy Rose is not a role model for the young."

"Oh Joy, ten years into the library profession and now I have to be a role model; it's all very complicated. Well, I've already started; I joined the Association of College and Research Libraries and have asked to get involved with their Western European Section. For no better reason, I suppose, than that I read French and Norwegian."

"I didn't know about the Norwegian," said Joy, "which Norwegian do you read with? But I certainly approve of the scholarly involvement. By all means do that, and no more leading teenagers astray."

"If I meet someone a little older than that, can I lead him astray?"

"Amy, now that you're in a research library, you should develop your academic side. Otherwise, how do you expect to get ahead? It can't all be done on committee work and SRRT Task Forces."

"Indeed, Joy dear," said Amy, "I've thought of that. I've talked to the graduate English Department at Berkeley—"

"Hope you can get in," said Joy.

"And at Davis," said Amy.

"Wherever *that* is," said Joy. "But you majored in philosophy?"

"A Mills girl can do anything," said Amy. "I minored in English. I'll do late seventeenth-century stuff, age of Dryden. I've thought of a thesis topic already: 'Sense and Sensuality in Susannah Centlivre.' "

"I'd emphasize the sense," said Joy, "and lay off the sensuality. A Ph.D. thesis isn't a personal memoir. And after all, Amy, what do we really *know* about the early life of Mrs. Centlivre? Wasn't she married three times? And is the life of a Restoration dramatist a fit subject for the pen of one who is about to reform?"

"I'll reform when you do, sweet," said Amy. "After all, you're settling down with another woman—which is more than Mrs. Centlivre ever thought of doing."

"Well, one never knows," said Joy. "There are many events in the seventeenth century which its diarists dared not reveal. Fortunately, we live in a less secretive age."

"Then you can be assured that I will keep *your* secret, Joy," said Amy.

"Oh, I have no secret. Laura and I are going to live together quite openly."

"I see the lifestyle up there has changed. Well, I'm glad you've found a loving woman at last. I'm looking forward to seeing you at Thanksgiving."

"Then we can talk about everything—your progress, the Restoration drama, and love."

"The subject of eternal fascination. Take care, Joy."

"Love to you, Amy."

"And to you."

NOW IF YOU, gentle reader, think that this is the end of the story of Amy Mary Gregory Rose and Will Newcastle, then you must think that this is a tale told by an incompetent. For it is not the end.

Instead, this is the end: Amy was elected to SRRT's Action Council, all the while working hard at her library job—she was given some time off, to pursue a Ph.D. program at Berkeley. The necessity of keeping pace with her work and keeping track of Mrs. Centlivre, kept her from any social activities beyond the local; her intercourse with Will was enforcedly epistolary. Will graduated from Pomona College with a B.A. in music, *cum laude,* which meant that he had no time for any organs except the ones fitted with *stops.* He finished off his education with an M.L.S. from UCLA. So it was with shrieks of relief, as well as passionate encounter, that Will and Amy met at ALA's Midwinter conference at San Antonio, whither Will had gone to seek a job. Over drinks, at Gambits on the Riverwalk, they discovered that with Will twenty-four and Amy nearly forty-two, their age differences no longer mattered as much; and they formed a plan. The would meet again at the annual conference in New York, arrive a day or two early, and enjoy each other's company.

And that is exactly what they did. They checked into the Plaza, as Mr. and Mrs., on *his* credit card; dined at the Russian Tea Room, on *her* credit card; rode a carriage in Central Park, at twilight; heard Itzhak Perlman in Carnegie Hall; shared a king-sized bed, rumpled it thoroughly with loving, and had breakfast in it the next morning; held hands at The Cloisters in the forenoon and at the Museum of Modern Art in the afternoon; and over dinner in the South Street Seaport, Amy said to Will, "Let's send Joy a postcard."

"Oh yes, Joy! I'd totally forgotten about Joy! Where is she now?"

"Oh she's still back there. Happy with her job, and with her woman lover. She never had the ambitious itch, the way I got it—right this moment, I expect they're shopping. You know, she never believed we'd get together again."

"We're together now," said Will, "so let's tell her about it! One moment, I'll be back." He left the table and returned immediately with a postcard from the revolving rack by the cashier's desk. It showed the Statue of Liberty, floodlit by night.

"How shall we compose this?" Will asked Amy. "Shall we try a poem?"

"Why not? 'By the light of Freedom's statue—' "

" 'We'll eat and drink our fill—' "

" 'For at last, we are—' "

" 'Together!—

        Love, Amy,' "

                " 'and her Will!' "

Part II

AMY ROSE,
FRIEND OF THE CHINESE PEOPLE
(with excerpts from Amy's diary and Joy's journal)

The action takes place the year before the repression in China, which began with the massacres of 3-4 June 1989.

"So he decreed, in terms succinct,
Whoever flirted, leered, or winked
(Unless connubially linked),
Should forthwith be beheaded."

—The Mikado

The quotations from the *I Ching* are from the edition by Gary G. Melyan and Wen-kuang Chu, under the title: *I-Ching, the hexagrams revealed* (Rutland, VT, Charles E. Tuttle Co., 1986). Reprinted by permission.

Amy Rose, Friend of the Chinese People

THE OLD BERKELEY HOUSE was a horror. The upstairs bedrooms had lost much of their interior paint; rain had seeped down to ruin chamber, closet, and bathroom; shingles were curled up like bat wings, ready to fly off; and downstairs the rooms were a dreadful dark brown, like the color of a room in which someone far too old is found dead at five in the morning after a long illness. Amy Rose, former school librarian from Washington, now librarian and Ph.D. candidate at the University, had bought the house for a song after coming down from her Puget Sound home, and had hired a Mexican contractor, who, with his family, was stripping the house of all that was awful. Amy stepped round the stuffed and mounted head of a moose, face up on the living room floor; avoided stepping on a snail on the hearth—they were everywhere; and watched as vines, Angkor-Wattish, fell away under Mexican fingers and light poured into the room. "Something smelly in the corner," said Amy, wrinkling her nose: "what is that?"

"I do not know," said Jorge Ramirez, head of his family, turning down the Latino music on his boom-box. "But I will find out."

He pushed aside a rolled up carpet, brown with dirt, and tugged with a crowbar at a loose post in the corner. As the house quivered, a stream of termites poured out, like dead white cells from a terrible boil.

"*Mira,*" said Jorge, "I think it is the sewer pipe. It is no good. See, in there."

Amy had no wish to see. Surely the pipe had stifled all previous occupants, one by one, beginning with Great Grandmamma, to *death*. "What can we do?"

"The post must go out, and we need a new pipe, I think." The family had downed tools and looked at the corner as if they had just discovered a prehistoric atrocity scene. "I think it costs a lot of money."

Amy began to think that if she had bought this house for a song, it was a very sad song indeed. Maybe she should have just had the house demolished and replaced by a new townhouse. But it was too late now; Joy was coming down to visit. "Can we finish the job in six weeks?" Amy asked. "My friend Joy de Grasse and I are going on a librarians' tour of China. I could help you," she said, picking up the crowbar and testing its weight doubtfully.

The family looked bewildered. Jorge was mournful. "I think we do it—but you do not need to help," and Amy realized that he was thinking of the contractor's fees, as well as his insurance.

"And there has to be time for me to move in from around the corner," said Amy, "and then Charlotte will have to stay in the house when I'm away, to feed Olivia the cat." (Charlotte was Will's younger sister). "So it has to be ready sooner—five weeks, maybe?"

"Maybe so," said Jorge, and Amy handed him the crowbar reluctantly. Olivia the cat, who had followed Amy from their present home, came and rubbed against Amy's jeans. "There's nothing to eat here, darling," Amy said. The part-Siamese was no longer young: undeniably, that was arthritis in the right foreleg—and she had become very dependent; she mewed even when Amy shut herself in the bathroom, and wanted to crawl between the blankets at night to make a cat-sandwich of herself. Amy started to carry the cat upstairs to inspect the attic, when the telephone rang. It was Joy, who had left her school library, and was now head of reference at a university in the Pacific Northwest.

"It's you!" said Amy into the phone. "How are things at Tumtulips?"

"I'm ready to leave," came Joy's soprano voice; "my AUL is a sexist bore. Never mind, there are other positions up here—and dear Laura is ready to leave, too. We could all come down and join you, or lure you up here. But I have the latest itinerary for China—have you got it? and a surprise letter."

"I have the itinerary, yes, and a booklet with Chinese language tapes, and I just bought a copy of the *I Ching*."

"Oh Amy, not *that*. My new book on Chinese printing puts it all down. 'Unscientific, superstitious,' they call it, 'a book of divination.'"

"Joy, I tell you, it's quite fascinating. It tells you what to look for in travel, in love, even where to look for lost articles, in the southwest or in the northeast…"

"I know, I looked into it once. 'The wise man crosses the stream. On the way he stops to pat an alligator. Prudence is the better part of wisdom.' Amy, *ma chérie*, it'll be utterly *useless* in the People's Republic."

"But it's magical!"

"You're magical yourself, you don't need a book. Meantime," came the firm voice, "we have a *project*."

"To visit China, and see 'more-than-oriental splendor.'"

"More than that. The chair of the Art Department here at Tumtulips has asked me to deliver a letter to a missing person!"

"How can we deliver the letter if he's missing?"

"He's supposed to be in Shanghai. We have an address."

"What? Are we going to be sneaking through the streets of old Shanghai in trench coats? You know, I've never owned one. Maybe I'll look like the woman in the Nagel prints—my hair's the same color, but longer."

"No need to buy a heavy coat, dear. It'll be hot in China. Settle down and listen: here's the story."

Amy sat down on the stair, the only place to sit, while Olivia wandered around hoping for mice. Panels were being ripped away and the carpet rolled outside: there ought to be a mouse *some-where*.

"Way back in the thirties, a young potter, whose father had come to this country from China, came back to the land of his ancestors to learn from a master potter in Shanghai. The young man's name is Wang Shou-yi, and he wanted to learn the secret of making celadon ware. Apparently it's dangerous to produce because the beautiful gray-green color comes from carbon monoxide—I've forgotten the whole explanation."

"I couldn't understand it if you remembered it," said Amy. "I just squeaked through school chemistry at Foxcroft."

"Anyway, he was producing marvelous stuff very soon, and shipping it back to this country, and collectors were snapping it up like mad. But as soon as war was renewed in nineteen thirty-seven, he disappeared; he's been presumed dead for fifty years."

"Then he is. Nobody could live through all that's happened over there. I've been reading Su Kaiming's *Modern China*, and...."

"But now," Joy interrupted, "he has reappeared—and he must be eighty-something. The celadon ware came first: it's been seen in Friendship Stores, and my friend at the Art Department has one of his ceramic sculptures, of a lovely Chinese lady—quite seductive."

"How do they know it's his? Maybe it's like those second-rate Italian paintings that get attributed to *scuola di* somebody famous. Or maybe the old guy really is dead, and his stuff is still being peddled around because some collector had to sell it."

"We have his address, as I told you—and he's been *seen*."

"Like Elvis?"

"He addressed a group of art historians on a tour—just as we'll be. Anyway, we're supposed to seek him out, and arrange to get him out of China and bring him home. So he can teach—at Tumtulips."

"Maybe he doesn't want to come. Joy, if he's got a passport, he could have come home at any time. Maybe he's forgotten his English. And why would Tumtulips want to hire someone that old? He's well past retirement."

"I suppose, because he's that famous. Come on, aren't you up to searching for a mysterious man?"

"Not if he's eighty, darling. Octogenarians are like octopuses; they take a lot of pounding and heating up, and even then they're quite rubbery."

"Not even a famous artist who does discreetly erotic sculptures in celadon ware?"

Amy laughed into the phone. "No, darling, by no means. Actually, he sounds ghastly. Look, I'm more concerned about the paper I'm to present: 'The Human Side of Reference Service.' I expect they could use some reference service over there; our students coming from Asia seem to need a lot of help. Meanwhile, I've got to work on this house before you get here; the place is absolutely *sick* with termites."

(FROM AMY'S DIARY: The plane is somewhere over the North Pacific Ocean. I can only pray, though I don't do much of that, that it doesn't get tired and decide to fold its wings and rest. I'm deep into Blunden's *Cultural Atlas of China*—all about Chinese inventions and why they stopped—it's a good thing to have something big to read on this long, long, tiring trip.

(From Joy's journal: Dear Amy is certainly a librarian; she has brought along a whole library, not just paperbacks, but entire albums. She is copying Chinese ideograms into her journal. If they lose her checked luggage she'll have virtually no clothes at all to wear—and she loves having lovely things and showing them off. I'm glad I'm small, so I can just curl up on these dinky little seats and try to get some sleep.)

AMY WOKE FIRST in the vast new hotel in Beijing. Joy, who with her lighter body weight needed lots of sleep, was a golden-crowned ball in the other bed. Amy lay back on the pillows and thought: This is China. The unbelievable had happened: the inaccessible country had opened, and opened to her and her dear friend.

A plinking sound was heard outside. Persistent, it forbade sleep; Amy glanced at her watch: it was time to get up and be ready for the first library visit of their tour. Were those voices, too?

Amy, in silk trimmed with Alençon lace, rose and parted the curtains slightly. A young worker, building the hotel garden, raised a friendly hand and greeted Amy with a warm smile. Amy pulled the curtains tight.

"Joy," she said softly, "are you awake? There's a man out there—I'll hold these curtains closed." Joy opened her blue eyes, thrust out a white hand with a gold watch on the wrist, rolled out of bed and scurried to the bathroom.

"Joy, we must both hurry. The bus leaves at eight-thirty!"

WHEN ALL THE LIBRARIANS were in the bus, Ralph Lamb, a stout gentleman with snow-white hair, counted heads, and then introduced their guide, who stood beside him. Ralph said, "I can't pronounce his name in Chinese, but he says you can call him Jack."

The guide was young: a tall rangy North Chinese with high cheekbones and an angular grin; Amy liked him at once. "For those of you who want to learn Chinese," he added, "my name is Zhang Mian-min."

Amy's phrase books suggested that many Chinese names mean something, and she liked her men to be tall. "What does your name mean?" she asked him, in the moment's silence.

"Zhang Mian-min, that means: commander, encourager of the people."

"I must get his autograph for my journal," said Amy to Joy, "in both pinyin and English. We won't call him Jack, will we?"

"Me too, and never. Let's encourage him to find us some jade; I have lots of commissions for it." The bus swung out of the hotel parking lot and moved through long alleys of cottonwoods. All Beijing rolled past them, going to work on bicycles.

"I've been reading about jade," said Amy. "It comes in white, or amber, as well as green. And it has meanings: the jade stem is something exclusively male, and the jade mountain is the breast, and…"

"And when you see a piece of jade, and look at the price, suddenly the abstruse meaning of the thing dawns on you," said Joy.

"Take my advice, and stay away from jade stems. And look; here comes the National Library."

(From Amy's diary: The word for jade is *jü,* pronounced with a sudden downward tone. We sit in reception rooms, drink tea in tall glasses, and are told how many books they have here, which I immediately forget—it's Joy's turn to take notes anyhow. Everybody is very pleasant, but it's all very formal. The American delegation is almost entirely women; there are no flirtable men on this trip.)

In the foreign languages reading room, Joy found the 1987 *Best of Library Literature.* "We must get them to subscribe to *Alternative Library Literature.*"

"Too far left-deviationist" (Amy's deprecating nod).

"Decadent bourgeois influences!" (Joy's raised gold eyebrows).

"Irrelevant careerist concerns" (chin lifted scornfully).

"Uncultured humor!" (mouth downward).

"To be condemned to the flames…" (sternly).

"And its editors to a lifetime of labor on the Great Wall." (Decidedly). *(Exeunt).*

IN THE AFTERNOON the bus sped out of the city to the Great Wall.

(From Joy's journal: We are in the city on the way to the Great Wall. Beijing is a sidewalk city; people play billiards on wide dirt sidewalks, a carpenter finishes a bookcase, someone repairs a bicycle. It's hot out there. Amy is studying Eberhard's *Dictionary of Chinese Symbols,* and leaning over the seat in front of her to seek interpretations from the guide.)

(From Amy's diary: The countryside is gold—grain, cottonwoods, big stone buildings. The mountains remind me of California! Oaks in the valleys, and brown hillsides, and what looks like chaparral. And there's the Wall! It snakes across the hills just the way it does in the pictures.)

Yellow banners fluttered from the ramparts above the parking lot. Up and down its steps army men with their families, college students, Taiwanese getting their pictures taken, moved in happy crowds.

"Everybody likes it here," said Amy, in step with Zhang. "I thought this was remembered as a place of suffering."

"It was, but that was back in imperial times."

Amy looked north at the old frontier country: beyond a watchtower the land dipped away to a bright desert valley. Mountains were a blue shadow-line on the far northern horizon. "So now is there more freedom in China?"

"Perhaps. Not much; in some ways."

Amy thought: he's being cautious, there are all these people around. "Here, you two," said Joy, "back up against that parapet. I want to take your picture."

Having your picture taken with someone new is important, Amy told herself. Her light blue shirtwaist dress swished behind Zhang's legs and the west wind made her hair a black banner behind his head. They were not touching: not quite. Amy was humming, "Getting to know you."

Then it was time for Amy to bend over the camera, while Joy and Zhang stood together, and then for him to photograph the two distinguished foreign ladies. "Mian-min," said Amy, passing him between "takes." "Is that how you pronounce it?"

He pronounced it, and she repeated it until she got the right intonation. Then both ladies held out their diaries, to have it written in hanzu and pinyin romanization, and Amy peeked over his shoulder as he did it—she did want to learn how to write Chinese. (Also, he had a nice clean white shirt on).

"We need your advice," said Joy, when she caught her breath at the top of the Wall. They were inside a watchtower; further progress was barred by a locked gate. Through slits in the wall, they had an archer's view of the barbarous distant mountains. "Two things. One, we've both been commissioned to find jade. Should we start here in Beijing, at the Friendship Store?"

"It is very expensive at the Friendship Store. The best place to buy jade is not here. The best place to buy jade is in Wuhan." He looked from one lady to the other.

"Thank you, that does for one," said Joy, "and now—problem number two. We have to find somebody in Shanghai. We have a personal letter for a Chinese-American scholar. He has lived a long time in China, and we have to bring him home to the States. We have his address—can you guide us to him? His name is Wang Shou-yi. Perhaps you have heard of him."

Amy said, "Apparently he's quite famous—a maker of celadon ware."

Zhang was silent: looked out at the desert. "There are many people of that name in China."

"Our university president has invited him to come, and we have an invitation to bring him personally—he didn't reply to the first one. We will need a guide." Joy's voice was high and clear, above the crowds milling in and out of the tower.

Amy reminded him, "We don't know anything about finding our way in Chinese cities."

"There may not be time," said Zhang. And, after a pause, "In Shanghai the signs are in Chinese and English. You will find your way."

Amy and Joy glanced at each other. Zhang added, "Perhaps someone could take the letter for you."

"But we want to see him personally," said Joy, "to make sure he understands."

Zhang suddenly glanced at his watch, and gave what Amy thought was a carefully staged gasp. "We must hurry! The bus is leaving soon. Come, I will lead the way." But Amy needed the support of his shoulder on the steep steps; and sometimes even Joy, with her lower center of gravity, needed it too.

(From Joy's journal: This afternoon through the Forbidden City, much of it grass-grown, pigeons strutting in the parts still being repaired: not all of it is like that "Last Emperor" film. One room is entirely furnished with European clocks, with a great throne in the middle. Amy is taking pictures of the wooden carvings under the eaves, of bronze cranes, brass lions, the whole works, and I—or the guide, or even someone else in the party— have to be in every one. She's such a people person!)

BACK AT THE HOTEL, Amy spread out the huge map of the People's Republic of China she had bought at the Friendship Store, along with two pocket dictionaries. "If Beijing means northern capital, and Nanjing means southern capital," Amy said, her raven hair falling over one cheek as she knelt at the edge of the map, "then I can learn words and build up a vocabulary. Everything has a meaning in this country."

"Learning geographical names won't help you with our guide," said Joy, who was propped up on pillows on her bed, writing a postcard to her lover Laura. "They aren't *real* conversation—the kind *you* need to know. For example: what's the Chinese word for *flirt?*"

Amy consulted Ramond Lau's dictionary. "It isn't in here. Probably something they don't feel like encouraging."

"Well, *you* don't need any encouragement; you were very obvious."

"Joy, I barely touched him."

"You nudged him on the Wall, and coming down, you clutched him the way a drowning man clutches a spar. You've implicated him; now he'll be executed in some barbarous oriental fashion."

"I shall save him by rolling him up," said Amy, "like the Old Person of Pinner, and putting him in my handbag." She sat up. "Joy, do you think we could bring him home? He'd make a good librarian—he knows so much—and he's so nice."

"We'll be lucky if we bring Wang Shou-yi home—he's the one we're supposed to fetch, remember? So get back to your Chinese *characters*—please! and let me return to my postcard."

Amy knelt over her map, and her little books. A half-hour passed. "I've got the names of at least some of these provinces; the Eastern Mountains, the Western Mountains, the Cloudy South, and the Black Dragon River. And the names of the last six dynasties are the Vast, the Summer, the Gold, the Chief, the Bright, and the Pure."

"We're none of us pure," said Joy, writing, without looking up.

"*Hu* is lake, *jiang* is river, *shan* is mountain. Three up-and-down strokes on a level one."

"You've learned a lot," said Joy, swinging her legs off the bed, standing up and surveying her friend's map and books. "Seriously, Amy, how are we going to find this man, without a guide, and bring him back to Tumtulips? We'll incur suspicions of espionage. We'll have to detach your M-n-M..."

"That's not his name!" Amy sat cross-legged, and laughing, brushed the long black hair from her sweating brow. "Now I'm hot from crawling all over the floor."

"I wouldn't be surprised if Wang Shou-yi had moved, or had been liquidated," said Joy. "Who can tell?"

"Easy, as I told you! The *I Ching!*" Amy scrambled, found her purse, with the three silver dollars she had paid a lot for in the States. "Heads are *yin*, tails are *yang*." Amy flipped the coins over, kept a tally on the hotel stationery, and (with Joy, arms akimbo, watching) came up with the answer: "Number thirty-one: everything will come out all right. Love: you already have his affection. Definite chance of success."

"Projection," Joy said scornfully. "Self-deception. Disappointment inevitable. Return to the Pacific Coast of the United States with a distinct feeling of humiliation and a resolve never more to rely on Oriental oracles. Amy, come on!"

"If you're waiting for someone...he will come, bringing smiles and good times. See, I've already made Zhang smile! Now, what's the next: if you're looking for someone...This person is already tied up in some sort of sexual complication...Oh-oh!"

"Then it is your *métier* to untie him. Remember your school librarian days? How many you so graciously untied?"

"Joy, let's not speak of that. You know I'm a serious Ph.D. candidate." Amy closed the book on her lap.

"Your greatest challenge is this Wang person. We are commanded by the president of Tumtulips. Consult your book, or indeed your library, darling Amy, and devise a plan."

AT XI'AN, an immense wall warded the old city, with its wooden balconies and swallow-haunted temples, from the new, with its factories and smoky horizons. Joy declined to join the others; she had an upset stomach, soon as she woke up. "I'll just curl up with some hot tea, Amy," she said, as Amy hovered tenderly. "You go out and beguile M-n-M, while I get some rest."

On the city wall at sundown, Amy found herself inside a guardhouse turned into a tourist shop; Zhang, ahead of the group, followed her: "These are the textiles of this province," he said.

"You know this art well?"

"Shaanxi Province: this is my home."

Amy bought a textile hanging, embroidered with dancers, so as not to seem too proud to buy. "Let's go out on the wall," she said, trying to think of where at home she would put it. Light blue it was, the figures were gold and red.

Zhang followed Amy out on the wall. "Four chariots could drive on this wall," he told her, and above them, the swallows wheeled; below the sunset smoked to the ground. Amy imagined the rumble of the chariots, and quadruple hoofbeats on the pavement.

"Walls—every city seems to have one. What's the Chinese for wall?"

"*Qiang*. In older times, many walls in China. Kingdoms and warlords built walls against each other."

"I should like to follow the Long Wall to where it comes to an end;" she looked at him curiously—"where is that? In the desert?"

"It ends at a place called Yangguan. It is a lost city. There is a buried army out there. The soldiers were caught in a sandstorm. If you go out at night, when you are there, you can hear drums and bugles under the sand." Amy listened for the sound.

"Walls keep good people in as well as keeping bad people out," she said at last.

"Warlords and emperors like walls. Thousands of Chinese died building the Long Wall—maybe some died building this one. Now China is opening, and some of us have a chance to get beyond the walls."

The swallows were circling the tower, nesting in the eaves, their cries faint above the city's traffic. Zhang was urgent: "People are poor here in China. We students live very close together. And every Friday there is political education. No regular classes." He put his hand on his heart. "We have to say what the Party political officers want us to say. Not things in our hearts."

Amy looked up at him: she was receiving a message, something to take home, more important than statistics about libraries, more precious than jade. "It's very hard, isn't it?" she said, to encourage him to go on, and nearly took his hand—dropped it when she remembered the Chinese prohibition of touching.

"We want to be free to speak out," he told her. "Many people are not contented. There is much corruption. People watch us everywhere," he dropped his voice. "Here on the city wall it is better. Only foreigners come here, to buy things in the shop."

"I hope you can speak out, soon," said Amy, feeling uncommonly brave, a young librarian from America defending intellectual freedom in China. Her black hair floated in the sudden wind that sprang up as the sun settled down—a decadent banner on the walls of antique Xi'an. She watched him anxiously, drew near to him instinctively: "Zhang," she said, as if he were one of her students, a lover, "when you do speak out, you must be careful. Please be careful!"

"I am strong," he said, and Amy thought he spoke harshly. Had she overstepped a small boundary? Perhaps the message was that women are not to be too anxious about men, here; it betrays a want of confidence in the male. She stepped back, to repair the damage. "You *will* win," she said, "I believe it!"

"Yes, but it will take a long time," Zhang answered. "But we must do it for ourselves. No one else can speak for us." The sunlight shrank away from behind the smog. "The bus will be going now. It must not leave without the guide," he said smiling, "and not without Mrs. Rose."

BACK AT THE HOTEL, Amy found Joy dispirited, listless; an open book was face down on the blankets. "Joy, darling! You're so pale! I should have stayed at home. Here: let me stick this thermometer in your mouth. Have you been suffering? You look so dehydrated."

"I've been drinking tea," said Joy, weakly; "I'd appreciate it if you'd get some more. I've used up all the hot water in the carafe, and soft drinks from the mini-bar don't do me any good at all. And we're not to use the tap water. Tea, please, *pour l'amour de Dieu!*"

Amy picked up the receiver, dialled the number for room service, gave the message. "What's this note by the phone?"

Joy took the thermometer out of her mouth long enough to answer: "It's for you—for both of us." Thermometer in again; then out. "And two letters for you—the bellboy brought them up. Very helpful of him." Thermometer in again.

"Who would be calling us?" But Joy only hummed the "padlock music" from Mozart's *Magic Flute*, while Amy read the letters. One was from Will; he had given it plenty of time to arrive, marking it "hold for arrival": it was all about his music studies— he made no mention of his private life. Was this to reassure Amy, whose lover he had been, or to give her nothing to guess at? The other was from his sister Charlotte, who was staying in Amy's house, while it was being repaired. "The Ramirez family hasn't been seen for a week," cried Amy, "and Olivia misses me dreadfully! But I can't been in China and Berkeley at the same time! And Will tells me nothing about his social life—although the dear man does, at least, remember me."

"Hmmm?"

"Oh, poor Joy, I forgot about you! Here," and she took the thermometer out. "One degree of fever; you stay in bed until you've had a day without."

"That's what Laura would say, except she isn't on a tour of China. Amy, Amy, I don't want to be left behind in a Chinese hospital! I don't *want* moxibustion!"

"I don't know what that is; it sounds like some kind of bad investment. Look, take these aspirins, and if you aren't better tomorrow, well, thank heaven Doctor Crane is with us. Now, let me prop you up, before the tea comes—what was this phone call?"

"Well! The phone rang, and it was the people at the desk, and then a little tiny voice said, 'Joy Degla?' and I said, 'This is Joy de Grasse,' and the little voice said, 'Amy lo?' and I said, 'Amy Rose is not in; she will be back this evening. I am Joy de Grasse; who is this?' Then Little Voice said 'I am Jiang'— sorry, Amy, I can't remember the other part of the name, I'd have to see it written out—'and Wang Shou-yi will meet you at your hotel in Shanghai.' And I said 'when?' and Little Voice said, 'I not sure; I leave message when you come.' And I couldn't get anything more out of Teensy Speech, so I said goodbye—she wouldn't give me her number in Shanghai or didn't understand—or maybe they don't have a telephone—so I hung up."

"How frustrating! Joy, I think the mysterious East is overdoing the mysterious bit, don't you? And how did she get our number here? She sounds not an instant over eighteen."

"We sent the old guy our itinerary, remember? And probably she is his granddaughter. At all events that proves he's alive, and that he got the letters from Tumtulips; we should have no trouble finding him and persuading him to return."

Amy, for once, was the skeptical one. "That only proves that she got them —this Jiang person; and getting him out might be risky in this country—like fishing a pearl out of a giant clam." There was a knock at the door, and Amy rose to admit a lad with a carafe of hot water, and a small teapot. Some tea was already in the pot: good hot tea, with leaves swirling in it in a long brown dance.

"At all events, the old man isn't entirely mythical," said Joy, swinging her legs out of bed and gathering her robe about her, to join Amy at the table. "Unless the address is impossible to find, we can at least meet him."

"You belong back in bed," said Amy.

"It'll spill. Tea, please, *pour l'amour de Deng.*"

SHANGHAI. THE CONFERENCE ROOM of East China Normal University Library was filling up rapidly. The first wing of the monsoon had spread its northern tip over Shanghai, and Amy and Joy had experienced the relief of a temperature drop of fifteen degrees Celsius on arrival at the seaport. Everyone was shucking off overcoats as they filed into the room; there were chairs, a long table, and a view of a corner of the city's skyline. The Americans wore bright colors; the Chinese wore quiet ones. Amy wore a red dress with a white rose embroidered on the breast pocket; her hair swung free in a ponytail. Over there, Amy spotted a man in a typical green army shirt, but without tabs. The absence of tabs gave her an idea. She nudged Joy: "Watch this."

She caught the man's eye. "Amy Rose," said Amy Rose, bowing every so lightly.

"Long Quansheng." (No bow).

Everyone sat down. The head librarian spoke, and the interpreter turned his bell-like tones into English. ("See that man I spoke to?" Joy looked in his direction. "I think he's the political officer.")

Mr. Lamb gave the order of the speakers. Mrs. Strong talked about circulation systems, while bottles of warmish lemon pop were brought around by boys in white shirts. Each sentence in English was followed by the translator's Chinese. Amy listened to only part of the English; she was more interested in the sounds of Chinese: rustled papers, bird-talk, bells of silver or bronze.

Susan described cataloging for an art library, and then came Comrade Long's address. It consisted entirely of statistics of China's book trade: production, circulation, export. Amy noticed that the figures were all quite large, and given without sources, and without qualification in time, space, or circumstance. She barely kept herself awake, but at the end she roused herself to nudge Joy:

("That does it. Now I *know* he's the political officer.")

("Doucement!") from Joy's rose lips.

"…and our next speaker, AMY ROSE!"

Amy had cast the three silver coins and consulted the *I Ching* that morning: Number 51: careful conduct—step by step—sudden fame or fortune, trust of many. That was enough, but right now she was less interested in prediction than in the fact that at Mills she had learned how to project her voice to the back of an auditorium, to speak in public without shyness or strain. Anyway, there was not time to think any more about oratorical style, here was the mike, she was at the edge of the waterfall, and down she went!

"My subject is 'The Human Side of Reference Service,' "

began Amy, standing very straight in her red dress. She paused to
let the translator, a pretty girl with a black pigtail, make lovely bell
and rustling sounds out of her English words. "I am not talking so
much about CD-ROMs, or any kind of automated service"
(pause), "as about the persistent parts of reference service—the
human contacts." (Pause; I hope this doesn't disappoint them;
they do say they want to modernize.)

"The beginning of the reference interview is the smile," Amy
continued, smiling. (Pause. I'm proud of my smile—I've an oval
face, so I don't look witchetty, even with long black hair). "The
reader should be made comfortable, and the librarian should be
like a gracious hostess, willing to help the reader" (pause: patron
would never do in the People's Republic, and user suggests drugs)
"with his or her problems." (Pause. Good idea to remind them
that women read too; there don't seem to be any male directors
here). "Markham has shown that self-disclosure on the part of
librarians made readers more comfortable in the reference interview, but it had no effect on whether their questions were understood." (Pause: of course there are many things you don't disclose
on the reference desk—and certainly not in China). "McMurdo
has shown that a librarian who does not appear busy will be
approached" (pause: for what purpose?) "between seventy percent
and eighty percent more often than a librarian who does appear
busy" (pause; aren't we all of us busy?). "However, the sex of the
inquirer and the nature of the inquiries, in terms of their complex-
ities" (sex? complexity? what am I saying?) "are seen to be inde-
pendent of the librarian's busyness." (Pause: they'll translate that
as business, but that can't be helped. Amy looked over the vast
Chinese audience; they were all drinking tea or lemon pop; none
of them seemed put out). She went on to describe other studies,
most of which she had only skimmed; listening to the bells and
whispers of Chinese.

"Devlin," continued Amy, "has demonstrated the effectiveness of a technique she calls 'neutral questioning,' " (pause), "in
which the reader is in control of the direction that the inquiry
takes." (They won't like that!) "And Woodrow has conducted suc-

cessful workshops, to teach this skill." (We'll be all day at this [Amy realized] but if I cut, the poor translator will get lost. She looked to her right, and saw that her double-spaced typing had been interlined with delicate penciled characters, traceries by some slender hand working [no doubt] late at night: surely, a woman's hand. She felt a sisterly compassion for the writer, whoever she might be).

"There are two requirements for good reference service," Amy continued. "The first is that the librarians actually know something." (Pause). "It will not be good reference service if," (pause), "when the student asks about the history of China, the librarian cannot remember which came first, the Song Dynasty or the Tang Dynasty." Pause. Amy suddenly realized that she herself couldn't remember which came first: she brushed a lock of hair back from her hot forehead, hoped no one would come up and check up on her afterwards, and went on: "The second necessity for good reference service," (pause), "is the right to ask questions, and to get correct answers." (Pause: here I go!) "Varga has described the Freedom of Information Act, which gives United States citizens the right of access to governmental files." (Pause. They've never heard of anything like that!) "Access to sources is generally described as the 'freedom to read,' and there is a foundation by that name attached to the American Library Association." (Pause: she caught a glimpse of Joy, sitting three rows back in a pink dress, sipping lemon pop through a straw and looking wondrous round-eyed). "This freedom to read is not just the freedom to read romances; it's the freedom to question authority" (pause: did I hear a murmur?) "to criticize sources" (they'll think I mean their blessed Party, and perhaps altogether, dear reader, they're right) "and to take control of what a book by an American women's collective" (maybe they'll like that) "calls *Our Bodies, Our Selves.*" Amy reflected that she had put her own copy into the hands of her friend Will's younger sister, Charlotte, aged twenty. Perhaps the dear girl was reading it now, with Olivia the cat securely perched on her lap).

"And finally we come to the last requirement of good reference service," here Amy paused, "the one we started with." (This ought to go down as smoothly as a rum eggnog). "The smile. *Weixiao.*" (Was that intonation right?) "The smile, as we say in America, breaks the ice. It creates trust; and it makes the reader unafraid to approach the librarian. And let us not forget, the reader must be in charge of the situation from the start, whoever he or she must be: professor, student, worker." (At last! That's over). "Thank you!" And with her most gracious smile, Amy Rose left the platform. (Applause: which she had hoped would be "stormy and prolonged," was only applause). The chair of the meeting called, in Chinese and English, for a tea-break.

Joy hurried up to her through the slowly filling crowds. "Amy, it was wonderful. I think you made the Party man nervous—he was frowning—but I'm glad you put it all in."

"We will see—if I'm detained at the border—" Mrs. Strong, a tall silver-haired lady was behind her, saying in a low voice: "You gave them a taste of freedom, now maybe they'll want more."

"May I have a copy of your paper, please?" said a stout Chinese lad, and while Amy found an extra one in her tote bag, a Chinese lady introduced herself as a reporter for *Beijing Review,* and might she have a copy too? Amy fished out another one. "I'd be delighted!" she said, and reflected, as the reporter thanked her, that her paper would doubtless end up in the drawer for documents by the politically unreliable. She looked around for Long, the political officer (identified on the mimeographed list of speakers, though only by name), but couldn't find him.

Amy stood in line for a glass of tea, and then drifted over to the window, to view the rainy skyline. Behind her a small Chinese lady came up and waited till she had Amy's attention.

"Thank you for your presentation," she said quietly. "It went to the heart of our concerns here in China. You see, people come here and tell us about computers. But we already know about computers. We have other concerns."

Amy was astonished. She had expected incomprehension, even hostility; but this welcome made her day. "Do you think it was well received?" she asked at last.

"No doubt. There are many people who liked it, but they will not say so. It will be widely discussed."

"Thank you!" said Amy, still too astounded to say more, when she noticed that the Chinese scholar suddenly seemed confused, smiled briefly and hurried away. Amy turned around, and sure enough, Long in his green shirt was watching them both.

Amy moved away quickly, looking for Joy. When she found her, she hugged her for simply existing. "I'm so glad you're here! Joy, let's get out of here, as soon as we can. Listen, the political creature was watching us when a Chinese lady said she liked my speech. We're caught up in something—first your friend Wang and his friend on the phone, and now this. Is Zhang going to guide us to Wang—how funny that sounds!—or will we have to do it ourselves?"

"I spoke to your M-n-M this morning. He said he must stay with the tour—reasonable enough, I suppose, but I think he'd have enjoyed showing us around old Shanghai. Especially you."

"Perhaps, but now we'll have to trench-coat it alone. And we don't really know, other than by an address, where he lives nor how to get there!"

THEY FOUND OUT SOON ENOUGH when they came back to their huge whale of a hotel, an acre of lobby with vast vases, and Chinese making deals with American businessmen over drinks and snacks. They noticed the concierge pointing them out to someone, and here came a small young woman in the Chinese classic style of beauty: oval face, cherry mouth, arched eyebrows, full dark eyes, well-proportioned figure. She was dressed in simple light blue: high collar, long skirts; neither old-fashioned nor Maoist, her light figure so costumed had the perfection of simplicity. She would certainly inspire "willow thoughts" in any young Chinese man, thought Amy, as the lady extended a hand and introduced herself: "Jiang Jing-cai. Very good to meet you."

She certainly does have a teeny voice, and Amy thought her own contralto growly by comparison. "I'm Amy Rose."

"And I'm Joy de Grasse," said Joy, also taking her hand. "I'm the one who was sent to find Wang Shou-yi. We came together, that's why our names were on the letter."

"Ah, I thought you were the younger sister. I was confused!" (embarrassed giggle).

"No, we're just friends. You see, I was sent from my university in the state of Washington—and here, let's sit down." They found a small round cocktail table and Joy explained the whole story.

Jiang Jing-cai waited patiently, hands on her lap, sitting bolt upright (to show, thought Amy, socialist discipline and modesty), until Joy had finished with: "And so that's our story, and why we wanted to see Mr. Wang. Now, have you news? and by the way, are you his granddaughter, or some other relation?"

Given the limits of the girl's English—and indeed, she looked to be about nineteen—Amy wondered how much of Joy's speech she had understood. "Oh, no," came the answer. "I am not his granddaughter. I am his *friend*."

Jiang said this with such a special emphasis—little smile, slight tilt of the head, faint blush—that Amy, who had begun to wonder if anything in China was not connected to either politics (approved) or sex (concealed because disapproved), was unsure which explanation to select for this gesture. Fortunately, Jiang supplied the hint. "What we call in China *ai-rén*. That is special friend."

Amy had come across this word in Quo's *Concise Chinese-English Dictionary Romanized:* trust her to find the word for lover on page two. But then why had Jiang come, and not brought Wang? And could this girl not yet twenty really be the companion of a man in his eighties?

Jiang had her own explanation to give. "You see, I am his student. His very *special* student. I have learned everything he had to teach, almost, nearly." Even for Amy, the lessons were hard to imagine. "How to make beautiful celadon ware. Now Mr. Wang is old. He is so old, he may not be able to come to America."

"But he was born there," protested Joy.

Jiang Jing-cai shook her head sadly, almost as if she were in a play: Amy noticed her gestures were stylized, her little voice the voice of one reciting a part.

"No. It is not likely he will come. He has forgotten so much. But—" here she brightened up again, "here am I! And because I have learned all the secrets of celadon ware, I come and study with you." She smiled brightly, as a teacher does at her students, expecting acceptance and understanding on their faces. When she found none—only open-mouthed amazement from the Americans—she did not hesitate, but opened a tiny handbag and drew from it a folded paper, handing it to Amy. "This is my resumé."

Amy opened up the paper and found a neatly-typed resumé: her birth, parentage, education; a school of art in Beijing, a technical school in Shanghai: she was "able to do ceramics in both the art and technical applications fields." Wang Shou-yi's name was indeed mentioned as the latest of her private teachers for postgraduate work. Amy handed the paper to Joy, thinking: this young lady is nobody's fool.

"You see, you two sponsor me in America, I could come to work in the place of *xiānshéng* Wang. I could teach either in an art school or in a ceramics laboratory." She was smiling most charmingly.

"I'm the one who works at Tumtulips," said Joy, "but I've never sponsored anyone. I'm just carrying a message: I was instructed to find Mister Wang."

"I do not know if *xiānshéng* Wang comes." Again the slow shake of the head.

"But surely we could see him. We have his address; can you take us there?"

Doubtful face again. "I think he moves."

An idea occurred to Amy. "Do you know if anybody here in China told him we were coming?"

"You are here!"

Impasse. Joy rephrased the question: "Did any high official in China tell him not to see us?" It was a bold stroke, but there seemed little else to do.

"I do not know" (spoken mournfully; same slow shake of the head). Then, brightening up, before the foreign ladies could probe further: "You see, if he come, I come too. I am his special friend. And if he cannot come, then I come in his stead, and you be my sponsor."

"This is rather difficult," said Joy. "The position is not an open one, teaching art at Tumtulips. Nor is there more than one position. Nor am I the one doing the hiring. The offer comes from the Art Department: they sent a letter some time ago, and he hasn't responded: I am merely the bearer of a personal invitation." Jiang looked very grave at this.

Amy had been studying the business card attached to the resumé, and had been discreetly looking up the meanings of Jiang's name in Quo's pocket dictionary. "Jing-cai" evidently meant "skillful accomplishment," and Amy, who had a number of these herself, realized, for the first time in her life, that she was being outmaneuvered. It was time to rescue the dialogue. "Of course, you could come with him. But then, he would have to come."

She got a thoughtful smile for that, then finally the "commander of skillful accomplishment" answered, "But *lāo* Wang is over eighty. I think he forgets English. Your Art Department wants to learn celadon ware, not?"

"The University would have to negotiate that," said Joy, taking the resumé gently from Amy, and looking at its recital of "skillful accomplishments." "You certainly are talented." Here the cherry mouth really smiled for the first time, and Amy realized that they would have to pretend to promise something in order to get any help at all. "We could telephone them, couldn't we, Joy?" Come on, Joy, catch my drift. "Then they could telephone you, if they wished---your number is right here on the card." Of course, it was important that they not make promises for Tumtulips University.

"If they wish?"

"We can report the situation."

Thoughtful pause. "We will consider this very carefully."

It was the first time Jiang had said "we," and Amy, who had

never been in the Foreign Service, realized that she was not simply dealing with a reluctant guide, but negotiating in order to avoid hostilities. "In the meanwhile, we have his address, could you guide us there?"

"It is hard to find. This Art Department person, would he come out to talk to us, to me?"

Obviously we are low-level emissaries, unworthy to meet the Lord of the Forbidden Interior, thought Amy. "Possibly."

Joy, less patient of the two, seized the initiative. "We will not be going on a tour of the harbor with the other librarians. We will try to telephone Tumtulips University but we cannot be sure to do so. In any case, will you please meet us here tomorrow? And take us to meet Mr. Wang? At two, please." Joy stood up, taking her purse with her, and Amy followed suit. "Fourteen hundred hours. Here, let me give you my card." She found it quickly, and handed it to the astonished Jiang, who also stood up. "We will expect you," here both the Americans bowed slightly, and the Chinese lady did so with a little smile, "here at two tomorrow. It was so pleasant meeting you!" And Joy stepped quickly away, so rapidly that Amy had to take long steps just to catch up with her.

"The little minx!" cried Joy, and her face was pink with irritation. "She'd have kept us there all day, until she had got us to get her a job in America. For all I know, Wang may not even be alive."

"I think he is," said Amy, as they made their way across the marble floor of the hotel, past the gift shop full of enormous screens and jade pagodas so huge, that they could only fit in another hotel lobby as big as this one. "And I think she understands more than we realize. Did you hear her gasp when you said 'personal invitation'?"

"Yes," said Joy. They had reached the elevator doors. "I noticed that."

"She thinks you want to be Wang's 'special friend'."

"At this point, I wish he'd drop dead," said Joy. "Really, I'm enjoying this trip, but I wish I'd never heard of Wang Shou-yi."

They were back in the hotel room. The afternoon sun was

breaking through the clouds. Amy pulled the blinds. "It's half an hour to dinner. Let's have a drink from the mini-bar."

Joy shed her shoes. "Very little for me," she said, "because I'm very little, like that very little bitch with the very little voice. Didn't your *I Ching* say that the lost person would be sexually involved with someone?"

Amy found her favorite bookmark at just the right place. "Yes, but it says, 'Can be found soon.' "

"That's the part I don't trust," said Joy, pillowed on her bed. "If Miss Jangley-jingle doesn't turn up, we can always hire a taxi."

"Or walk, if you're feeling up to it and the weather is okay. I always buy maps from hotel bookstores, and I made sure to buy one yesterday."

TWO O'CLOCK found Amy and Joy waiting in the hotel lobby, an umbrella for them both, a map of Shanghai just in case, in Joy's white hand. "We'll give her a half an hour," Amy suggested, "and then if she doesn't turn up, we can leave. Are you up to walking? Is the address on the map?"

"Twenty minutes," said Joy crisply, "and yes, I'd rather walk, and with you, not her. The concierge said it's right here, on a tiny cross street, crossing a street with the name of Ju Lu. It should be about ten minutes, if we don't get misled by some would-be helpful person trying to get foreign exchange money out of us. The concierge wanted to get us a taxi or a guide, but I thought, this whole episode is complicated enough as it is."

They waited, quietly, keeping an eye on the lobby clock. No Wang, no Jiang. At twenty minutes after two precisely, the two foreign ladies left the hotel's wide door, and swung out into the city.

The streets of Shanghai were cool and leafy when Amy and Joy set out without any guide save their map. So while Amy held the umbrella high against occasional showers, they passed an enormous park, and an open square, and plunged into a complex of old streets shaded by plane trees. In a little alley they came across Shanghai's goldfish market, and Amy was so delighted by the gold and black fish, and the gadgets to amuse the goldfish with—tiny pagodas and little clams that opened and shut when you pressed a lever, that Joy had to remind her: "We'll run a risk of his escaping, if we don't find Wang now. Remember what she said? 'I think he moves.'"

Amy turned away from Goldfish Alley with reluctance. "I don't know what she meant by that. If she's his 'special friend', doesn't she know whether he's moving or not? Isn't she moving with him?"

"I think that was just a remark to put us off the scent. Probably he doesn't want to come, or more likely she's talked him out of it so she can come instead. Minxish creature!"

Fortunately street signs in this part of Shanghai are marked with *pinyin* English subtitles, and Amy and Joy soon found what they were sure was the right address; like other townhouses in the East, Wang Shou-yi's building was arranged in a U around a courtyard. The apartment numbers were in Chinese, but Amy had learned and written out the characters for "thirty-five," and the two foreign ladies began to mount the stairs at the back of the U, while the children in the courtyard stopped and stared at them. One girl began to follow them, and when Amy knocked on the door, she realized that every head in the building was, or soon would be, watching them out every available window.

There was no answer. "We never even considered what we would do if we found them not at home," said Amy. "We could leave our business cards, but that scarcely seems worth it, having come all this far."

"There's no place to stick them on the door," said Joy, "unless you brought a thumbtack in your handbag. Probably that would violate some old Chinese superstition. Wait: I hear someone coming."

The door opened, and Jiang Jing-cai peeked out. When she saw the two foreign ladies, she gasped, put her hand over her mouth, called out something in Chinese, and fled to the back of the house. Amy and Joy could hear excited babbling somewhere in the cool dusk.

"Why don't we go in?" asked Joy.

"Let them argue it out," said Amy. "He must be here, or somebody; I hear a man's voice."

Presently a very old man came to the door. He was dressed in a faded gray suit, without a tie, and with a big Chinese apron around his middle. He had tufts of white hair above his ears, but otherwise was bald, and stooped badly. His walk was slow, and he smiled with difficulty, as if he had been out of practice for a long time. He opened his door wide; the "minxish one" was nowhere to be seen.

"My name is Wang Shou-yi," he said leaning on his staff, as if reciting an old lesson. "I live at number thirty-five, Gansu Lu. This is my home." Then he stood aside to let them enter: "Please come in. I cannot let you stay long. I have to move to the country. I have been assigned to teach school far away, in the province of Qinghai."

Amy and Joy stepped inside. Amy had expected a wonderful old home, full of teakwood furniture and hanging scrolls and celadon ware. But the room was almost bare of furniture; there were two kitchen chairs with metal frames, a low table, and the only celadon ware was a bowl of flowers on top of the television.

"We have very little," Wang said. "I lost everything in the Cultural Revolution."

"I am Joy de Grasse," said Joy, "and this is my friend Amy Rose. I come from Tumtulips University in the state of Washington. We sent you a letter!" she finished brightly.

"Miss Jiang has gone somewhere," said Wang Shou-yi. "I am very glad to welcome you to my house, but I must get the tea myself." He disappeared into another room, where presently the whistling of a teakettle was heard, and Amy said, "I think I hear her talking."

"I hope she doesn't come out at all," said Joy in a low voice. "This is truly ghastly. He's a Chinese Doctor Manette."

The old man came out again, making several trips with a tray, two cups, a third cup, and presently a teapot, held with difficulty; the other hand he needed for his staff. "Here, let me help you with that," said Amy, who was afraid he would drop the teapot, and then they would all have to *die* of embarrassment.

"No, thank you, I can do it." The foreign ladies sat on the kitchen chairs while their host dragged an old wicker fan chair over to them, step by step, like a snail dragging its shell. He sat down rather suddenly in the chair, and leaned over to pour them tea. "Is this your first visit to China?" he asked, just as if he was a Chinese dignitary entertaining foreign business people.

Joy was the kind of lady who liked to get to the point, and she did so as quickly but as carefully as she could. "Yes, we have never been here before, and we are touring with a group of librarians, as I explained in my letter. You did get a letter from me, didn't you?"

The old man sighed, as if he had received a large invoice, instead of a letter from a young lady. "Yes, I did. It is very unfortunate that the authorities have told me I must move to Qinghai."

"The University where I come from," said Joy, in a clear voice, so that he would not fail to understand, "wants you to come and teach ceramics. Tumtulips University, in the state of Washington, in America."

"I used to live in America once. In fact," and he announced it as if he had just discovered it, "I used to be an American."

"And we want you to come back," Amy put in. She was going to rescue this old geezer, even if she had to carry him out on his back, as Aeneas carried Anchises through the gates of burning Troy. He looked so frail, she could have done it, too, she thought, but he probably would be too feeble to hold on. She would probably have to carry him in her arms, belly-up, the way she carried Olivia. She was just wondering if he could be induced to purr, when Wang Shou-yi, who had evidently been trying to think of an answer, said, "It has been a long time. I am eighty-six, did you know that?"

"We thought you might be advanced in years," said Joy, trying to sound respectful.

"Miss Jiang calls me *lao* Wang. That means old Wang."

"I am the bearer of this personal invitation," said Joy, fishing in her handbag for a letter; she drew out the envelope with the University's return address and seal (a star over three little waves).

"From Doctor Philip Van Horn, president of Tumtulips University." Joy handed it to the old man. "He wants to give you an appointment as teacher of ceramics—indefinitely." Joy said very loudly, as if talking to someone whose English wasn't perfect, "He will pay your airfare."

"I am very old," said old Wang, and Amy thought, 'You are old, Father William,' the young man said, 'and your hair has become very white.' "I do not think the Chinese government would grant me an exit visa."

"No doubt the State Department could negotiate that," said Joy.

"Anyway, you have an American passport," said Amy, sipping tea. "You were born in America!"

Old Wang put a finger to his lips. Amy thought she heard the young lady moving something around in the back of the apartment. "I lost it. It was taken away at the Cultural Revolution. They told me, 'You have lived too long in this country, and you are Chinese. You cannot be a foreigner any longer. We cannot let you be foreign. You are Chinese now.' "

"Why, I never heard of anything so ridiculous in my life!" said Amy, setting down her cup with a clatter. "The Chinese can't take away your nationality unless you give it up."

The old man looked at them, and shrugged his frail shoulders. "This is China," he said.

The two foreign ladies gazed at him, and then at each other, then back at him. "I look Chinese, I speak Chinese, I have lived sixty years in China, *I am Chinese.*"

It made logical sense, in a way, Amy thought, if you accepted the premises. The premises seemed to be that all Chinese were *Chinese,* before they were anything else, and that they all belonged in the same country, namely China, and they all had better follow the same rules. But she remembered what Zhang said about the Wall, and said, "If you really wanted to come, there would be ways to make it possible." She realized that she had no idea what those ways might be, but she had to keep her hopes up.

The old potter looked at her in dismay, but just then Jiang-cai came out from the back of the apartment. She was in a lovely slinky dress with a peach-blossom pattern. "How very nice to meet you again," she said, hands clasped before her, just as if there had not been that embarrassment at the door. "Previous engagement did not let me come to your hotel."

Amy glanced to Joy. If Joy's looks could kill, Miss Peach-blossom would have dropped dead that instant. "I did not have a chance to telephone the University about your coming," said Joy, and Amy knew that she hadn't bothered to. No American university would accept such a deal for a moment. "I have just given Mr. Wang a letter from the president, inviting him to come to America, and now he tells me that he must go to the provinces instead—I forget which one."

"I come to America too," suggested Miss Jiang.

Joy was about to reply, when Wang replied, half-turning toward her, "No! You come with me, to bury me in Qinghai."

The girl start to say something to him in Chinese, and the old man angrily interrupted her. The conversation went on for some minutes in Chinese; evidently this was a topic that had been broached before, and not very successfully for Miss Peach-blossom, who at last fell silent.

"I am very sorry that I will not be able to come to America with you," said Wang at last, "and I cannot accept your president's kind invitation." He handed the letter back to Joy. "But I am under suspicion because I once was an American. That is why we are packing to move to Qinghai."

"What's it like in Qinghai?" asked Amy, desperate to make any conversation.

"It is a high, cold desert," said the old man. "It is the kind of place where you go to learn how to get along with the government. *You* will never go there."

"I don't want to," cried Amy, "and I don't want you to go. Why can't we do something about this? We must get you over the Wall!"

"Nobody gets over the Wall," said Wang. "I will die in Qinghai, far from America. And my friend will bury me there. I am her teacher, she is my student: it is her duty."

This old man is trapped, thought Amy; they've put the trap inside his own head. "Lord, send us a miracle. Somebody's got to do something."

"Miracles don't happen in China," said the old potter. "Nothing happens here without blood, sweat, and tears." He said something in Chinese to Miss Jiang, who turned on her heel and disappeared to the back of the apartment. "You must excuse us; we will have to finish packing." Miss Peach-blossom came back with two little boxes, holding them out stiffly as if they were to be sacrificed. He took them from her, and gave one each to Amy and Joy. "These are for you," he said. "They are all of me that can go back with you to your beautiful America."

The two young women opened the wooden boxes, untying the cloth ribbon and lifting the little brass hinges, and there, resting in straw packing, were two little celadon bottles, curved as nearly as possible like teardrops: one in each box. "I made them when I could get a kiln," explained old Wang. "I do not think there will be a kiln for me in Qinghai."

"Thank you," said Amy. Her eyes were wet. "But can't we help you?" She looked around the bare room, desperately. "Can't we get you out of here?" He rose unsteadily, and looked from one to the other; both foreign ladies stood up too. Miss Peach-blossom, Amy noticed, was standing apart from them, her hands clutched in desperation. It was obvious that she wanted to escape from China, even if he couldn't; and it was also obvious that she realized that she had made a mistake attaching herself to a suspect person. Amy thought: she'll desert him the minute the train starts to leave. She'll find a younger, more politically correct lover.

"Everyone will be desolated at Tumtulips," Joy went on, dropping into her occasional French English. "I will bring them your personal regrets."

"No. I shall not survive Qinghai," said the old man. "I grew up in Oakland, California. Do you know Oakland?" Amy nodded. "I will never see Oakland again."

Amy thought of all the people who want to get out of Oakland. This man wanted to get back to it. "Now you must go," said the old potter. "It is good that you should go. Do not worry about me. I shall not live long. I have done nothing wrong, but they want me to go to Qinghai. Give my regards to your university president."

"Thank you for being here, and being with us," said Amy helplessly, and Joy added, "And for the tea." She turned to Jiang Jing-cai, and bowed slightly. "How pleasant to have met you."

Bowing, the two foreign ladies found themselves outside the door, and nearly pushed a gaggle of girls, who were waiting outside, down the stairs. They made their way carefully down the stairs and out into the courtyard. It had just stopped raining. The sun filled the courtyard and drew a light vapor up from its stones.

"This is simply awful," said Amy, when they were out on the street again. "We bring a personal invitation to a man, and he turns out to be a political prisoner."

"I think something is wrong with your blessed *I Ching*," Joy replied. "Can be found soon'? 'Sexual complication'? Yes—but we can't have him!"

"I must try those coins again."

"Do. And tell them to come up with better luck for Mr. Wang—and for us."

(From Joy's journal: Total failure with Wang Shou-yi—The Chinese have brainwashed him and taken away his passport. His girlfriend, who's about eighteen, wants to come instead, and of course we wouldn't stand for any nonsense. I *don't* feel well, and I *won't* feel well, until I'm on that big plane home.)

WUHAN. *(From Amy's diary:* We're fourteen stories right above this huge river, and right below it is a river steamer, in English marked *Xiling*—I can't figure out what the characters are supposed to mean. People coming in and out, hurrying figures with things wanted on board—sometimes a barge noses down the river, it's all fascinating, this river life:—Joy and I watched it for *hours.)*

Morning, and the river was misty, a dawn pink and gentle rising out of the half-seen bridge, the longest one in China, about a mile downstream. As the foreign ladies watched, *Xiling* gave two toots and swung down the river. Below the hotel gardens, sat a young Chinese, smoking a cigarette.

"Is that Zhang Mian-min?" asked Amy. "I dreamed about him last night. I have a plan in mind for his benefit."

Joy was drying her golden curls with a blow-drier. "I don't doubt that you do. Whether he will see it that way, is an entirely different question."

"Not a romantic scheme, silly, I want to bring him to America—if we can't get old Wang. I want to make Zhang Mian-min a librarian."

"But he never said he wanted to be a librarian, did he?"

"Of course not! I never said he did. Joy, the idea never entered his head. The point is, you have to put ideas into people's heads, that they never would have thought of by themselves. The point of making him a librarian, is to keep him as a *friend,* don't you realize? So I can meet him at conferences, and introduce him to all the people on the Action Council of SRRT, and take him to parties! Joy, come here, look at him down there, isn't that him? He's cute."

Joy peeked through the curtains. "I can't tell. After all, they all smoke. You'll have to break him of that, if you expect to introduce him to Action Council. They're all *non-fumeurs militants.* Anyway, you haven't even got him out of China yet. Maybe he's devoted to the Party. Maybe he can't leave his aged mother."

"You just keep any eye on him, while he sits there, and I shower and dress. If he starts to leave, open the glass door and whistle real loud. I'll be right back."

Shower, breakfast, and Amy emerged from the hotel in a shirtwaist, gray with a pattern of silver leaves. He was still there.

"Good-morning, Zhang Mian-min," she said, with the smile advocated in 'The Human Side of Reference Service.' It had greeted small children for story hour; inveigled older boys and girls; and charmed grumpy supervisors. Why shouldn't it work for a Chinese university student? And it did.

"Good morning, Amy Rose," said Zhang Mian-min, smiling.

"We watched the river steamer loading last night," said Amy, "it was beautiful."

"I saw it leave this morning."

"We saw it leave too, Joy and me." There was a pause. Zhang stubbed out his cigarette. Silently, Amy approved.

"We went to see old Wang Shou-yi in Shanghai," said Amy. "Do you know, he cannot leave China! They took his passport away and they're sending him to Qinghai!"

Zhang looked serious. Amy was thinking: he probably wants to know as little as possible about a person under suspicion. But Amy had to go on: "How can they do that? He was born in California!"

"China is different."

"Anyway, he couldn't come, and his 'special friend' wanted to come to America instead. But he is making her go with him to Qinghai. I do not think she will stay with him. I think she will run away, instead. What do you think?"

"I think you are right. I am sorry she cannot come to America. I am sorry for him, too." Zhang stretched, and looked at her. "I am sorry for one other thing. You do not know, but there was a big demonstration at the East China Normal University in Shanghai the day after we left. It seems that a foreign lady made a speech about freedom of speech in America, and now everyone at the university wants it, too."

Amy gasped, "That was me!"

"Yes," nodded Zhang, "just so."

"They had a riot? On my account?"

"Ten arrests were made."

"Will I—will we be arrested?"

"No. You are only a foreigner, passing through. But you will not come back again."

"No? I want to!"

"The students want you to. They proclaimed you 'Amy Rose, Friend of the Chinese People.' That is a great honor. Only a few foreigners have ever been given that title. But this time it was not given by the government. It was proclaimed by the students of East China Normal University."

"Which means it isn't official."

"But it means something more important. Because it is *not* official."

"Still, I will not come back to China."

"Because the government does not like foreigners whose speeches make students demonstrate."

There goes the whole trip, thought Amy. I've created an international incident. Now I'll never come back to China, Wang Shou-yi will never get out of it, and Zhang Mian-min will never be a librarian and meet the people on Action Council. "It was that political officer," she said at last. "He doesn't like me." A sudden thought struck her; she looked at him earnestly. "Do *you* like me, Zhang?"

He did not look at her. "I am not the political officer." The detachment in his voice was saddening. Then he added: "I am one of the Chinese people. I attend East China Normal University." This was heartening. "And I," he said slowly, turning to her with a shy smile, "am your friend."

Amy was delighted. Hope rebounded like a tennis ball on a trampoline. She never let an opportunity slip, and this one had returned. Time to open her campaign. "Zhang," she said, "what are you doing after college?"

"I am studying engineering," he said, and looked away from her, at the river, already beginning to glare in the morning sun. They were half-facing each other on the bench above it. He turned to her. "I will help build super-computers for China," he said proudly. "Just like your CRAY."

"I'm impressed," said Amy. But if he really wanted to do that, obviously China would need him desperately, and she would never get him to be a librarian. "I know nothing about super-computers. You must have wanted to do this ever since you were very young, surely?"

"My father told me that this was the way to succeed in China," he said, and Amy noticed that he had not quite answered her question. "And in China, they tell you what to study."

"Maybe you could come to America to learn about super-computers." Amy added, "then you could tell librarians about them too."

"The librarians on this tour are…all very beautiful people," said Zhang, smiling; "you are all very fortunate."

"You are fortunate, too, to be able to learn about super-computers," said Amy. "You will rise to the top of your profession in China!" This, with a big smile; although she realized she was hiding her disappointment. He'd be a super-computer expert in China, and she'd never see him again.

Zhang's face, instead, showed dismay as he answered: "I will tell you something. I really wanted to be a librarian! I love old books—I saw so many of them destroyed in the Cultural Revolution, it hurt my heart." He placed a hand on his chest. "What I really want: I want to come to America and be an old books—how you say it?—old books librarian. You librarians are all such good people—and I do not like computers!"

Amy sat open-mouthed. The little speech she had prepared at breakfast, about librarianship and its modest pleasures, had been totally forestalled by this heartbroken confession, and the wind was taken out of her sails. She looked up at his handsome, high-cheeked face; his eyes were wide, and the sunlight from the river showed tears.

"My dear Zhang—Mian-min," she said tenderly, "I never realized…"

"The only way they will send me to America," Zhang went on, "is to send me to study super-computers." His hands were folded in his lap; he had regained his composure. "That's the only way I can come and see you and your friend."

"So you really want to be a librarian," said Amy. "Look, perhaps you could work in a library while learning about super-computers. Libraries could always use another Chinese cataloger, and perhaps" (indeed, her generalization swept far too broadly) "we could find you a library that had rare Chinese books in it" (where?) "Berkeley, Princeton, Harvard—while you continued to do your computer work."

"But I am not yet a librarian. It is very difficult to do work and to study too."

"We could work that out," said Amy, who was accustomed to

making things work out. "I'm sure you could get into the library school at Berkeley. I'd be delighted to recommend you!" She realized suddenly, that she scarcely knew the lad. "You must get the people who are sending you to let you study library science as well as computers."

"The super-computers are for Chinese defense," said Zhang gloomily. "I do not like this 'defense'. I do not like war."

Amy was silent a moment. "We must get you over the Wall," she said finally. "You will have to persuade your teachers that what China needs is librarians to preserve her cultural heritage. You are a leader; you must do it. Remember what I said? When the time comes, you must stand up and speak. Be careful: but speak out. Tell them that you wish to undo the evil effects of the Cultural Revolution by learning how to preserve the old books. We have courses on conservation and preservation. Tell them that you love peace," said Amy, trying to think of a hundred suggestions at once, "and that coming to America is a good way of preserving peace and preserving books. Oh, do come!"

"It is very difficult," said Zhang, smiling. Amy thought: at least I'm making him feel wanted. "You will help me, please?" he continued. "It is much harder than finding good jade."

Amy was delighted with what she hoped was her success. She moved closer to him. "Please give me your card," she said, rummaging in her purse for hers. They exchanged cards. "I know people at Berkeley, at Stanford. You can come stay with me," she said, rashly; "I have this big house in Berkeley that they're fixing up—if they ever get through with it—and you don't mind cats, do you? You're not allergic to cats? *Māo?*"

"*Māo?*" Zhang looked puzzled, but he was smiling at her; they were smiling at each other.

AMY AND JOY were among the librarians who had brought along presents for the national guide, to give when they left China at Canton. Amy had brought along a pocket volume of new American poems, making sure that the book contained a good selection of poems by women. Of course the book was in English, but she assumed that any guide would be able to read English, and she wanted to introduce the Chinese to Emily Dickinson and Diane de Prima. Joy, less inclined to proselytize, had brought a little cloisonné pin in the shape of a dragonfly: a girl could wear it on her collar, a boy could wear it as a tie-clip.

The hotel was pre-war, but a huge addition, with the bookshops and gift stores and offices, was a cool refuge from the tropical heat. The two distinguished foreign ladies cornered Zhang before the other librarians quite found him. They stopped him in the corridor on the way to the lobby where all the luggage was marshalled.

Amy hurried up to him, touched him lightly: "Zhang, we have something for you." She opened her purse, fumbled for the brightly wrapped book. The young man said, "Thank you," and as he unwrapped the gift, Amy searched his face for a sign of disappointment. He looked through the gift carefully, and then said: "I am very grateful for these poems. I am sure they are beautiful. I will learn them all by heart, I promise."

Joy presented the little pin, and he smiled again when he opened the box. "You wear it as a tie-clasp," Joy explained. Amy looked around at the Chinese men in the lobby, and it occurred to her that no one wore ties in China, at least not in summer. "Thank you!" said Zhang.

Moments were precious; Amy wanted to be sure to make the best use of them. She drew close to him. "Now you *will* write, and you *will* speak to the right people; and you *will* come, to America, and be a librarian, won't you?"

Zhang began to say, "Yes," when Mr. Lamb called him, "Jack!" and several other distinguished foreign ladies came hurrying up to him. Amy took his hand, and held it an extra moment; he turned red, dropped her hand, and moved away among the crowd.

(From Joy's journal: I was ready to *die* of embarrassment when Amy said good-bye to the guide. I thought she would give him a passionate embrace right there in the hotel lobby. It won't be sanity time again until we get her back to the States—but living in Berkeley hasn't done much for her sanity, I must say. I must get her

back up north, somehow—if I can find a new job, maybe I can find one for her too. I *do* love Amy, but she needs a steadying hand, sometimes. And I wish she'd stop believing in that crazy *I Ching!*)

HONG KONG stood on its white office buildings, as if on silver stilts, to get a last look at the sea before the "hand over" to the Red colossus. Amy and Joy found themselves in a hotel still being built, and rested long enough to unpack and then set out to explore the city. They came back, and hour later, by a different route, and "Oh, look, a real bookstore!" cried Amy. She came out lugging a history of Hong Kong, a street map, and a book on the Great Wall. "I thought you said you wouldn't be allowed back here?" said Joy.

"I'm not sure of that," said Amy, as they rode up in the elevator. "There are other possibilities. Wait:" and the moment they had put down their packages, Amy was kneeling, unlocking her purse, finding the three silver dollars, and the *I Ching.*

"Oh, not that again! Amy, promise me that when you get back you'll toss that book in the trash. I can't let my best friend run her professional life on the basis of some Oriental oracle!"

"Just these last times," pleaded Amy. "This one is for Zhang," and she bit her lip as she scattered the coins, tallied the results, and then came up with the answers.

"Mutual expectations," Amy quoted, "wishes will be realized; and if we're awaiting someone, he or she will come, bringing joy and laughter. And here: he'll find a job. I knew it, I knew it, I knew it!" Amy clapped her hands. "I'll find him a job at the Bancroft, soon as he gets to the States."

"Amy, your Peking duck hasn't even hatched yet!"

"My dear, the *I Ching:* it *knows.* Now for you and me."

"Isn't it usual to do people separately?" But Amy was already tossing the silver coins.

"Our fortunes, darling, are forever linked. Wait a minute…possession in great measure…you are by nature healthy: long life; employment, propitious; a good job with prestige for *you!*" Amy looked up, brushed the long black strand ever in the way, back from her forehead. "That's for both of us. Joy, I haven't told you; there's a rumor of a department-head job opening in a college library in Washington."

"But you've never headed a department."

"My dear, I ran three school libraries, all with real brats in them. What's the Chinese for 'unflappable'?" Amy demanded, sitting erect, her long hair black as a pirate's flag.

"You're the one who's learning the language," Joy answered her, sitting on the edge of her bed and sipping her soft drink. "Now go on and do it for the other librarians on this trip."

Amy rolled and calculated. "Hexagram eight: contact with others will go well; all will be smooth. Travel…let me see…safe journey, you will gain something from the trip. There!"

"At least, they'll get the income tax deduction for professional expenses. How about the Chinese people? They've named you their friend!"

Amy rolled the coins, kept the score, consulted the tables. Her face, at the end, was grave.

"Hexagram twelve: stagnation. No meeting of minds between government and people—petty people may inflict harm—lost article: fallen into someone's hands, who will not return it." A soft Amy-cry of dismay; Joy looked up. "What?" "All those people—what could they lose—suddenly—and not get back?" Amy swept the silver dollars into her purse, closed the book, and brushed her raven hair back over her shoulders.

Joy sat on the bed, composed, drink in hand. "Freedom, the little they have." She tossed the empty soft drink can into the wastebasket. "They will ask for more, and receive less. Amy, let's go home before it happens."

THE HOUSE WAS NO LONGER A HORROR. Charlotte Newcastle, twenty, long gold ringlets, met Amy at the door with wide blue eyes and a torrent of story:

"The Ramirez's finished it all! They went away for two weeks, then they came back! They worked overtime! They were painting in the middle of the night, 'cause I told them you were coming back, and Olivia got sick from the paint fumes, and she's in the cat hospital, 'cause Will took her there, and she's waiting for you there now, and the house is completely finished, and the Ramirez family said they had to go down to San Diego 'cause somebody's having a difficult baby, I mean the birth was difficult, and I didn't see them, and then they came back, and they said for you to pay this!"

Amy set down her two pieces of luggage, slung the overnight bag off her shoulder, and sat down in the chair to look at it. A column of penciled figures cascaded down the right side of the invoice to form a great swelling pool of numbers at the bottom: "total parts and labor, $15,967.45."

"More than four thousand dollars over estimate. I suppose that's the overtime," said Amy wearily. "It better be. When did Olivia take sick? I wanted her here so!"

"Just after they started painting the inside," began Charlotte, "but here comes Will."

They swept into each other's arms. "You must be exhausted," Will said. "Let me get your bags upstairs. We've done everything we could. We brought the books from the other house and put them where we thought you'd like them. We'll move 'em around if you want things different. We're sorry about Olivia." He placed the suitcases by the dressing table. "Come on, Charlotte, let's wait downstairs while Amy changes and unpacks her luggage. We'll be fixing you a drink for when you're ready."

Amy was sick at heart that her own little half-Siamese cat wasn't there to greet her. There was a new paint smell everywhere, but the Newcastles had left windows open, and Charlotte had placed a bowl of daisies on the table.

"I ought to go out and look at Olivia," said Amy, forty-five minutes later, accepting a small glass of bourbon and branch water from Will's brown hand.

"Sit down first, Amy," Will suggested. "You must be exhausted. Tell us just a few things about your trip."

"Oh, tell us everything," said Charlotte. "Did you take slides?"

"Yes, and I think I've inveigled our Chinese guide to come to America. He's studying computers but what he really wants, as it turns out, is to be a rare books librarian. But I don't know about China. The people there are very friendly, the food was marvelous, but I don't know how long it will stay wide open like this."

"You mean you want to get your friend over here as quickly as possible?" asked Will, smiling.

"Yes, that's it. What hospital did you put Olivia in?" Amy asked with a start. "I have the feeling that she needs me just terribly."

THE WEEKS THAT FOLLOWED were a nadir for Amy. The China trip was over, there was a ton of mail to get through, there was the fall semester to get ready for, and it was back to the old reference desk schedule. Olivia, faithful servant of her lady, was clearly awaiting her *nunc dimittis*. The toxic shock to the little cat had triggered a metastasizing cancer, and after three weeks of struggle and agony, Amy let the veterinarians persuade her to let the cat go. Returning home, she saw the little water dish, the untouched dry food in the bowl, and cleaned it and put it, with tears, away.

It was Will she wrote first to (perhaps because the little cat had rested beside them both, once); and Will, coming back down from the end of summer vacation up north, stopped off in Berkeley. She had no idea of his coming, but she answered a doorbell one evening, and there were Will and Charlotte, she with a cloth-covered basket which trembled when she moved it. "Surprise-surprise!" they both cried, and Charlotte giggled.

"Come in, you silly kids," said Amy flinging the door wide. "Why didn't you tell me you were coming? I might have been out visiting, or shopping. Well, don't just stand there!"

Quickly Will brought his sister in the doorway, and said, "Let's close the door quick," said Will, "I don't want him to get out."

"Who to get out?" asked Amy, backing away, her hand at her throat; she watched with apprehension as Will carefully laid the wicker basket on the hallway floor. Something was under the white napkin. "What's in there? What are you bringing into my house?"

Will whisked off the napkin, and over the rim of the basket appeared the head of the smallest kitten that Amy had ever seen away from its mother. It had gray fur with black stripes, tan nose-leather, tiny white forepaws, and two gray-green eyes. Amy could have cupped it in the palm of one hand. "*That!*" she cried, trembling with delight.

"That," said Will, helping the kitten climb out of the basket and step carefully into its new home, "is *The Molecule!*"

"Oh, Molecule!" cried Amy, her heart assuaged for the first time in three weeks. The kitten indeed sat in the palm of one hand; she cupped both around it. "Where did you get it?"

"Charlotte's friend Belinda has a cat, and this is the runt of the litter. He—it is a he, isn't it, Charlotte?—needs, like, *love.*"

"And he shall have it! Come, follow me into the kitchen, where's that milk dish?"

They sat around the kitchen table, talking summer pleasures and autumn plans, and watching the kitten explore the corners of his new home. Suddenly Amy said, "I have a letter from Zhang Mian-min."

"Who?" asked Will.

"The guide—the one who wants to come here—I think he may be in love with me. He says that it is very 'strainful' living in China now. Everyone thinks that something is going to happen. He wants to get here quick, and asks me to pull strings with the immigration people—of course, he doesn't put it that way. If he comes to this house, of course, he'll have to give up cigarettes, or smoke them on the porch."

"In short, you will have to get him trained, like The Molecule."

Amy stood up and put the kitten in a sandbox on the porch, so that he would know where it was. He was too small to be able to push the cat door open, so she brought him back when he was finished. "Well, I certainly won't neuter Zhang, as I will have to do with The Molecule," said Amy. "After all, he might prove to be entertaining." She put the kitten back down on the floor when the telephone rang.

Joy's voice. "Hello, Amy? He's landed."

"Landed? Who? Zhang?"

"No, Wang. Wang Shou-yi, the man we were sent to find in Shanghai. He's here, at Tumtulips. With his 'special friend'."

"Good heavens! How did he get here? I thought he was being sent to Qinghai!"

"Apparently when we left, she panicked, thinking they were both doomed, and then went to the American consulate, where she talked them into giving him a new passport. I suppose the consul must have cabled Washington for records of his passport back in the thirties; and his Chinese papers would have identified him as the same person. Anyway, the consul gave her a visa, and the Chinese gave her a passport, so she could get out too, and now they are here."

"Not staying with you and Laura, surely?"

"Not with us, no. We're too unimportant. They are the guests of the President, until they can find an apartment in the city. They're being wined and dined and made much of. He looks as if angels carried him off, and she looks pleased as Punch."

"Then our visit was crowned with success. The *I Ching* was right after all!"

"I do hope you've put that thing away, Amy. You'll be collecting a Ph.D. in a year, and you don't want it to be known that a distinguished scholar of English literature does fortune-telling. If you apply to work for Rhododendron College, would you want that on your resumé?"

"It shall be done in secret, Joy, I'll roll the coins on the carpet at home."

"But what good will it do you? You can't do it every time you're faced with an administrative decision!"

"It's likely to prove correct with Zhang Mian-min, anyway," said Amy. "He wants to come here—I've just opened a letter. As soon as he gets here, I'll clap him into library school. And he can stay at my house. Listen, Charlotte and Will are here; I can't neglect my guests."

"Very well, Amy, but remember, you can't rescue all the people in China. There are a billion of them."

"Not all? But isn't just one a good faith effort?"

"That depends on the power of faith. You have the heart, darling, but not the house room. A billion Chinese on your porch? Love, *ma chérie,* extends just so far."

Part III

HOW DO YOU MANAGE, AMY ROSE?

> There was Tullibardine and Burleigh,
> And Struan, Keith, and Ogilvie,
> And brave Carnegie, wha but he,
> The piper o' Dundee?
> > [Anonymous]

> Ceremony's a name for the rich horn,
> And custom for the spreading laurel tree.
> > —Yeats.

The action of the story takes place in the year 1997. Part of the calendar for that year, with phases of the Moon, is subjoined for the reader's convenience.

Sun	_Mon_	_Tues_	_Wed_	_Thurs_	_Fri_	_Sat_
APRIL						
20	21	22°	23	24	25	26
27	28	29(	30			
MAY						
				1	2	3
4	5	6•	7	8	9	10
11	12	13	14	15)	16	17

How Do You Manage, Amy Rose?

AMY ROSE, LIBRARIAN, sat at her desk in the College Librarian's office in the northwest corner of the library at Rhododendron College, Washington. The spacious study was paneled in canoe-cedar; her desk was of the same wood, the writing surface with a veneer of Sitka spruce under glass. Through the windows came the scent of firs and the sea, and the "shook-shook-shook" of a Steller's jay. On the desk was a crystal vase of red and white tulips brought her by the College gardener, Giuseppe, whose daughter, Anna, Amy had hired to do the payroll; and beside it, a portrait of her late predecessor at this desk: Miss Willow Goldfinch, a small, spry lady who had died in her sleep, suddenly: just one month before the new library was to open. Now Amy Rose, formerly a school librarian on the eastern shore of the Sound; then reference librarian and Ph.D. candidate at Berkeley; had at last come to Rhododendron College: first as head of reference, then Assistant, then Associate College Librarian for Readers' Services: was, today! Acting College Librarian at this desk.

There was a knock! and Judith Brown, a slender lady with a limp, entered. Judith's late husband had been pastor of an A.M.E. church, and Amy, a widow herself, had rescued Judith from the campus security office, where she had been the butt of racist and sexist jokes. "Dr. Rose? Mrs. Kay McNeil to see you; you remember, she's the College engineer."

"Show her in, please, Judith," said Amy, rising—what, a woman engineer? Amy was not astonished. Rhododendron College was doing affirmative action long before anyone coined the phrase. Originally the oldest college for women in the state, Rhododendron had been accepting men back in the nineteen-thirties, for financial reasons, and even now there are twice as many women students as men. Not that the lads have their choice of girlfriends; Rhododendron women are choosy, knowing it's really *their* school, and they came there to *study*, preparing for professional careers. The school's reputation for excellence is unequalled in the Pacific Northwest.

But nowhere equalled—look around you!—by its beauty. In summer, the aspens blow green-and-silver and the Sound sparkles with light. In fall, the aspens spiral blessings on the heads of nearly a thousand hurrying students, scattering more gold medals at the feet of the professors than they could earn in fifty years of teaching and research. In winter, when the snow burdens the firs and spruces in great crests and drifts, and the College chorus marches into Wood Hall of Music to begin the annual Christmas concert:—flutes, oboes, trumpets: girls, boys: and students and parents rise to "O come, o come, Immanuel,"—in all the Pacific Northwest there is no more solemn yet festive scene. Spring, and tulips sprout from their beds: red and white, the College colors. But May! In May, the rhododendrons bloom everywhere in raised beds, planters, and hedges. Then city people come out to stroll the paths, and girls in flowered dresses and boys in jeans and red sweaters with the block "R" on them, walk, holding hands, to class, or to sit on the benches to admire the flowers. Rhododendrons ring every campus building, waves of rosy light lapping the old granite: here the Gordon Hall of Social Studies, there the Stevens Art Building, and above all, the Library, faced with warm red brick, heart of the campus. Were you there, at Rhododendron College in May, you would have to admit, whatever your own *alma mater* might be, that Rhododendron is the most beautiful college in the United States.

Yet all was not well at that Library. The handsome Carnegie building, finished in 1936, designed to hold one hundred thousand volumes, plus ample study space, conference rooms, and offices for Technical Services and Administration—paneled in spruce and cedar and fitted with cedar shelving; carpeted in forest-green and brown—was simply overwhelmed by three hundred thousand volumes and over sixty years of heavy use. The cedar bookshelves were bolted to the floor. Conference rooms had been converted to stack space. Some Technical Services desks spilled into the hallways. Some stains in the forest-green carpets were beyond removal. And the students were frustrated, the faculty furious!—that one hundred thousand volumes—one-third of the collection—were currently housed in an ugly steel building called The Annex, at the edge of campus, where all but the newest and most heavily used volumes were locked behind moveable shelving: compact storage. Sure enough, someone has used in a murder mystery the device of squashing a disliked library administrator between the heavy steel racks. Amy wondered whether it might not happen here, at Rhododendron, and in her time.

The final straw: yesterday, Professor Lloyd, bald-headed historian, stormed into her office, grasping a roof slate. Amy had never fought a duel: was this his weapon of choice? "Do you realize, this thing nearly hit me on the head? Several of these tiles have been loose since last February's big wind. That walkway has got to be closed off!"

Amy had no choice but to comply. Professor Lloyd, author of the three-volume *Maritime History of Puget Sound*—was not a man to be brooked. Amy telephoned Physical Plant, and in half an hour, the north side of the walkway fronting the College Library had been cordoned off with a string from which flourished little red pennants.

Now today, it was the turn of Mrs. McNeil: a small, silvering woman, with a direct approach.

"Mrs. Rose, this library is a danger to man and beast!"

Amy thought: two-thirds of the students were women, and

none (as far as she knew) were beasts. This calculation gave her
the time to gather the sense of humor that had long ago gained
her the title, "The Unflappable."—"Which men," she asked quietly, "and which beasts?"

"Professor Lloyd was nearly decapitated by a falling slate—
from *your* library!"

"I know that," said Amy; "I've just had that north walkway
cordoned off. Now then; you're the college engineer; you know
what I know about this library; we all know that it will be replaced
by a new building. The question is, Kay, how soon must I close
off the present building for remodelling? Before I open the new
one? What will that do to the students and faculty?" Her long
black hair a tight braid behind her, Amy stood erect before her
desk.

"The County," said Kay McNeil, "has already condemned it.
The building is to close in eight days. Second of May." And she
raised her eyebrows briskly.

Amy was appalled. "That's not in their jurisdiction. Who has
been doing this?—Ah, Professor Lloyd?"

"His wife is a County Supervisor," said Kay, "and it *is* within
their jurisdiction. Sorry, my dear. I think you had better move the
books on reserve into one of the classrooms, and close the rest of
the building, until we can move all of the books. Just to be on the
safe side. It isn't my doing, but you know we're all liable in the
case of injury."

"But the new building isn't ready, yet! What am I to do? See
here, I can't close the place down, and I can't move books into a
building that hasn't been delivered to us! Oh, *damn* Professor
Lloyd! Why, it hasn't had time to get into the local paper yet!"

"Then we must refer this problem to Dr. Collins," said the
engineer, and at that moment, Judith put her head through the
doorway. Amy looked up in surprise, but was very quiet when
Judith announced, "Dr. Collins to see you all."

Dr. Mildred Collins, B.A. Radcliffe '48, M.A. Chicago '53,
Ph.D. California/Berkeley '58, was an erect lady of seventy summers, in a light gray dress, who supported her slowed steps with a

four-foot staff of ash. This staff, familiar to everyone on campus, was topped with silver and shod in an iron point. For thirty years her waking hours had been devoted, as President, to the welfare of Rhododendron College. Senior professors, multiplex of degrees, honors, and awards, trembled before her piercing eyes and shock of glacial-white hair. Her principal interest, after the quality of education of Rhododendron, which was the school's greatest asset—was the Capital Improvements Fund; and this fund, since few alumnae and alumni were wealthy, she had slowly built up by visits to the local business and professional community, which had learned to rely on Rhododendron for the best graduating students available. True, Rhododendron was a private college, and many students sought jobs and graduate training far away. But so excellent was the quality of those who did stay in the Puget Sound region, that fat greedy merchants; lawyers, lips curled skeptically; overstuffed pastors of supine parishes:—all learned to dread the triple step-*tap*-step of Dr. Collins and her ashplant.

"I have come," she would state, with dramatic pauses—she had played Antigone at Radcliffe to her Harvard boyfriend's Creon; the relationship broke up after the final performance, and Mildred Collins had never married thereafter—"I have come, to discuss, the *needs,* the *future,* of Rhododendron College." And, as if at the command of Pallas Athena of the glittering spear, the businessmen, attorneys, and clerics, wrote out huge sums which guaranteed the continued existence, and excellence, of the most beautiful campus in the Pacific Northwest, or (as some insist) in the United States.

But Mildred Collins also had her milder side. Once a week, she obtained the names of all the students obliged to spend a weekend in the College infirmary. Taking a friend or two (once Amy), she visited those ailing students on Friday afternoon at half-past four. Girls with mononucleosis, boys who broke their legs skiing in the Cascades, heard the same triple step-*tap*-step, and the grave, ancient voice: "My dear, I heard you were ill, so I came."

As you can imagine, the loyalty of Rhododendron's alumnae

and alumni is legendary. For thirty years now, the percentage of each class contributing to the Alumnae-Alumni Fund has exceeded ninety, every year. No other college in the United States can make this claim. Only Rhododendron.

Such was the lady, this the College President, who now appeared in the office of Amy Rose, Acting College Librarian. Amy remained standing, her hands folded before her, not daring to raise her eyes higher than the hem of President Collins's light gray dress. Kay McNeil also stood away from her chair. Timid reader, would you not have done the same?

Judith held the door wide for President Collins, who advanced, *tap*-step-step, until she stood before Amy's desk, and then settled into a chair Judith wheeled in for her. President Collins sank into it slowly, grasping her upright staff, the way a great dirigible descends its mooring mast. "Thank you, Judith," she said. "Amy, has Kay McNeil told you, of the decision, of the County people, to close, this building? I wished, if possible, to forestall, the announcement."

"She has just given me the news, President Collins."

"I have known," President Collins continued, "that it was *possible,* these past two years. But I fear, I have not done enough, to foresee the details, and to prevent them. I greatly fear, indeed— that some faculty member may have exceeded his authority!— one, as it were, beyond his sphere of influence." The strong New England voice paused for breath.

Amy said: "Perhaps the same faculty member who sent me this—" and she turned to point to a sign on the south wall, hanging from a hook. "I don't know who sent it; it came in the campus mail in a new envelope. I guess librarians are fair game!"

Mildred Collins peered over her trifocals at the blue board. "Read, I pray."

" 'HISTORIC SITE,' " Amy read aloud. " 'ON MAY 8, 1768, THIS WAS DECLARED THE FIRST CONDEMNED BUILDING IN NORTH AMERICA.' I looked up the date, and it can't be true; the eighth of May, seventeen sixty-eight, was a Sunday. People didn't make laws on Sunday back then, and they don't now."

"In seventeen sixty-eight," said President Collins gravely, "this part of the country was unexplored, save by Snohomish and Snoqualmies. The County supervisors, rather than the Amerinds, are our problem. I must *intervene.*" There was a low *boom!* in the distance. Amy thought it might be a gunboat off the coast.

Kay McNeil raised a hand. "If I might suggest...?"

"Surely."

"That you might consult the campus architect, Alexander Ogilvie. He might persuade the contractor to expedite the completion of the new building."

"If we don't pay, the workers, time-and-a-half for overtime, we might, consider it," said President Collins. "You may *attempt*, that approach; while I shall essay, the other. As for Mr. Ogilvie; Amy, the initial contact lies with you. Report, please, on your discussions with him; Kay, can you follow me, please? I shall return, to my office." So saying, she raised herself with the aid of her staff—she never laid it down—and stepped out of the library office. Watching her go, Amy thought: if tough old Andrew Carnegie, who had donated this building, had met Mildred Collins, even he would have been glad to see her rigid, retreating back.

AMY HESITATED before telephoning Sandy Ogilvie. He had given her, the day after poor Miss Willow Goldfinch died, a complete tour of the new building; taken her into his confidence; shown her every detail. True, she had seen the plans in staff meetings, explored the place before; but she had not worried about any area not hers at the time: lobby, circulation, public catalog. Now the moving schedule, worked out and agreed upon, had been knocked aside overnight. Amy would have to ask her best friend for the impossible.

While she dialed (as an architect, he was on retainer; would he be there?) she asked herself: what was Sandy Ogilvie really like?

Take a thistle glass: one cut to a thistle's thorny shape. Fill it with a hand-made single-malt whisky. Warm it, turn it slowly, before a November fire. Notice how the cut-glass cuts your fingers (not really); how the single-malt cuts your tongue (a shaving of ice?) and then feel how the liquid slowly warms your innards, all, the, way, *down*. Then it radiates up; and a little more sends you into a lovely daze, too much to bear.

Fortunately, Amy thought, a man is not a drink. Nor did the thought of Sandy Ogilvie make her dizzy (not *that* much, not *all* the time). He was more like her long-lost husband, George: before everything, a tender, trusted friend. She was shy with him; she wished to please him; she (come on, admit it!) loved him. The phone rang, and rang! and was finally answered.

"Is Sandy Ogilvie there?"

"One minute," said his secretary, confusingly also named Sandy, and then his "Ogilvie here!"

"Sandy, this is Amy Rose, they're going to condemn the old building before I have time to move the library books. I have to close the place the second of May. President Collins says she will intervene, but the County people have done this to us, because Professor Lloyd has a wife on the County board, and a falling slate nearly killed him, and *can* we get the new building open ahead of schedule?" A long pause.— "...Sandy?"

Silence. "Aye, I'm figuring." At last. "What date did ye say would suit ye?"

"Day before yesterday—no, really, we were to open May six-teenth, just before finals; and now it'll have to be the second. I will have to come up with a new set of schedules, and alert my whole staff; and the sooner I know, the easier it will be on them. And today's April twenty-fourth—can you do it, *please!?*" And then, having learned to make her questions constructive, "what *can* we do?"

"I'll see to it, as best I can."

"But what can I tell my people?" Amy was thinking of the hurriedly convened staff meeting.

"That Alexander Ogilvie is talkin' to the *con*tractor," putting the accent on the first syllable; "and that he is makin' whisky out of a turnip, seeing as a lady requires the same."

"Thank you," said Amy. "I don't want to be unreasonable, but the County people have done this to us—I think, out of spite. It's as if everything were coming down at once."

" 'Tisn't the fifth act of *Macbeth* yet," said Sandy Ogilvie. "Let me tak my gate, and talk to John Caird, and President Collins will do what she can, and ye'll meet with your staff, and all's weel that ends weel. Will that do for ye?" adding, "I think it will have to."

"I think so; please, and thank you!" Amy thought: the man more deserved the title of "The Unflappable," than she did, this morning.

"Then bye noo:" and he hung up.

Amy's mind ran on words unusual in the lexicon of love: *terse, taciturn, laconic*…Lovers were supposed to be voluble, but this man was more valuable: he had never let her down. His background, as she had listened to it on dinner dates (for which he was always punctual), had been unlikely, after all, to produce a loquacious man. The son of a joiner—which meant something quite other, as he explained, than a clubbable gadabout—he had grown up in Strathmore, the "great valley" of eastern Scotland, and finding little work for a furniture-maker's son there, had emigrated to America, to become a student at U.C. Berkeley's School of Architecture. He rarely mentioned the American wife he had lost fifteen years ago, and Amy suspected he might be looking for comfort.

And after nineteen years, wasn't it Amy's time, too? Silver had appeared in the long raven hair (which she still would not put up in a bun, nor [yet!] cut short). She stepped out to Judith: "Call the ACL's, please; we need an emergency meeting."

IN THE CORNER, by the window, was a coffee table and a semi-circular couch. The couch enabled three women to see each other: Amy at one end; at the other, Araminta Vane, tall, red-haired, the Assistant College Librarian for Readers' Services; and in the middle, her dear friend, Joy de Grasse: small, golden, mordant. Joy had been (by Miss Goldfinch) appointed head of Technical Services and Personnel a year before Amy came to Rhododendron. There was coffee in the Library's Minton china cups.

Amy began: "Sorry to have to call you away from desks and

meetings, but I have difficult news. The County has condemned this building—yes, the one we're in—and it must be closed a week from tomorrow, before we have a chance to move into the next one. They'd really like it closed now. I'm afraid that we'll have to move the reserve books into some classroom, if we can find one, and shut the place down."

"An outrage!" cried Araminta. Her high freckled cheekbones were scarlet. "Who has done this to us?"

"Professor Lloyd, whose wife is on the County Board, was nearly cloven in twain by a falling tile," Amy began. "However, there is hope—"

"That the tile may not miss next time," said Joy, softly.

"Joy, please! President Collins has said she would intervene with the Board of Supervisors, and I'm sure you can guess what that implies. And Sandy Ogilvie told me that he would try to expedite the completion of the new building."

"What kind of a time gap are we talking about?" Joy asked.

"Unless the contractor can get the work done faster, not less than two weeks."

"Then close it," said Joy, "and let the students and faculty wait. We can operate Reserves and Reference out of the Annex. 'T'isn't *our* fault; and the campus will have to endure it."

"I'm unlikely to be confirmed in my present position, Joy, if I take that view; nor you in yours."

Araminta: "We should organize a demonstration outside the county courthouse!"

Amy: "With the same result, Araminta. No, the important thing is to keep quiet about this for—let's say, forty-eight hours, while Sandy talks to the contractor, and Mildred Collins stamps her silver staff at the County people."

"I think the campus community is entitled to a full explanation," Araminta declared. "As a member of the ACLU..."

Another [Acting] College Librarian might have lost her cool, but Amy knew her Araminta. "Civil liberties have nothing to do with this case. All we have to do is not alarm faculty, staff, or students."

"Cover-up!"

"Rubbish."

"If it comes out with the rest of the county news, in the *Express?*" Joy wondered.

"The office of the *President* negotiates with the County, not the College Librarian. Dr. Collins has a very good staff—I mean the people who report to her. After that, I call the movers, and find out how flexible they are. We may have to draft students to help, if they can't come."

But before Amy could begin her conscription plans, Judith Brown knocked quickly and slipped her head in as she barely opened the door.

"Dr. Rose, a Mr. Edwin Murgatroyd to see you, ma'am."

"Can he wait?"

"Federal Bureau of Investigation, ma'am."

Araminta: "What on earth...?!"

"Mr. Edwin Murgatroyd," Judith Brown announced, her eyes big.

Edwin Murgatroyd was a shortish man, in navy pinstripes, with slicked-back hair, and small brown eyes; but what Amy noticed first about him was his mouth, which turned down all the time. He repeated his name, and flashed a shirt-pocket badge as quick as a wink. "I'm sorry to disturb you, but I am here on an urgent mission. May I take this chair?" He dropped into it, and opened his attaché case, handing out position papers.

Amy said, "We would have preferred an appointment. This is an emergency meeting of the Library Administrative Council." She glanced at her companions and made a quick patting motion with her hands: Let me handle this. Then she rested her hands on her dark blue dress (with small white roses) and let him begin.

Amy guessed, from her reading of *Library Journal* and *American Libraries*, what he was going to say; and so her mind raced ahead of him as he slowly intoned his memorized phrases: "no one here under suspicion...general concern...The Department...Bureau...*Library Awareness Program*. We are asking you to keep an eye on the use of the Library's facilities and collections by foreign scholars, especially those from China, Libya and Iran.

Intelligence-gathering capabilities have greatly improved in recent years, and some foreign countries have a great interest in our technology, despite easing of tensions…" The man's monotone is putting me to sleep, thought Amy; he sounds like a deacon reading the lesson at a small-town funeral, and that's the danger, right there. "…patriotic duty…visiting students…" He can't believe all he's saying; this is Rhododendron College, not MIT. "…thank you for your cooperation."

"We can't do that, it's against the law!" Araminta burst out, but Amy said, "Please remember, Mr. Murgatroyd, Rhododendron is a very small school. We're twice the size of Bennington, almost half again as large as Pitzer, but only three-fourths the size of Reed. Our faculty depend on the University for research materials. Our Science Library is—well, rather larger than microscopic."

"What made you select Rhododendron?" Joy asked, tilting her head: Amy guessed that Joy must be trying to sound casual.

"That rests with the Bureau." The mouth shut with a snap.

Amy thought Joy's question hit home. Perhaps Mr. Murgatroyd was a young agent on a fishing expedition, hoping to look zealous in the eyes of his superiors. "One last point," she said, rising: the tension must not proceed further. "Ms. Vane is right. The State of Washington has enacted privacy of circulation records legislation for libraries. And privacy is also College policy—never bent. I shall make President Collins aware of your visit, and she will doubtless consult with College counsel. In short: the College will be in touch with you later."

The young man—Edwin Murgatroyd was surely no older than I am, Amy thought, and I'm nearly forty-seven—looked startled: he was supposed to be the one to conclude the interviews. He reached into his attaché case and withdrew a card, and handed it to her. "This is your office?" Amy asked. (Why, the man's not even a regional deputy director).

"Yes."

"You report to a deputy director?"

"Pacific Northwestern region, yes."

"The College adjourns for lunch at noon," said Amy. "During

the course of the afternoon, I shall bring this visit to the attention of the President of the College." She hoped that the regal bit would work; Murgatroyd's sullen mouth seemed ready to announce a blockade. "Colleagues?" Amy led; Araminta and Joy rose and followed; over the swish and rustle Amy thought she heard: "full cooperation." She beckoned him forward, leaving him no chance to linger in her office. Seeing him out, she said to Judith, "Be sure to lock the office for lunch:" a precaution announced for his benefit only, since the office was always closed for the noon hour. Let him get out, Amy thought, with no further attention than that garnered by his passing, with all his imagined weaponry, through the Library's security system. It might just set off all the alarms in the building.

LUNCH AT THE FACULTY CLUB was the high point of Amy's day. At the corner table—the hangout of regulars—she could hear all the academic-political gossip, and soothe the faculty who were upset by small changes in the Library. Today, however, she and her two colleagues secured a table by the window, where under the cedar rafters they could watch a varied thrush hopping about at the foot of a rhododendron hedge almost ready to bloom.

"I can't believe this!" said Araminta, flouncing out her great paisley dress. I used to wear dramatic clothes like that, Amy thought: that was when my life *needed* drama. "This is the most outrageous morning in thirteen years of librarianship! First the County closes our building, then this Library Awareness Program rises from the dead!"

"I know, I thought it had died years ago," said Amy, "but like this morning's other outrage, as you call it, we'll just have to sit on it until Dr. Collins can handle it. Fortunately, in this case, there's no deadline involved."

"I wonder if this isn't just something young Mr. Murgatroyd has thought up," Joy said, *"pour nous épater.* And to get a promotion."

"He might find more spies at the University," said Amy,

working on her potato soup.

Joy: "Perhaps he's already started on them, and on other schools in the area. We could always ask around."

"No need to get people scared," said Amy. "I'll put in a call to the WLA Intellectual Freedom Committee: just ask if anybody's reported other little visits from the Bureau."

"And the ACLU," suggested Araminta. "And 'People for the American Way,' and…"

"And the Longshoremen's Union, and the Trotskyites, and the Sierra Club," said Amy, spluttering in her soup. "My dear Araminta, there is nothing to get alarmed about. The only foreign scholars *here*, are some Japanese working on plant genetics—rhododendrons, I believe. *They* hardly constitute a threat to the security of the United States."

"The man did say, 'grand jury,'" Joy reminded her.

Amy raised her eyebrows. "I didn't hear that, I'm afraid; his speech put me almost to sleep."

"Eternal vigilance is the price of liberty!"

Amy smiled: "Araminta, you said it yourself: the state statute on confidentiality of records says it all. The FBI will have to take the College to court, not me. What I want you to do, is to draft a memo to Readers' Services, and Joy, to draft a memo to Technical Services, saying that if anyone asks about circulation records or people's use of materials or reference questions, they aren't to answer, but to send them in to me. I will harmonize the two messages later; I'm sure there'll be plenty of time." Amy was thinking how Joy and Araminta did not get along very well: Joy, observant, skeptical; Araminta, passionately involved, talkative, inclined to fear the worst and to face it with a direct attack. Of the two, Amy decided, Araminta would burn out in ten years, while Joy, mocking, smiling, would survive.

AFTER LUNCH AMY placed a call to President Collins's office, checked her schedule, and noted that she had half-an-hour before Joy came in to discuss the budget. She had no idea, even as late as April, whether there would be any end-of-the-year money;

and Joy, who also served as what Amy called "Minister of Finance," had a better grasp of figures than she did. Amy had a moment of time, therefore, to think about how she had got here.

Amy's life: born in Cambridge, Massachusetts, where her father was a teacher of philosophy; then a girlhood in Washington, D. C., to school at Foxcroft, then to Mills, library school at Berkeley, marriage to a young physician who took her back to his Evergreen home. A few years of love, then his early death when another doctor took him up in a light plane. Black years that followed, she had put away. Then there were the discreet young lovers (Joe, the sculptor with a stammer, was the first; Will the last). A new career at Berkeley, a Ph.D., and in the meanwhile the trip to China with Joy. Back to Washington State, to Rhododendron College: first head of Reference, then Associate College Librarian for Readers' Services, now [Acting] College Librarian. She'd expected to be a happily married school librarian all her life, time out for kids. Alone, she was running (with, admit it, Joy's help) the library of the most prestigious small college in the country.

A light rain was blowing in from the Strait. The island home she had loved, and sold twelve years ago, was irrecoverable, but she had a big clapboard saltbox house, with a field stone chimney, and the portrait of her ancestor, Lieutenant Gregory, USN, hero of the battle of Lake Champlain, hung once again over the mantel. City lights glowed far to the southeast, beyond the hills' elbow; white peaks showed east and northeast; the Strait was full of foghorns and looming vessels; and a cat named The Molecule welcomed her home, with a big salaam, every evening. Still: Amy felt desperately alone.

Certainly: there were professional friends: at work, and once or twice a year, at ALA's Social Responsibilities Round Table. But she sometimes wondered whether the rest of the world ever heard of its resolutions and boycotts. As for loftier steps, she had never been elected to ALA Council, never become president of ALA, never got to choose (as Librarian of Congress) which color of limousine would be hers. Nor had any lover, since Will Newcastle, taken her any farther than the opera, or a sail on the Sound. No man had been her confidant, since George died. But now, she had found herself actually *talking* to, not merely making conversation with, Sandy Ogilvie, campus architect.

The very fact that he was terse, Amy considered, told her something about herself, as well as him. Fifteen years ago, she would have expected a nonstop conversation about everything under the sun:—a hundred in-jokes, little things you say in bed, ways of touching feet and hands. Now she was quite content with a man who was quietly, solidly, *there*. She could confide in him: and he would listen.

" 'When the whirlwind has stripp'd every leaf on the mountain,' " Amy quoted, " 'The more shall Clan-Alpine rejoice in its shade.' "

Perhaps their friendship, that of acting College Librarian and College Architect excepted, began when she found that he had a prodigious memory for the works of the Scottish poets. How he came by this, he never told her (or hadn't decided to inform her just *yet*, thought Amy). Sandy Ogilvie could recite the whole of "Tam O'Shanter" and much of the introduction to "Marmion," he knew the difference between "M'Pherson's Farewell" and "Mackrimmon's Lament," and he could sing , "The piper came to our town," "O, waly, waly," and "The lass of Patie's mill." And he knew so many tragical ballads, that at last "aye she loot the tears doon fa' / For Jock o' Hazeldean." All this was, in an admirer, a singular accomplishment; any lover might take her to *Trovatore* once more, but who else knew *all* the words of the "Canadian boat song," or "Over the sea to Skye"? True, these were not accomplishments she could ask him to share with others. She could scarcely invite friends over for tea and a recital. But, "Billows and breeze, islands and seas, / Mountains of rain and sun" danced in her head as he sang them, until it was dark in his small apartment, and time to "tak her hame."

So the half-hour before Joy came in, she employed in phoning Sandy. She had to find an excuse—she hadn't had to do something like this when she talked to other men; it hadn't been this way since she was (way back then) falling in love with George. What should she tell Sandy? Oh! it was too late now; and here he was.

"Look, Sandy," she began, "President Collins is going to lean on the County people, so maybe it isn't so bad after all. I just got panicky at the first news. But I do need to be prepared, in case she fails. Can we move the date up a couple of weeks—to May second, as I asked you—just in case?" Amy realized that she sounded schoolgirl-breathless. Hope he doesn't notice, or doesn't mind.

Silence. (He *does* mind?)

"Och aye. But the heatin' will no be on."

"By that time the weather may have warmed up."

"I hae me doots."

Amy laughed, trying not to: "Let's pray that it does."

"God's will is not to be moved aboot these things. We maun suffer whatever comes our way."

Amy had her doubts about that last sentence: if they married, and if she were ill? Then she recollected that he was a widower, as she was a widow, and forebore. "If the heat is not on, it will still be spring. We could move the books—"

"If it doesna rain."

Amy was about to invoke the Deity again, when she recalled that she had just now been forbidden the same. "Surely not," Amy continued, "and anyway, Joy has laid in a set of plastic bags to carry the books in. The point is, can we get the building open by the second, heat or no heat—in case Dr. Collins can't persuade the County people?"

"I seriously doot it," said Sandy. "I talked to the contractor, and he said there was no way he would keep his people workin' by Lochiel's lantern. What I can do, if President Collins desires it, is to be at her side when she addresses the County. But that depends on her."

"Lochiel's lantern?"

"The müne, lady," Sandy answered. "The Camerons o' Lochiel did a' their fechtin' by the licht o' the müne. John Caird willna be keepin' his folk to wark thataway."

If I marry this man, thought Amy, I'll have to get a pocket Scots-English dictionary, and a small flashlight, and read it in bed, the way I did when I was a girl at Foxcroft, after "lights out." There was a providential knock on the door: Joy peeked in, waving spreadsheets. Over the phone, Amy asked, "Can we have lunch together tomorrow?"

"I'll survey me buik."

"Do that, and please come anyway. I *need* you." Hope that wasn't too dependent.

"I'll be in contact with ye," said Sandy. "Bye the noo," and hung up. He was so brisk, Amy still had the receiver in her hand.

Joy slipped in, spreadsheets under her left arm. "I can see you've been on the phone to the College Architect again, Amy; you're blushing."

"And what of it?" The black eyebrows arched.

"You know I warned you, long ago, when you and I were school librarians, you would have to give up romance when you took up administration." Joy sat down in the guest chair. "Here, take a look at these—the French Department is out of money again—and I hope, for our sakes, that you aren't having your conversations taped."

AT LUNCH THE NEXT DAY, Amy wore a green velour dress with a silver and malachite clasp; her eyes looked very green, and her hair hung down in two black braids, threaded with "natural silver" (her term: age was now an inevitability which Amy wished to render to advantage whenever possible. [She also admitted that she wouldn't have thought any nonsense of that sort, twelve years ago: but here she was]). Amy had reserved a table under the wide yellow-pine rafters of the Faculty Club, and there she sat until Sandy Ogilvie arrived to meet her: brown tweeds, white shirt, and the complicated tartan of the Ogilvies adorning his tie.

"I regret to report," he said, after the usual courtesies, "that I canna get the new library opened any sooner than the end of next week. The building is no to be considered safe, until all the ventilation systems are tested an' inspected, and if it is no safe, ye're forbidden to move into it. As I'm sure ye must know by noo, if ye'd had a chance to scrutinize your contract."

"Yes, I realize that now, but President Collins has been after the County people. She has won an extension to the ninth of May."

"The second was when ye wanted it opened. Still, it is barely possible that we maun be ready by the ninth. Fortunately, the men are anxious to finish the wark. How did President Collins convince the County folk?"

"By threatening to secede from the County, I think; anyway, she must have had quite a challenge, because Rhododendron is seen as a hotbed of liberals, and it pays no taxes."

"I rather think she did it with her staff—the ashplant, surely. Are ye sure ye can use the old building yet?"

"There's this one entrance. Kay McNeil is to rig a steel awning over it, to protect people coming in, from falling tiles. And everywhere else along the roof line is out of bounds." Moving wasn't Sandy Ogilvie's problem, but it was nice of him to inquire. Sandy's warmth moved Amy to confide in him. She went on: "I don't think I've seen you, since the day the FBI man came. He got Araminta Vane all upset."

"What did he come to visit *you* aboot?"

"Their Library Awareness Program. They claim that the Chinese are getting all their engineering ideas, for planes and other things, from doing research in American libraries. We've been asked to watch for foreign scholars using science books and periodicals."

"Canna the Chinese get those things by their ain sel'?"

"No doubt, but the Bureau thinks they do their spying here."

"At Rhododendron College?"

"We think it's the zeal of a young loner—one acting without specific orders, on a fishing expedition. His business card doesn't even say he's a deputy regional director."

"Then perhaps he's no important at all," Sandy suggested. Amy began to cheer up, which was a common occurrence when she was with Sandy Ogilvie. He went on: "Did he send a letter saying he was coming, or did he just drop by?"

"He just dropped in—I understand that's the way they do it—while I was meeting with the other Library administrators. (By the way, I can't decide what to call us: if we're the Library Administrative Group, that spells LAG, if we're People, that spells LAP, if we're a Movement, that's LAM, and if we're Council, which is what Miss Goldfinch called us, we simply LAC). Anyway, I'd heard about the Library Awareness Program—that's LAP again—in *Library Journal* and *American Libraries*—and even so, I can't imagine why he should pick on us. We've nothing to offer a spy!"

Sandy looked up from his corned beef and ale. "Perhaps that's only part of his approach. I remember that your Library Administrative Staff—that's LAS? —they're a' women."

"No harm in that, surely? And very appropriate for Rhododendron."

"He supposed that they might be easily intimidated."

"I?" Amy raised her black eyebrows. "Then he's *wrong*. And Araminta had to be practically held down in her chair."

Sandy smiled. "Tak his point of view: if Rhododendron does-n't have any spies, so much the better. You could be cajoled into inducin' other libraries to gae alang wi' the Bureau."

"Edwin Murgatroyd is just one little man. The state has a policy on confidentiality of library records. He won't get very far. More than thirty other states have similar laws, and they've never been challenged in federal courts, so far as I know."

"Dinna underestimate these people. The federal government has got aroond the states before. I trust ye got him oot of the meetin' withoot incident?"

"Barely. I managed to appear poised, without being deferen-tial. You learn a lot about that in library work, especially when you've started out as a mere school librarian."

"There are no minor Scots poets," said Sandy, "and no mere librarians." Amy smiled happily. "Guid it is, that ye're at the helm. Did he give a day when he'd return?"

"I didn't give him a chance. I told him that the College would be in touch with him later, and that we adjourn for lunch at noon. We had to continue our Library Administrative Whatever—that's LAW—over lunch, here at the club. It took a roast beef sandwich to calm Araminta down."

"She is carnivorous when wrothy, nae doot." Sandy had finished his meal. "But noo, ye've nae idea when he'll return. It could come at any time."

Amy looked up in surprise. Sandy went on: "Seriously, ye'll be keepin' in touch wi' me on this. It's nane o' my business, but—" he paused and reddened, but looked at her steadily: "it's the true and tender regard I hae for ye."

Amy smoothed her skirt down: she hadn't heard those words from him before. "Thank you. I'll keep you informed." She looked up: "I'm new at this. I need all the help I can get."

"It shall be yours." Sandy Ogilvie pushed back his chair; Amy rose, his hand was out to her. "And noo, I maun return to my wark."

IT WAS THE WEEKEND, and Amy and Joy were strolling through the College's Botanical Garden. The work of three generations of devoted plantswomen, it spread through five acres of second-growth forest: aspen, hemlock, and an abundance of fern, with brambles always carefully pruned back from the sandy paths. (The summer students raided the berries). Amy was in gray tweeds—which she wouldn't have been caught dead in twelve years ago—and Joy was in white cords and a cheerful yellow sweater.

"I'm concerned," Amy said, "that's why I dragged you out here, away from Laura and your kitchen goodies. I can only decide things by walking, and now I've got to decide whether I want to be a *real* College Librarian."

"Like a real Queen; you sound like *Alice in Wonderland*. However, you haven't got to the eighth square yet, so there's plenty of time. Have you consulted your *I Ching*?"

"Oh, Joy, *please.*" The tall dark-haired lady looked down at her golden-haired ACL; some silver was beginning to show there, too. "This is *serious.*"

"But you were quite taken with the *I Ching*, when we were in China. You never made a move without consulting it."

"And didn't it always turn out right? But this isn't China, and I've mislaid the silver coins somewhere when I moved back up here from Berkeley. The question is, I'm 'Acting' now—"

"And a very good act it is—"

"Oh, *please*—and you and I know that as long as the College gets any federal funds, for anything, we will have to go through a nationwide talent search for the new College Librarian. And I don't know whether I was right to try for it."

"It sounds like a screen test at Paramount—which, no doubt, you could pass. However, it's worth looking down that lonely road. It is one, you know. Here, everybody knows you, as in a small town. And if you have to give up a lot of fun things, like running collection development, if you want to be an administrator."

"CD is the funnest of all!"

"And then," Joy continued, "you have to fit administration in with personal plans. Vurra personal plans," with a sly smile at Amy.

"Oh, you mean Alexander Ogilvie," Amy said briefly. She was conscious of a reddening sensation—it would never do for the perhaps-soon-to-be College Librarian to be caught blushing in the College Botanic Garden. "That—poses a difficult question."

"Architects and head librarians both have very demanding careers," Joy reminded her boss. "They fly hither and yon. They rarely see each other. They bid farewell at airports."

"His career is pretty well based in this area," said Amy, and they rounded a grove of hemlocks and came in sight of the Strait. There they found a small cedar bench placed to front the view. "There'll be time for us to love, I'm sure."

"And both of you have lived long enough to have a past," Joy said.

"If you're thinking of George," said Amy, spreading her skirt as she sat down, for there was a sea breeze, "my husband has been dead twenty years. If you're thinking of Will, he got married, last month, to a girl named Bettina somebody. The newspaper clipping showed them hugging—she's plump and curly. She'll give him babies—I'm sure he wants some."

Joy was silent. Then she said, "There are so many 'ifs.' I think you should marry Mr. Ogilvie. You've been alone with cats too long. But he has to ask you first, and you say he's very taciturn."

"He has a 'true and tender regard' for me. He said so last week."

"*Bon.* We are making progress. Has he ever talked about his last wife?"

"Elsie? Scarcely mentioned her existence."

"A help—perhaps. He can't have forgotten her; but maybe he isn't making comparisons all the time. You've seen his apartment. Are there pictures of Elsie all over the house?"

"No. A miniature; he let me see it once."

"*Pas mal.* Perhaps he can put it in a treasure chest. You'll have to be less diffident, if you don't want to see him fade into the wallpaper. You know how to do it: you did it with—those teenagers of yours."

"Please! I've left all that behind. You told me to."

"Quite right: and now the College Librarian thing." They watched a distant schooner sail close-hauled out the Strait. "Let me reassure you: I'm not in the running myself. I have enough to do with being Minister of Finance. But I love working with you—you're easy to get along with, and you take all my excellent suggestions. And you don't mind being teased."

"Then you'd better pray that I get it, because most administrators don't like to be teased. And if I don't get it?"

"Two disappointments would be far too many."

"You're too pessimistic. The faculty makes recommendations, Mildred Collins decides—and she keeps her thoughts to herself until she's ready to speak her mind."

"If I'm pessimistic, it's because you could lose it all by not speaking out. You have to let Mildred know that you want to stay here—that you're not about to run off and try to be head of Bennington."

"I knew the man who had *that* library job," said Amy; "he was irreplaceable. Joy, it's not that I've lost my decisiveness; I just thought life would get simpler as I got on."

"*Erreur, ma chérie*," said Joy. "It wouldn't have got simpler if George had lived. You'd now be the mother of three teenage boys."

Amy put her long hair behind her shoulders. "Joy love, the problem is this. If I marry Sandy, he's enough of a male to want me to be his—angel, whatever. (Not servant, surely). And if I become College Librarian, then I'll be the ruler of the Queen's Librairee, perks, problems, and all. I'll be middle management—a word that derives from training horses—but the staff will expect me to pull off miracles. And so, between five and eight, I'll be one person; and between eight and five, another; and it's really too much like Alice in Wonderland. And the whole thing could collapse, and shut up like a telescope."

"Which is why I turned to Laura, and abandoned administration—except that I'm lower middle management anyhow. You've forgotten the students, and the faculty, and all *their* expectations. *Aimée ma chérie*, maybe you shouldn't have left school librarianship, after all!"

"No way. No more illiterate brats for me. But then there's Mr. Murgatroyd."

"Ah, your FBI man."

"Yours, perhaps, my dear, not mine. *I* never asked for him! You didn't get him with a coupon in a cereal box, did you?"

"No, but he *is* your problem. You shouldn't even have talked to him, beyond 'Go away, I have nothing to say to you.' That's what it tells you in the underground papers."

"But I can't live underground, I'm the 'Acting'. Suppose he returns with a subpoena?"

"Leave the room as quickly as possible, and slam the door behind you. If he drops it at your feet, you've been served."

"What if I'm in my office?"

"Tell Judith you're not in."

"How do you know all these things?"

"I was reading the *Berkeley Barb* when I was in public

school—while you were at *Fox-croft*," said Joy, spelling out the syllables preppishly. "Then you go talk to your lawyer—in this case, the College counsel and Queen Mildred."

"What if Murgatroyd turns up, before I can get an appointment with our dear Queen, barges in, demands that I help him, and then drops the subpoena on my desk?"

"On that your survival as 'Acting' depends. You were, I believe, one of the 'Foxes' at your blessed school?"

"Yes," said Amy, preening at the memory.

"Then he's a 'Hound'. Fortunately, the back window opens easily from inside, if you can manage to remove the screen, and don't mind heel prints in the tulip bed. We all cross bridges—you decided to go for a Ph.D. instead of remarrying, and then to come back up here—and then someone behind us pulls them up and burns them—so we can't return. You'll never be a school librarian again. So assume Murgy will come back, and avoid him with what skills you learned at school."

EDWIN MURGATROYD RETURNED on Monday, April twenty-eighth, but for Amy, only as a subject of discussion. Around the big walnut conference table in President Collins's office, with its fifth-floor view of the Strait, sat President Mildred Collins, Amy Rose, Joy de Grasse, Araminta Vane, and Freya Holm, vice-president for Academic Affairs—a large gray lady, and Amy's supervisor. Facing these five women from the end of the table was a slender middle-aged man in a brown suit: William W. Williams, the college counsel. (Amy had never found out what the middle W. stood for: Walter? Wilbur? Warranty? She tried to focus, as W.W.W. read from a paper):

"...and then Agent Murgatroyd said that the Library could instruct its student assistants to note which books and periodicals in critical areas were most frequently re-shelved, and who had been using them, and that such observation would violate no confidentiality of library records statutes, as no such records would be used in such a process. I thanked him for his suggestion, told him I would refer it to the office of the President, and concluded the interview." Mr. Williams looked up from his paper at the women. "That was this morning: I typed these rough notes myself just now on my p.c."

"An out—" began Araminta, but President Collins uplifted her staff—a signal which all at Rhododendron comprehended. "The activity, which our visitor requests, is quite out of the question. Even if it were lawful, which I know that it is, *not*, it would be totally ineffective. As if our boys and girls, were to notice, what books had been left open by someone, who looked like Leon Trotsky!"

Amy wondered how many students knew who Trotsky was, let alone what he looked like. (Was he the third baseman for the Cincinnati Reds?) "What do we do if he comes to the Library first?" she said aloud. "We're drafting a paper telling our staff not to talk to him, but to refer him to us—" her hand waved toward Joy and Araminta. "But that doesn't let us off the hook."

"What if he brings subpoenas?" Araminta asked with rising excitement. "What if he brings us before a grand jury?"

"Call me as quick as you can," said William Williams. "Then you better let President Collins and me work this thing out together. If he serves one on you, he might serve one on others of us. We'll just to have to take it as it comes. Mr. Murgatroyd may elect to do nothing."

Amy answered: "But I can't be coming out of the ladies' room, to find Edwin Murgatroyd waiting with a paper in his hand!"

"What I can't promise," said President Collins, "is to stand guard over the ladies' room, while you hide. Don't forget, the state confidentiality of records law, is on your side. As long as you obey it, you have nothing, to fear."

AMY AND JOY walked back together to the library. The rhododendrons were just beginning to open; the day was clear, but the ocean had laid a fog bank like a foundling at the Strait's doorstep. There was a cool wind coming over Amy's left shoulder, and she turned her collar up. "I certainly hope that's the last we hear of Edwin Murgatroyd; he keeps turning up, like Doctor

Miracle in the opera—you shut him out the door, he comes in through the window, you shut the window, he comes through the wall."

"I don't think he's Doctor Miracle, I think he's a nut. President Collins will write a letter to his supervisor, and that will be the last you hear of him."

"What if he comes to my house?"

"You look out the window and refuse to answer the door. What you don't do, is say, "Ooh, is that a Treasury note you have in your hand, just for me?' And remember, you're 'The Unflappable Amy Rose.'"

"It's a role that's getting harder to sustain, as time goes on."

" 'As time goes on.' Amy, look at Mildred Collins. There she is, with her staff, erect, and seventy. She'll support you, and we'll support you. You can delegate things to me—or to Araminta," Joy added with a mischievous smile.

Amy said nothing to this last. "What do you think is their real motive? We don't have technical information no one else has; we don't have any connection with Hanford; we haven't had any student demonstrations—we cleared out of investments in South Africa without being asked; why us? Why Rhododendron?"

"I don't know; he's a young agent, trying to make his mark. President Collins will straighten it all out with a wave of her staff. Don't worry! Heaven will protect the working girl!"

"I think it's more than a cop making a mark. I think it's Rhododendron: something a small college stands for. We aren't accountable the way a tax-supported school is; we don't try for defense contracts like a big university; and we harbor dissidents."

"Like you. And me."

"We stand for academic freedom," persisted Amy. "That's it; we're a mark because we don't play the game. We're not part of the military-university-industrial complex."

"I don't think that's it," said Joy, holding the door open for her as they passed under the columned entranceway of the old Carnegie building, now protected by a steel apron from falling roof tiles. "There are plenty of small colleges that don't get hassled—Reed, Lewis and Clark, Whitman, the Claremont Colleges, don't have Federal gumshoes on their campuses. Perhaps, we've done something to attract their attention."

"Maybe Araminta—or one of her friends—has protested the Library Awareness Program. That's the way to get on their list." They had come to the door of Amy's office, and Amy swept in, flung herself down in the big chair, and picked up a snowy glass paperweight left there by her late predecessor, Miss Goldfinch. Amy inverted the paperweight and let the snow fall upside down into the little world's sky. "How do we deal with it?"

"The way people always do in a political situation," said Joy, at ease in the visitor's chair. "Find out what's going on, line up your support, and fight it."

The tiny Swiss chalet was upside down, and the deer held on by its hoofs, while the snow settled in a pool in the heavens. "What you don't do," Joy went on, "is assume you're oppressed, because you're pure. No one is *that* pure," this last with a wink.

"Oh, but I *am,* politically," said Amy, hand above her breast, but at that moment Araminta knocked and entered, without waiting, walking up to Amy's desk. Amy saw Joy bite her lip.

"I've searched the literature on the Library Awareness Program," Araminta announced, "and here are the printouts. And I've found something else: why the FBI is after us."

Amy: "Because we're little, and free, and vulnerable."

"When I checked some titles on OCLC, the Acquisitions staff said they had a message: there's a hacker, who's been using our computers to get into databases where he shouldn't be."

"Not into Fort Lewis," said Joy, "surely the military are inaccessible. And how do they know it's *our* system?"

Amy looked out the window, swinging her chair around to see the emerald lawn, the tulips red and white, the little red flags where the walkway had been cordoned off since Thursday. She turned back, set the glass ball on the desk right-side-up, watched the snow start to fall around the deer and the chalet, and looked around at her colleagues. "It falls into place. We have to find out who the hacker is before the FBI does—if we can. Araminta, call

Samuel Diamond in Systems. And be discreet, please; don't start a panic."

AMY HAD A RED HARD HAT for such times as she inspected the progress of the new library. She had decorated it with a small decal: a white rose, her personal emblem, which she had picked up at the Pike Street Market. Sandy Ogilvie's hard hat was white, and that of John Caird, a tall man with a fringe of black beard, was white too. He was directing workers where to put steel shelving. Some of them, Amy noted with satisfaction, were women.

"You said the men were anxious to finish the work," Amy said, glancing up at Sandy, "but it might just be that the women will have to finish it for them." She felt light, comfortable with Sandy, more so now that the building was nearing completion ahead of time.

"How so?"

"Women work faster than men. They have a better sense of detail. Ask any of your workers—that one," and she glanced toward a worker whose blonde hair stuck out from under her hard hat: she was carrying the frames for steel shelving, two at a time.

"Sally's a—verra gude warker," said Sandy. "Here's the staircase: ye'll enter here, by the east door, and your offices will be to the left of the top of the stair."

Amy said merrily, "And that's where we'll have the champagne for the reception, and the string orchestra will be over there, and we'll have Mildred Collins cut the ribbon, and then you and I, and Amy and Araminta, will go down a red carpet, and then the party will start!"

"It sounds ower much like a procession," said Sandy. "It's no for me."

"A procession, yes, with assorted deans, and Freya Holm, and— well, I'll let the President's office handle it. Undoubtedly they have someone to arrange these things. But you will be in it—won't you?"

" 'T'is nane o' my business," he reminded her. "I'm only an architect—on retainer at that. It wadna do."

Amy had met this latter phrase before. "But you're *the* architect. And you're special—two ways. Remember?"

"I do indeed. But the others maun never know, until the time."

"But nobody knows, about us, except Joy. And your sister Margaret. And we haven't settled on a date yet."

"Aye, that we have not."

"How about next Sunday, the fourth of May? We could do it very quietly, just you and me, and Joy, and President Collins, and I suppose Araminta—"

"My sister lives in Toronto. I fear we couldna get her here in time."

"She could fly."

"Margaret boards nae aircraft."

Amy had a vision of a tall lady in a bonnet, nay-saying at the foot of a flight of steps. "She could come on the train."

"She'll need time to be ready."

"If she leaves tomorrow, should could be here by Saturday at the latest."

"She has always said that she'd rather be ready to gae, and no' gae than gae and no' be ready."

Amy looked around at the nearly-completed building. A lass on a ladder was spraying a wooden-beamed ceiling with polyurethane. "We must telephone your sister—tell her not to wait—everything will be ready for her arrival. The most important thing is to walk down the aisle with you on Sunday, and to walk through this library and up these stairs on the Friday after that. I want you to be with me. I *am* proud of you, you know."

"We'll hae but little time next week."

"You're right," said Amy, "any time next week may have to do. The wedding needn't be Sunday. It could be Wednesday the seventh—"

"Ye'll be supervisin' the movin' of a' those buiks."

"Araminta can supervise for an hour or two, while we slip around the corner and down the road to the First Presbyterian."

Amy watched Sandy: looking straight ahead of him; before him the impressive stair now being laid with carpeting: a sturdy pile of imperial blue. "Very weell," Sandy answered, "but nae processions. I'll speak to Mr. Auchtermuchty, if he will marry folk on ony day but the Sabbath. But I doot it."

Amy followed Sandy up the stairs to where the office would be, where she would work; and looked around. "My desk will go here," she said, looking out at an aspen that was talking to itself in the light spring breeze. "Of course, I'll have the best room in the house—if I get to keep it. You remember, I'm only 'The Acting.' "

"I canna remedy that," Sandy said.

"Darling, I know you can't, but please pray for me. Or not, if you don't think it's right," catching a blue glance. "Joy, at least, says she's not in the running. I don't know about—"

Araminta came in, hastily, followed by Samuel Diamond: tall, stout, curly-haired; friendly grin. "How—?" (Amy). "I have a key, remember?" (Araminta; hiding something under her blue sailor coat with brass buttons).

Samuel Diamond: "You've got a problem, all right. There's a hacker loose, and he's on campus. If you don't mind, we'd better make this entirely confidential."

Amy almost bowed, led the way. Sandy said: "I'll tak my gate, and be in touch wi' ye tomorrow." Amy threw him a kindly glance—the man did have tact, and so few men do—and her glance, in passing, saw a small head peep from the buttons of Araminta's coat. "Now what is that?"

A small gray and black tabby kitten: "This," Araminta announced, "is the well-known speaker for women's suffrage, Carrie Chapman Catt."

"Then *please* take it outside. No food, drink, or animals in the library—even if it isn't moved into yet."

"But I *found* her outside. And she was *mewing*."

"They generally do. So take her home—off campus, *please*."

"She stays. There have to be exceptions, sometimes."

"NONE," in the tone that students way back in Amy's school librarian days, had learned to respect. "Take the cat outdoors, and leave me with Sam Diamond." She looked around; Sandy Ogilvie was gone, so she led the way out of the new building. Samuel Diamond followed her back to her old office. They lost sight of

Araminta, and Amy forgot all about the cat, as Sam explained that reports of disrupted programs had come in from several defense laboratories, and that the FBI had been asked to investigate. The military installations, as they both had expected, had proved impenetrable to the hacker.

They got back to Amy's office. "The situation is getting worse," Amy said, both elbows on the spruce-topped desk. Out of her immediate gaze, a Kwakiutl mask showed an alarming leer; it had been a collector's item from the Goldfinch Era. "Anyone could hack their way into a computer—save me and my AUL's. I know Joy couldn't, and Araminta only knows enough to buy the right CD-ROMs—I hope. You know, of course, that the FBI has been down our backs on the Library Awareness Program."

"No, I didn't."

"A Mr. Edwin Murgatroyd has been hovering around the place all week," Amy said. "Sam, do they already know about the hacker, or don't they know, and wouldn't they be glad to find out? We're about to be blackmailed, Sam, into conformity with the plans of those gumshoes." Amy felt as if she was in a story, or on television. "Your job" (and she felt her inner voice saying 'she said tensely,') "is to catch the hacker, or hackers, before the FBI charges in here and pins me to the wall!"

WEDNESDAY MORNING: last day of April: fog late to lift, sun a disc of latten—silver alloyed with copper—behind the clouds; but fresh tulips in the crystal bowl, and to Amy, suddenly, Araminta: "The hacker has come in, and she's one of our brightest radical students!" She waved a printout like a flag.

Amy put down a pencil—she had been editing a paper, "Dissidence and the Electronic Network; or, The Scarlet E-mail Letter," and looked up at Araminta, who had burst in, wearing a tight blue dress, but without waiting after knocking. She certainly has knockers, thought Amy, but she doesn't really knock.

"We have to defend this woman."

Amy looked up in silence, eyebrows raised.

"This is *our person*," continued Araminta, feet apart in

(thought Amy) a fighting stance.

"Who has disrupted…"

"The databases of warmaking corporations!"

"For which Rhododendron College will be…"

"Already *is*…"

"Responsible." They said it together. *"Dio mio,"* said Amy.

"The FBI need never know," said Araminta, taking a chair, and waving the printout at Amy. The white flag certainly didn't mean surrender.

"As if they didn't! Don't be naive, Araminta. Where's the woman now, and what's her name?"

"Her name is Sue Love, and she's in the Dean of Women's office, 'cause she got scared, and came in from the cold."

"She confessed to Mrs. Frankenstein?" Amy thought of the homely, worthy dean, who had never handled anything more complicated than a pot bust or a student about to flunk out because she had lost her boyfriend. "When I was at Mills, we never told *anything* to the dean. Certainly nothing political; the dear creature wouldn't have known what we were talking about. Araminta, you must have made this whole thing up; you've been writing sitcoms, to break into television. Why didn't Mrs. Frankenstein call me?"

"Her office called our office, and you were out, so I took the call. Amy, this is serious. The College has to protect her from the FBI!"

"I doubt that we can," said Amy, and a proper knock, followed by a wait, introduced Samuel Diamond. He, too, had papers in his hand.

"The reports from other libraries are in," he began, "and several of them, which are in the Strait-Sound network with us, have experienced interference with their computers. They think the disruption started *here*." He turned the papers over to Amy.

"It did indeed!" said Araminta. "One of our students, unfortunately, confessed." She confronted Sam directly. "We're *involved*," she told him.

"I can see that we are," said Sam, easily; it took more than this to get *him* upset, Amy had noticed. She thought better of people like that.

Another knock: Mrs. Frankenstein entered, her hand on the shoulder of a tearful young woman of twenty, with shoulder-length straight blonde hair, blue eyes, and a nice figure. Sue Love was dressed in a blue sweater and jeans. "Mrs. Rose," said Miriam Frankenstein, "this is the student who says she abused your computer system. I thought you might wish to talk to her." Judith Brown was bringing more chairs through the door.

Amy saw to it that everyone had a seat. "Thank you, Mrs. Frankenstein," she began. "Sue, this is serious. It could result in a felony charge. What I want to know, comes down to two things;" Amy brushed her long hair behind her ears: "one, did anyone in the library, on the library staff, help you to do whatever you did, and two, if not, how did you learn to do it?"

The girl looked sullen and scared, but the questions were evidently not that threatening to her. "No. Nobody helped me."

"No one on the library staff—that you know to be a library person?" Amy knew that to students, anyone working in the library was a librarian.

"Nobody helped me at all!"

"Then how did you find out?" Sam asked her.

"I—I just read *books!*"

"Books?" asked Amy.

"Yes!" [snuffle.] "You don't forbid people to read *books,* do you?" [Defiant snuffle.]

"But *what* books?" Araminta.

"Books that I found in the *library!*" Two tears down each cheek.

"How in God's name did you find them?" Amy.

"I looked in the *subject catalog*—the way you're s'posed to!"

(I shall have to write a paper on "The Dangers of Bibliographic Instruction," Amy thought. This was getting more complicated every moment.) "But what did you look under, my dear?" trying to soothe her. If the girl burst into tears, she would never get to the bottom of this.

"HACKERS!" sobbed Sue. "I looked under HACKERS—and

it said something else—" and the sobs took over entirely. Amy looked at Araminta. "That's not an LC heading, is it, Araminta?"

"No, but we're not just using LC headings, remember?"

Amy gasped; put her hands to her cheeks. Those innocuous-seeming little packets of microfiche, from that library in Minnesota! They were so full of friendly subject headings, that made it easy for students to find delightful ethnic topics: ECDYSIASTS—CARIBBEAN AREA, or MARIMBA AND SHOFAR MUSIC. Now what were they leading students to?

Amy turned to the online catalog in the corner. At the command BROWSE SU HACKERS, she found one that aroused her curiosity: HACKERS—CORRESPONDENCE, REMINISCENCES, ETC. Could this be it? She selected the title for display:

HV   Playfair, Lucy Lively [pseud.]
6773   How I hacked my way to fun and profit /
P555   Lucy Lively Playfair [n.p., n.d.]
H65   180 p. illus. (diagrs., plans) 22 cm.
          Cover title.
   1. Hackers—Correspondence, reminiscences, etc. 2. Hacking—Handbooks, manuals, etc. 3. Computer crimes. I. Title. II. Title: Hacking for fun and profit. III. Title: Fun and profit through hacking. IV. Title: Profit and fun through hacking. V. Title: Fun of hacking. VI. Title: Profit by hacking.

Amy stared in disbelief. When such care had been taken to make the cataloging, through rotated titles, to be forever user-friendly; with that [pseud.] the crowning touch (doubtless they had search RLIN)—why had no care been taken in deciding if the book belonged in Rhododendron's collection at all?

"Araminta, would you come here a second?"

Araminta walked over to the online terminal, bowed her head, and read.

Amy, very slowly: "Araminta, you're Assistant College Librarian for Readers' Services. Did any of your people check with you before ordering this?"

"No, not that I know of."

"Can you guess who might have ordered it?"

Araminta blushed bright red. "No, I can't."

Next, it was Sue's turn. Amy beckoned to her, and the girl came over to the computer screen. "That sure looks like the book I used," she said, "but I can't be positive."

Amy noticed Araminta's blush, visible over Sue's shoulder. Time to get Sue out of here, and let her take the consequences. "Mrs. Frankenstein, you'd better take Sue back to your office. Thank you, Sue." They disappeared. "Sam, I think you'd better leave those reports with me. If you see Joy on the way out, could you ask her to step in, please?"

Exit Samuel Diamond, and enter (after a few seconds) Joy, ACL for Technical Services, Finances and Personnel—in a daffodil outfit: yellow blouse, green skirt.

"Joy," said Amy, "did any catalog librarian check with you about this?"

Joy stepped over to the on-line terminal. *"Mon Dieu!* How did this get in here? And no, nobody told me about it at all. Call it up on the INNOVACQ, let's see who ordered it, and when it came in."

But before Amy could switch over to the other system, there came another knock on the door. Tap-*step*-tap, and Amy knew who it was before turning round.

President Collins took a vacant seat. "Good morning, everyone. Miriam Frankenstein, has told me everything. Apparently, Miss Love learned her skill, from a book she found in the library."

Amy said, "There it is: on the computer. I've called it up on our local system."

President Collins stepped over, sat down in the chair before the computer, and surveyed the record briefly. "We cannot commute a felony; so the FBI is, or soon will be, talking to Sue Love in Mrs. Frankenstein's office. What I want to know, is—this book by the hacker—should acquiring it be part, of our collection policy?"

Araminta murmured something indistinct; Amy caught only the words, "intellectual freedom."

"It was *intellectually free*," said President Collins, "but was it *socially responsible?*" Araminta reddened, and stared at the floor.

"That's a good question," said Amy. She couldn't raise the title on INNOVACQ—the acquisitions file, as apart from the online public catalog—at all.

"Two librarians debated that question in a book," Araminta began, not looking up.

"I think I know that book," said Amy, "and it wasn't half bad. This 'Playfair' title doesn't turn up in our acquisition record; it must have come in before we closed out our paper files. That was before I came—and Joy?"

"I arrived here a year before you did, and the first thing we did, was recycle all the goldenrod order slips. They'd been purged down to the last hundred or so anyway, and there was no time to search for problem titles. Isn't it in INNOVACQ?"

"No trace of it at all," Amy said. Everybody looked at Araminta.

Araminta looked at her blue shoes. "I know nothing about it," said Araminta.

Another knock, and Judith Brown put her head through the door. "President Collins, ma'am, the FBI is waiting to see you in your office, ma'am."

"Then they had better see all of us," said Queen Mildred Collins, and staff in hand, she swept to the door, followed by her librarians three.

EDWIN MURGATROYD was waiting in President Collins's conference room, with a taller, dignified man in brown; bald-headed, even courteous, this man was clearly the senior official. The President's office staff had rounded up the other *dramatis personae:* Helen Frankenstein, Freya Holm, Samuel Diamond. Only Sue was not present; Amy guessed that she must have been remanded to the custody of College Security, until some decision on what to do with her had been reached.

All stood up as President Collins entered. When all were seated and the door closed, the senior agent handed President

Collins his card. "John Cope, Federal Bureau of Investigation."

"Thank you." Mildred Collins scrutinized the card as if to verify its authenticity, then put it away in her reticule. "Now, I will not forget." She looked at the new gentleman levelly, for a full minute, until he turned away and opened his briefcase. Amy recalled the tale of how dogs cannot outstare their owners.

"The facts of the situation are, I trust, well known to all," President Collins began. "We have ascertained, as, no doubt, you gentlemen have ascertained, that Miss Love had no assistance in the abuse of our computers, from any known library personnel. By her own account, she learned her skill by reading a book in the library."

"And *how* did the book come into the library?" John Cope asked, in a deep voice.

"We are unable to discover," said President Collins; "the acquisition records for that period were on paper, which has been discarded. And the online records show no record of the order at all. Is that not correct, Mrs. Rose?"

"That is correct, President Collins," Amy said, feeling very small and solemn. "All we know is, that we have the book, and it is cataloged."

"May we not see what records show who else has checked the book out?" John Cope asked. "There may be more than one person who has checked out this kind of material."

"Impossible, if I may say so," said Joy. "The system provides for the automatic cancellation of the record as soon as the book is returned."

"That is why we suggested you keep an informal note of who checks out books in sensitive areas," Edwin Murgatroyd reminded them. "That is the whole point—or one of the points—of the Library Awareness Program." He was fishing some papers out of his attaché case, he was pushing them toward President Collins; but Amy noticed that Mildred Collins was taking no notice of them at all. She must have gotten pretty good at overlooking impertinences, thought Amy; I shall have to learn to cultivate the art myself.

"The activity, which you propose, is forbidden by the laws of the State of Washington, and incidentally by the laws of thirty-eight other States of the Union, is that not so, Mrs. Rose?"

"What?—oh, yes," said Amy.

"And is, as Mrs. de Grasse informed you, impossible. What we could do, but what we will never do, is peer, over the shoulders, of every reader, to find out what she, or he, is looking up. Such an activity, besides circumventing the intent of the law, is beneath, all, *contempt.*"

The two agents looked at each other, and then back at President Collins. Amy saw that her Queen was deeply stirred: the lady was breathing deeply, and her knuckles were white around her ashplant.

"Inasmuch as you already have a hacker on your campus," said John Cope, "you may have more. We will expect your cooperation in all matters regarding domestic security, as citizens directing a corporation chartered under law. When did you first become aware of this woman's activities?"

"Two days ago," said a different male voice, and Amy realized that she had not noticed William W. Williams, sitting in a corner. He was handing a paper to John Cope, and other copies of his report were being passed around. Amy noticed that the agents were surprised that any report delivered to them should be shared with anyone else. "Mrs. Rose called in Mr. Diamond as soon as she became aware of the hacker, and we have no further information to impart beyond that contained in the paper now in your hand."

"Two days? That's quite a while ago," said Edwin Murgatroyd.

"You should have called us immediately," John Cope added. "However, we can reassure you that your cooperation with us will be appreciated should the matter come into Federal court. In the meantime, let us urge upon you the necessity of taking some preliminary steps to implement the Library Awareness Program."

Had silence a color, the air would be black, Amy thought. John Cope broke into her momentary confusion: "You sometimes work on the reference desk, Mrs. Rose, do you not?"

"I? Yes."

"Then you yourself, and your staff, can make any observations and communicate them to us."

"I forbid my subordinates to commit domestic espionage," said President Collins, raising her staff slightly. If the gentlemen from the FBI were unaware of the meaning of this signal, every-one at Rhododendron knew it as a warning. "This matter we will handle in our *own* way. Mr. Williams will be the one to commu-nicate with you. Is that clear?" The staff rose still higher, the voice became a trifle sharper. Any student, any faculty member, would have known it was time to leave.

"Your testimony, President Collins," said John Cope, "and that of Mrs. Rose, would be valuable in court."

If the Queen's staff had suddenly sprouted a pair of black-and-red hurricane warning flags, and if Saint Elmo's fire had sud-denly sparkled at the top of the staff, Amy would have thought such phenomena entirely appropriate. Instead, President Mildred Collins raised herself with the staff's support. "Neither I, nor Mrs. Rose, will appear in court," she said, in her high New England voice. "The College, will be represented, solely, by coun-sel. Is that clear? This conference, is at an end. Mr. Williams, kindly show our guests, out of the building. Let all depart; I must speak to Mrs. Rose *alone.*"

Amy watched all the ladies and gentlemen pass through the walnut-paneled door, and sank back into her chair. Mildred Collins also settled back into her chair, and looked at Amy fixedly.

"They will be back," she said at last. "You might have called them, earlier, but you did not; and, all things considered, it is just as well. You have not had evidence, that anyone else, has been doing this, since Miss Love confessed?"

"No, President Collins."

"The predilections, political at least, of your Assistant College Librarian, Araminta Vane, are well known to me. Did she know this student?"

"I have no way of knowing. She did not speak of her as a close friend."

"And the book whence she got her information?"

"It may have been that one, or she may have got her informa-tion elsewhere."

"Of course. The College may not be in the clear, but *you* certainly are. Now then: the Committee has concluded its labors, and a copy of them is in hand. You met with them, I believe, two months ago?"

Amy came out of her bewilderment, to realize what committee Mildred Collins meant. "Almost as soon as you appointed me the Acting College Librarian, yes."

"You were quick to apply for the position. You might not find it, were it yours, entirely, to your liking."

Amy remained silent. Certainly the past week had been difficult.

"I should warn you, therefore, that the Committee likes you very well. And, so do I."

Amy's lips parted slightly, as she waited.

"The time, therefore, has come: to withdraw, or to continue."

Amy thought fast. Another lady might have asked time for prayer, but Amy had not been raised in a nunnery. As quickly as the time you took to read this paragraph, Amy said,

"Yes, I will continue."

The staff was at parade rest, and Mildred Collins's smile was quick and tender: a slight hint of old spices, like the ones in Amy's grandmother's potpourri jar. "Then it's almost settled. There are formalities: the final report; the decision of the Board of Trustees. You're aware, no doubt, that you'll have the rank of dean?" Amy *was* aware, but it was all so new to her, that she could scarcely follow what Mildred Collins said next: "The Board will hesitate, of course, if there are any problems with hackers, and the Library Awareness Program—and that book."

Ah, yes, that hacker's correspondence, reminiscences, etc. Perhaps she better keep it in her office. "I see: it depends on how we handle it."

"How *you* handle it."

"I will," said Amy, very softly.

If Paris had been worth a mass, the paneled office was worth a book that shouldn't have been in the library anyway. Should she scrutinize those packets of subject headings from that library in

Minnesota? No; that would be exceeding her instructions. And, it would play into the hands of Messrs. Murgatroyd and Cope.

"I have every trust in you," Queen Mildred was telling her. "And now, I must bid you return to your labors; for I, must return to mine." The Queen was holding the door for her, and Amy, who had learned at Foxcroft, how to curtsey, did so, with a low bow.

"AND SO," AMY TOLD SANDY, "Queen Mildred raised her staff, and told Edwin Murgatroyd and John Cope, of the FBI, to stop questioning us, and they did!"

"'Hey, Johnnie Cope, are ye waukin' yet, And are your drums a'beatin' yet?'" sang Alexander Ogilvie softly. Amy looked round, but there was no one near them in his favorite bar and grill, Rum Cove.

"I dinna ken wha's that all aboot," she said, picking up on his Scots, "but Mildred Collins thinks they'll be back. She as much as hinted so."

"Battle of Prestonpans, twenty-first of September, seventeen forty-five. Ogilvies joined the Prince ten days after. The question is, what will ye do if the twa do come back?"

"I'm asking that myself," she was keeping her voice low. "Joy thinks they'll have a subpoena to a grand jury. She tells me to refuse to take it."

"That may not be all that easy." Sandy was working his way through a swordfish steak, a flagon of ale by his side. Amy contented herself with a seafood salad and a glass of the "house white." "Your man will have heard the hacker's tale. I'm sorry for her, though she seems to be a camsteerie lassie. But there may be others?"

"Of that, we have no knowledge—nor any evidence."

"So it may be," said Sandy, drinking ale, "and yet that may not be the end o't. Your men will be looking for conspiracies—that's their trade—and they'll be wanting to cross-question everyone—and the more blame they can cast on you, the merrier they'll be."

"President Collins doesn't want me to talk to them except in the presence of counsel. I can manage to do that, but Araminta isn't able to keep quiet. She's likely to blow off steam at them, just to prove how radical she is. And she thinks we ought to be defending the hacker."

"And the hacker-lassie took the information frae a buik . . ."

"Which she found in the library. And I'm beginning to wonder if Araminta didn't sneak it in there, years ago—just to be subversive. If it was a practical joke, it wasn't a very funny one."

Sandy was thoughtful. "I see your problem. Ye've a mischief-maker aboot ye. Time to get shent of her?"

"Not that easy," said Amy, studying the dim light in her wine glass. "She's here until we can prove something against her, and we can't. Meanwhile, I've the move to think about. We're supposed to be ready by a week from Friday. Can you...?" she hesitated to go on.

"Ye're askin' John Caird to finish in seven working days what he thocht, at fairst, he had three weeks' time for. He'd counted on being ready the sixteenth."

"You know we won an extension to the ninth; that's the best Mildred Collins could do."

"He's put extra men on. 'Tis a verra great expense."

Amy realized that this was a serious charge: but she let it go by. "Sandy, we're doing our part: Joy has alerted the movers, and the students would rather move books than study for finals. Now I really do have to ask you: *can* we move in, the ninth?"

She saw him ponder, frowning. It's as if the man hates to come up with good news, thought Amy; is it that he prefers not to disappoint me, or doesn't he trust God? He grasped his goblet; while Amy waited; took a sip of ale. Set it down. "Yes, I think ye can move in," was the answer she got.

Amy breathed a sigh a relief, and lifted her own glass. "Now that's settled. The ninth..."

"But dinna count on it."

Amy set down her glass and burst out laughing. "Sandy, love, *what* am I to do with you? How can I plan *anything?* The Goldfinch Library *has* to be open Friday, the ninth of May, at eleven in the morning, without fail. Even if the books are still in boxes and book trucks." She gave him the look she gave The Molecule, when he whined and decided he didn't want his cat food.

"As for what ye'll do wi' me," he replied, from under white eyebrows, "ye've said we'd wad."

"Wad?" Amy was momentarily puzzled: then she thought of the cognate. "I may assume, then, that your sister Margaret is on the train?"

"I am her younger brother. I canna speak for her."

"But you wired her money to buy tickets."

"On Tuesday, yes."

"Then on Saturday you pick her up at the station, and my cousins arrive from Spokane."

"As God wills."

Amy raised her eyes heavenwards. This man may make me religious, but not, perhaps, in the way he expects. "Sandy, if it wasn't that you always make things come out right, I wouldn't trust you with my little toe, let alone my hand. Mr. Auchtermuchty will talk to us tomorrow?"

"He will say a few words."

(Another taciturn Scot). "I trust you for him. I want him to be gentle."

(With deep emphasis). "Nane will be ungentle to ye, Amy."

"If it isn't too much speech, will you tell me if you love me?"

"I luve you dearly."

"Then *that's* settled, and that's the most important part." Amy looked round: Rum Cove was not her kind of restaurant. It was too dim; there were fishnets and cork floats around the windows, the lights on the tables were shaded, and a large mahogany bar sheltered a few men shaking dice. The music, at least, was low. Rum Cove was a place for older men, solitaries, conspirators; or much younger lovers. Amy preferred bright cafes and small chicken with wine. However, marrying Sandy meant learning to like this dusky ambience: so be it.

As Amy surveyed the nearly empty restaurant, she noticed, at a far table, two men, and even in the dim light she saw in a moment who they were: John Cope and Edwin Murgatroyd. They had apparently ordered from the menu, since they had clean plates before them, and were drinking coffee.

Amy let her fork clink on the table: open-mouthed, she watched, then turned back to her lover: "It's *them!*" in a whisper.

"I tak tent they're no drinkin' onything afore they eat," said Sandy. "Verra canny o' them."

"But how did they know we would be coming here?"

"They're buggin' your phone line, Amy."

"But they can't do that!"

"Suppose ye inform them o' the same."

Amy looked at her lover: he was as calm as if he was in his architect's office, seated at his drawing board. She felt a sudden welling of love for him; he was as reliable as she wanted him to be. Leaning forward, her long black hair shielding her face from the FBI men, she asked him: "What can we do? Is it true that they have tiny microphones in their watches?"

"I've heard the same, but never given a thocht to't."

"Do you suppose they'll turn up at the wedding? What shall we do then?"

"I doot it will provide them wi' muckle information, if they do."

"I can't stand the idea of their being at our wedding!" Amy forgot to speak softly, and glancing round, she thought she saw Edwin Murgatroyd raise an eyebrow. But it was only their sight of the dinner the waitress was bringing them: Dover sole and potatoes for John Cope, a filet mignon for Edwin Murgatroyd. "They certainly eat well," she said, more softly now.

"At your expense, and mine."

"Damn," said Amy, as quietly as she could manage. "Perhaps we should simply go over there, and demand to know what they're doing. And why don't they take the bugs out of my phone."

"Inadvisable."

"Or ask them over for a drink after dinner."

"Your ain risk. And the phone may not be bugged. Did someone overhear you makin' a reservation from your office?"

"No one in my office would tell them anything."

"Then it *is* bugged, and it's all a manner o' alarmin' you. That's the reason o' they're bein' here the noo." A pause. " 'T'other library will hae no bugs, oniegate."

The two lovers sat quietly, getting through dinner, while Amy's thoughts ran fast and furious. Why was she being followed, when she had done nothing against the law? *She* hadn't taught Sue Love how to break into computer networks; and as for the Library Awareness Program, she remembered President Collins's voice, high and clear: "I forbid my subordinates to commit domestic espionage!"

Then what were they here for? She remembered also that she was not to speak to them without the presence of College counsel, and it dawned on her: she was being tempted to speak to them—to rush up—to explain everything—to confess anything—to offer to cooperate—and that was why they were there, eating Dover sole and filet mignon, and waiting, waiting. What was to be done? They had to be made to go away, before she gave in.

Amy drew out of her handbag a small leather-bound brown book, stamped "A. M. G. R." in gold.

"Wha's that?" from her intended.

"My journal. Very private. I made the blank book in bookbinding class." And as innocently as if she were brushing her hair in her bedroom, she took out a little gold pencil and began drawing in it, glancing at the spies, who were munching their meal.

"Ye're temptin' fate," said Sandy, smiling.

"I'm a temptress," said Amy briskly; and then, looking up, "You're marrying a temptress, for your information. But of course, you're the only one I'll every really tempt—in that way," she finished in a whisper.

"Remember, they have those watches," Sandy was smiling at her. "As lang as ye're no eisin for some other body, I dinna care whose portrait ye draw."

"Eisin?" (still sketching).

"That's a private matter, whilk I'll explain later. Whisht noo!

Ye're *really* drawin' their pictures? You publish them, and that's against the law."

"I've no intention of publishing them;" as quietly as possible; "I just want to make them leave."

Sandy set down his fork—he had nearly finished anyway—and watched his bride. Amy was an indifferent draughtswoman, and the notebook was far too small for freehand drawing, but that was not the point. The point was to get the FBI to leave the restaurant, not to let them ruin the quiet evening of two gentlefolk who were about to embark upon a second marriage and a life of domesticity together. "Finding them here," said Amy, softly, intent upon her drawing, "is like finding a live toad under the teatable."

Presently first John Cope, and then Edwin Murgatroyd, took out little black books from their coat pockets and began writing in them. "Will ye luik at that!" said Sandy, soft as he might.

" 'They're putting down their names, for fear they should forget them before the end of the trial,' " Amy quoted. Finished with her drawings, she put the brown notebook and the little gold pen back into the handbag, and returned to her meal.

"Ye're forgettin' your salad."

"It never got cold, you know," Amy answered. "They came in earlier than we did. Shall we stand our ground, and have dessert, or shall we pay and leave?"

"If we sit, and they flit, we may be sittin' a lang time; if they sit, and we flit, they've won the high ground, if they care to tak it. We could go to a film on campus."

"We could got to your place, unless it's bugged."

"No likely. I'm scarcely that important in their buik."

"Then I want to go to your place," said Amy, putting down her napkin, "let's pay, and go. I want to be away from those people." More softly now: "Sandy, I want to be close to you. I just want to be alone with you, no one else near me."

And they flitted, and drove to his apartment, and under the blue woollen blanket they were douce together.

"I'M MAKING YOUR WEDDING PRESENT," said Joy, the next day. "A simple piece of embroidery. Actually I started it a month ago, when I was sure you'd do it."

They were having a tea-break in Amy's office. Amy leaned back in her chair: "But he didn't even propose until last week, and a week ago, you were saying we had far to go!"

"I've sized your man up," said Joy, setting down a teaspoon. "On insufficient evidence, from your point of view, but French women understand these things more easily than others. He's not slow to love: he just doesn't want to be hasty. It takes a long time for a man like that to give a woman his trust."

"We trust each other."

"I'm sure you do. And I hope *I* don't disappoint you: I'm bringing Laura to the wedding." (Slight gasp from Amy): "Yes, darling, you forgot to invite my lover. As for your Mr. Auchtermuchty? He'd better keep mum."

Amy recovered her balance. "If you don't come dressed in rolled-up jeans and blue denim shirts, with buttons with pink triangles saying "I'M ONE TOO," I'm sure Mr. Auchtermuchty will never guess your relationship. Anyway, I doubt that there's a word for 'lesbian' in Graham's *Scots word book.*"

At this point, they were both laughing. "The question in my mind, is (here Joy dropped her voice) "who will Araminta come with?"

"The entire membership of the American Civil Liberties Union," said Amy, "to protect us from government interference."

"You said you routed the FBI last night, at the Rum Cove," Joy went on. "If you left, before they did, how routed was the rout?"

"I made them nervous," said Amy, "that was the whole point. And I have plans for routing them at the wedding. The six cousins from Spokane have orders to bar them from the First Presbyterian Church if they try to enter on Wednesday afternoon."

"Bar them? With barbells? What if they have warrants?"

"They won't have *invitations,*" said Amy firmly, "and we can straighten it out later. Cousin Bill is an ex-stevedore, and his son

Tim is an attorney, and the younger boys can tickle the agents'—ballocks, is (I think) the word; that one *is* in Graham's."

"So then: you and Sandy, and the minister, and ME, dear Amy, and Laura; and after that, his sister, and your cousins, and President Collins, and your own dear friend Araminta, whom you wouldn't omit for the world: all seeking sanctuary from the Library Awareness people. Amy, *belle amie*, I wouldn't miss this for the world."

"I doubt that the FBI will come. I hope that they'd have too much sense to trouble a widow on her wedding day. Anyway, as Sandy says, they'll gather little information if they do. We haven't broken any laws, have we?"

"You're forgetting the subpoena to the grand jury."

"I haven't forgotten it. That's what the Spokane cousins are supposed to tackle. If the FBI comes near us, Sandy and I have them for a bodyguard. They are to snatch the offending document, crumple it up, and trample the fragment beneath their feet with haughty sneers." Amy sat up, smoothed back her hair, and viewed her surroundings—a librarian's office—regally.

"I simply can't wait! Laura will bring her video camera!" Joy laughed, sipped tea. Then she raised a blonde eyebrow, setting the cup down: "Of course, they could do it another time."

"Judith can always say to any visitor, 'May I ask who you are?' And when I'm at home, I can always look through the little peephole, and open to no one but Sandy or you."

"There's always the opening of the new building." Joy looked around: "Darling, you must start offering small sandwiches, petits-fours, if you're going to have afternoon teas when you're the official College Librarian. All you have is these Japanese thingies, and I'm starving. What happens if the two monsters turn up then?"

"As God wills—as Sandy would say," Amy answered. "I've picked up his habits, I'm afraid—and anyway, he was so steady last night—and so gentle afterwards—" her voice trailed off, and she sat gazing at the tulips in the bowl, while Joy watched, with bemused despair, the love-light once more in her older friend's eyes.

There was a knock at the door, and Judith Brown leaned in. "Mrs. Kay McNeil to see you all."

"The College engineer? Why?" said Amy, coming out of her reverie, but in stepped the lady, a girl of eleven at her heels.

"Are you ready to pack?" inquired the silvering shawled Kay McNeil.

"Kay, please. We've won an extension till the ninth, remember?" It was Joy, helping her out.

"You'd better move now," said the small slim girl, "the moon will cause an earthquake tomorrow night!"

"This is my daughter Tamara," said Kay McNeil. "She reads the *Old Farmer's Almanac;* then she extrapolates."

"Earthquakes," said Joy calmly, "are associated with the full, or new moon—this is the last quarter. The new moon won't happen till the sixth. And, as your mother surely knows, the Board of Supervisors have already extended our moving-out date."

"That's not what the movers have heard," began the engineer; "they're here now;" and Tamara added, "But the moon is in conjunction with—"

" 'The moon sleeps with Endymion,' " Amy quoted, and she could see that Tamara was trying to think what planet bore that name. To Kay McNeil: "Do you mean to say that the movers are at the door? I called them last week—"

"Yes," Kay McNeil started to say, but was interrupted by Judith Brown: "Two gentlemen with briefcases, Mrs. Rose, I think they're the ones who—"

"May go to the devil!" cried Amy, standing up, flinging back her black and silver tresses (still never caught up in a bun [nor with a pencil tipped with a date-stamp through them] but wild, and free). "You may tell those movers, and the gentlemen with their briefcases, to repair, with all possible speed, to the College counsel, Mr. William W. Williams, who will not only give them all the particulars of the move, but advise them whither *they* can move—"

And Amy Rose paused for breath.

"To the moon," suggested Tamara, coming out of eclipse behind her mother.

"You lead the way, darling," said Amy, as kindly as she could. "Now everyone, please leave (except you, Joy). I have some calls to make."

SWIFTLY AS THE MOON'S SPHERE the weekend and the week flew by. No gentlemen in three-piece suits threatened the wedding, which was celebrated in peace and joy. The newly-married pair spent the night under Joy's gift, a splendid coverlet of powder-blue, embroidered with silver love-knots joining white roses, red hearts, and gold thistles. ("Joy, it must have taken you weeks!" "I learned embroidery from my grandmother; once I'd made the pattern, it was no time at all.") As for Sandy's gifts to his bride, what was Amy to do with a man who brought his new wife: a crystal bowl, with dove-wings defending its four sides; a silver belt with a golden buckle; and a copy of Lorimer's *New Testament in Scots*? Living with this man, Amy concluded, would be what her Berkeley friends would have called "a learning experience."

Still, she embraced the experience, embracing him. She even obtained from Sandy a promise to accompany her, she on his arm, down the stairs of the new building, when it would be dedicated as the "The Goldfinch Memorial Library." Amy told Joy, "That name makes it sound like a bird cage," but Joy reminded her: "If the Academic Senate wants to call it that, it's the least we can do for the poor dear. She flitted herself to death."

Dedication day came at last: Friday, ninth of May. The air was calm and warm: rhododendrons in full bloom. Bees hummed about, workmen cleared space for the procession. Amy's dress was a turquoise satin; here came Sandy, in the same wool suit he had worn at their wedding (the dear man apparently has only one suit; I must do something about that, thought Amy). Araminta, in a paisley shirtwaist, and Joy, in goldenrod. Dignitaries, visiting professors, learned societies, deans, heads of departments, all in robes and mortarboards, a few faculty with exotic foreign robes to match their degrees. Over Amy's shoulders, the regalia of a Ph.D. in English from the University of California; the other librarians wore the lemon yellow of the M.L.S.

But where is President Collins? Surely she is not walking here, slowly, with regal pace, from her office; there must be something wrong with the limousine? The crowd under the awning, looking anxiously about, perceive two gentlemen, in navy-blue suits, carrying attaché cases. One is slender, but walks slowly, with a step which conceals arthritis under dignity. The younger, with a larger attaché case, walks behind him a pace, his doleful visage with downturned mouth instantly recognizable to Amy: the face of Edwin Murgatroyd of the Federal Bureau of Investigation, following his superior, John Cope.

All eyes: front. The two gentlemen, stalking up the red carpet, approach the roped-off enclosure. Within the building, the College orchestra is tuning up: and where is President Collins?

"Amy Mary Gregory Rose," Edwin Murgatroyd begins, and opening his attaché case, draws thence a large white paper.

Amy shrinks back, as if a black mamba snaked across her path. Remember what Joy said? "If they place it at your feet, you've accepted it!" Amy steps back, almost treading on Araminta's feet; she is about to lose her balance, in front of everyone…the black mamba approaches… "No!…"

She is dimly aware of a car sound on gravel, then tap*step*tap, *step*tap*step,* and President Collins's crisp New England accent, clear in the silence:

"Pray, who are these gentlemen?"

"John Cope, Federal Bureau of Investigation," and Amy suddenly stiffened: she put fear away, behind her long black hair. "I demand the cooperation of Amy Mary Gregory Rose, and Mildred Collins, as a patriotic duty, enforceable by law. The Library Awareness Program—" He paused; a seagull passed warily over the crowd.

"I *know* my patriotic duty," said Amy; "I had an ancestor in the U.S. Navy, War of 1812—"

"And I," President Collins cut her off, "am descended from a privateersman from Stonington, Connecticut, in the Revolution. Enough of this. State your business: you are interrupting an academic ceremony."

"This subpoena," John Cope was drawing another one forth from his attaché case, proffering it to President Collins: but that lady's iron-tipped staff flicked forward, quick as the rattler on the "DON'T TREAD ON ME" flag, and speared the subpoena as a custodian spears paper trash.

"No one serves a subpoena on us! You may direct your writ to the College counsel. Also, for your information, I am the chair of the President's Conference on Excellence in Higher Education." (Quizzical faces of the G-men). "I was appointed, because my younger brother, Stephen, insurance executive in Hartford, was a friendly classmate, of the President, at Yale. They still play golf together, whenever the *President,* visits *southern, New, England.*"

The FBI men looked at each other hastily, took several steps backwards, nearly lost their balance, gripped each other's arms. Amy could hear their mutterings: "You never said—" "It was your business to find out—" "Her brother?—The President?" "Yale? a Yale man?—"

President Collins had the fallen subpoena at her feet. Amy thought, she's still accepted it; what will she do now? "And since there is no occasion for it, I will have it *quashed,* gentlemen!" She swept aside the fluttering document.—"And now, gentlemen, you may withdraw. You are on College property; unless you can show a warrant, depart at once." And to Amy's astonishment, and that of everyone else present, the two FBI agents turned on their heels and left, waggling their attaché cases, arguing with each other: "But, a friend of the President! And, a *Yale* man!"—out the College gates, never more to be seen.

Such was the power, and the presence, of President Mildred Collins, and her staff, tipped with silver, but shod with iron.

THE PINK RIBBON WAS CUT, President Collins said a few words, and then touched with her staff a white linen cloth on the wall of the entranceway: the cloth fell away, to reveal a bronze plaque naming the library after Miss Willow Goldfinch. The procession formed up promptly, and as President Collins stepped across the threshhold, the orchestra struck up a TRIUMPHAL

MARCH OF LIBRARIANS, in E-flat, composed and conducted by Professor Johann Gottlieb Puffendorff, of the Music Department. Professor Puffendorff had scored his March for double string quartet, two flutes, two oboes, two bassoons, two trumpets, two horns, snare drum, cymbals and glockenspiel. Behind President Collins came vice-presidents, with Freya Holm, and deans, and finally Amy herself, with Sandy on her arm, Araminta, and Joy. Behind them came the library staff—but what was this?

With a bound, Carrie Chapman Catt emerged from somewhere, and in her trim short coat, gray with black stripes, skittered down the red carpet, before all the other dignitaries, and hid behind the feet of the second cellist.

["Araminta!"]—Amy.

[—] the reply was indistinct; laughter swallowed it up; and the glockenspiel tinkled merrily.

Carpets were rolled back, and Sandy led Amy out on the hardwood, for the first and last time to be used as a dance floor. The orchestra waltzed, foxtrotted, tangoed; President Collins sat in a great throne-like armchair and kept time with her ashplant. In the course of time, all troubles forgotten, all corks popped, the dance would be concluded—for the older dignitaries; the students and their friends would adjourn to the College auditorium, to continue celebrating with the College's own heavy-metal band, The Tungsten Trio.

(And Miss Love, the hacker? She was advised to stay home: out on bail, she was a heroine to some, a traitress to others. [She was eventually let off with a suspended sentence.])

LONG BEFORE THAT, watch Amy and Sandy go home, pack for their honeymoon journey, and drive to the airport. Hear their quiet conversation, as they line up to board the plane for Alaska, the great land now opening to its tender spring. The aircraft warms up, takes off surely and steadily, and Amy Mary Gregory Rose, widow, newly married to Alexander Ogilvie, widower, fly endlessly into the night, in the direction of the polar star.

Part IV

HER FINAL PROBLEM;
or,
THE ADVENTURE OF THE FOUR JAPANESE SCHOLARS

"Said Kutsugen, 'The Sages move the world.'"
—*The Book of Tea*

Accipe, Postume, ligneis et nunquam nummulis.
—Horace [attr.]

Her Final Problem

AMY MARY ROSE-OGILVIE, nearing retirement, heard the good news. From the front-row balcony of the Wood Hall of Music, whose paneled hall was decorated with holly and ivy, she heard Rhododendron College's most beautiful soprano, a tall blonde senior named Cicely Honeywell, sing, "I know that my Redeemer liveth." Amy, who had been College Librarian for sixteen years, sat, teary-eyed as a teenager, as Cicely touched the octave with the lightness of an angel's wing. For no close friend sat beside Amy, this Christmastide.

Amy's husband, Alexander Ogilvie, who had been campus architect, and whom she had married while still Acting College Librarian, was now an invalid: arthritis of the spine, deteriorating memory. Her friend, Joy de Grasse, companion of her earliest days here in the Puget Sound country, was dead these nine years, of a foudroyant cancer. Alas, the *I Ching* had been proved wrong after all; the beloved life was cut short at forty-seven. The lovely, teasing, golden one, so shrunken on the bed, her lover Laura beside her—*"Excusez-moi, mes amies, mon Seigneur m'attend"*—Amy could never forget it, could never bear to remember it. Joy de Grasse, at least, knew very well who lives forever.

Amy's mind went back to the last time she and Joy faced a challenge together, in the third year of the new millennium, the year before Joy died.

And Joy was the one who brought it in....

AMY WAS AT HER DESK, talking on the phone, in the office of the (no longer new) library, when Joy peeked in, holding an opened cardboard box, which almost hid her oval face. "Excuse ..." and Joy withdrew, seeing her boss and friend on the phone. Amy finished her conversation (it was with the president of the American Library Association, who wanted her on a committee), and beckoned the small, adored figure in. "It's nearly Christmas, and this is my present?" Amy asked.

"Perhaps. Would you like to see what we found (that's Patrick and me) in the basement of the old library?"

"You'd better clear everything out of that place before the contractors get in there. We've waited for years to get the money to have it remodelled, and they're due in January."

"It's from the Behaim collection. Aren't you curious?"

Mrs. Martha Edelstein Behaim had willed Rhododendron College a heterogeneous collection of artifacts from her family yachting cruises in three oceans. Amy had sometimes wished that the Behaims had attempted the Northwest Passage. Trailing abandoned souvenirs the way Sir John Franklin's crew dropped tins and equipment..."So open it, and tell me what it is, this time. I thought we had given all that stuff to the Anthropology Department."

Joy set the heavy cardboard box down carefully, on the floor, and bending over it, removed a green vessel, about a foot in diameter, rather like a large corroded wine-cooler. Tissue paper floated away from it and fluttered to the rug. Joy carried it to the blotter on Amy's desk. "Must I?" protested Amy. The container was not entirely free of dirt; Oriental calligraphy was incised over part of it, and a strange face appeared on one side. Inside was a small envelope, like a gift envelope. Amy drew out the card within. Small neat writing; the ink was faded. She read aloud:

" 'This Japanese bronze caldron from the Kamakura period *proves* that the Japanese discovered America two generations before Columbus. Unearthed by my gardener on Whidbey Island, May 27, 1949. Mrs. Martha Behaim.' —It proves nothing of the sort!" added Amy; "she can't prove anything by a caldron in the dirt; can she? How does she know it's Kamakura?"

"Mrs. Behaim—when she was alive—was a great traveller," said Joy. "She often said so herself."

"And with tales to match. Why was this not unearthed before, if it was so important? I mean, why has it disappeared until now, in the basement of the old library?"

"Perhaps," answered Joy, taking a chair in front of Amy's desk, "because it exercised the late Miss Goldfinch's incredulity."

"Miss Goldfinch believed everything," Amy replied; "she had this guru she visited every summer, down in southern California ...what was his name? Jhelhi Jham Something. The only thing she didn't trust was a man; that's why she remained Miss Goldfinch."

"Entirely right of her," said Joy. She came around to the other side of the desk, and stood behind Amy, who was still seated. Amy's long black hair, now well silvered, curled over the top of the vessel.

"Joy," said Amy, "I don't believe this thing is Japanese at all. You and I were in China back in 1988—that's how long ago?"

"Fifteen years—"

"And we saw bronze sacrificial vessels just like this. Only I can't recall ever having seen such things, when I went to Japan, years later."

The two women turned it round, tipped up to read the bottom. "I had an uncle once—" began Amy.

"Hamlet had one too."

"Oh, please! And this uncle was an appraiser. And some woman with nothing but money came in with a fake-looking Chinese vase, and asked my uncle, 'Pray, Mister Gregory, to which dynasty does this vase belong? I paid a hundred dollars for it.' And my uncle Richard turned it upside-down, and it said, 'CHINESE VASE COMPANY, NASHUA, NEW HAMPSHIRE.' So he handed it back to the lady, and said, 'Lady, this vase belongs to the *Stung* dynasty.'"

"So, turn the vase all the way upside-down, I mean the bronze caldron, and let's see what it says."

There was nothing there, and Amy admitted that it showed her ignorance of Oriental art that she expected to find any mark there at all. "Assuming that this isn't as obvious a fake as my uncle Richard's client's treasure," said Amy, "what do we do with it? It might be genuine—I hope so—but Mrs. Behaim might be wrong."

"You might be right."

"Can we assume that Mrs. Behaim was entirely honest? The card says it was dug up on Whidbey Island, and it looks dirty. What if she bought it at S. Nakamura and Sons, and afterwards buried it in the garden for a week?"

"Surely not," said Joy. "She wasn't that bright, or she wouldn't have collected all that junk—remember all the stuff we had to cart over to Anthro. Anyway, what's her motive?"

"The motive of the fellow who concocted the fake plate of Sir Francis Drake, and when it wasn't immediately accepted, picked it up and put it somewhere else. Then there was the Kensington runestone—some old Swede with a passion for numerology."

"The rich don't need that kind of notoriety—they're eccentric enough as it is. Anyway, we can do nothing without Patrick. He's the one who went over Mrs. Behaim's inventory with her."

"I don't know what Pat could tell us that we don't know," said Amy, "but I'll call Collection Development." She turned to the telephone, and a moment later Patrick Connolly stood in the doorway.

If I were still in the flirtation mode, Amy said to herself, I think I'd take on a red-haired Irish lad with sea-green eyes, a short fuse, and a warm heart. If he has a girlfriend, he probably satisfies her thoroughly: "He as bold as a hawk, she as soft as the dawn."— "Good morning, Patrick."

"Good morning, Dr. Rose-Ogilvie." This was the correct way to address her.

"Joy and I were wondering if you knew anything about this bronze whatever—"

"*Pot de chambre japonais*," said Joy. "She wants to know if Mrs. Behaim was putting one over on us."

"It came with this card," said Amy, handing the card to him over her desk. Patrick leaned over, took it and read it. "Somehow the bronze thingie didn't get over to the Anthropology Department. Can you tell us why?"

For answer, Patrick turned to the bronze caldron itself. He touched it, lifted it gently, turned it round, set it down again in its box. "Now that I remember," he said, "Mrs. Behaim wasn't sure about this thing. She didn't want to send it anywhere until she had consulted an expert about it. She thought it might be Chinese."

"But it says here that it's Japanese," said Amy. "She's very positive about it."

"That's because the Japanese did a lot more sailing in the open ocean than the Chinese did—that's the way she explained it, at first," Patrick answered. "So she thought it might have been brought here by Japanese traders visiting the Indians. She was less positive, the last time I talked with her."

"But did she know the difference between Chinese and Japanese?" Joy demanded. "And 'dug up by her gardener'—I just can't believe that."

"I don't think Mrs. Behaim was dishonest," said Patrick; "she herself was reluctant to send this along with the rest of her gifts until it had been authenticated." He was testing the edge of the caldron with a finger nail.

"Undiscriminating, perhaps—" began Amy.

"Lacking in taste, as a rule—" said Joy.

"Collector of dubious souvenirs—"

"—themselves banal to the point of ennui—"

"—herself naive to the point of absurdity—"

"But never, no never, dishonest," said Patrick. "Remember, the poor lady's dead." He stood with one hand on his breast, and looked down at the caldron as if it held the cremated remains of Martha Edelstein Behaim.

"One thing we do know," said Amy, "is that *we* don't know

the difference between Chinese and Japanese either, particularly on some bronze object over five hundred years old. We can do nothing without Dr. Kumagai."

"Why didn't she talk to Dr. Kumagai?" Joy wanted to know. "He was in the Oriental Languages Department while she was bestowing the treasures of the Orient on us."

"She was always going to, so she told me," Patrick put in; "but then she died."

"Of fear of being found out?" said Joy.

"Mercy," said Amy. "We can't read her motives." She reached for her campus telephone directory. " 'Kumagai, Jiro'—here he is."

TWO DAYS LATER, PROFESSOR KUMAGAI was seated in Amy's office, turning the heavy bronze caldron over and over in his hands. He and Amy were seated on the visitors' couch. A November rain beat against the library windows, and little birds sought shelter under the eaves.

"This is a very strange piece," said Prof. Kumagai, "very strange. But you must understand, I am a teacher of modern Japanese literature. Metal-work is not my field." He put the caldron carefully down on the coffee table, and blinked his eyes rapidly at Amy, who was fascinated by a small wart on his cheek, and by his thick glasses.

"But could you tell if it's fake or not?" said Joy from a chair opposite them.

"I am not sure," said Jiro Kumagai. "It certainly appears to be old. But there are so many ways of confusing the collector."

"Mrs. Behaim thought it proves that the Japanese discovered America," said Joy. "She said her gardener dug it up in her country-house garden."

The teacher of modern Japanese literature smiled and said nothing. Was he being cautiously noncommittal, Amy asked herself, or was all this more information than he could absorb and instantly react to? "We don't know whether the incised writing is Chinese or Japanese," she said.

"Hard to tell. Very early writing in Japan is all Chinese characters, but with Japanese meanings and pronounced like Japanese. That's before Heian period. After that they used *kana*—that's what you call a syllabary; *katakana* and *hirakana*. This has—neither one. Chinese writing only; but it does not seem to make sense in context."

"Then maybe it's Chinese!" said Amy, "and we should be asking Dr. Lu."

"Japanese artists only made bronze for household use in the seventeenth century," said Dr. Kumagai. "Therefore it cannot be very old. But a Japanese artist would have used *kana*—perhaps. Therefore—I don't know." He peered at the caldron, really only the size of a largish Dutch oven, about forty-five centimeters across. "What is always the wisest thing to say? The wisest thing to say is 'I do not know.' I have never seen anything like this before."

"In a sense it doesn't matter," said Joy, "we're librarians, running a library, not collectors of Oriental art. All we need to know, is where we're supposed to send it. If it's a modern fake, then we can store it; Mrs. Behaim wasn't specific about whether the library had to keep it, or whether it was all right to put it anywhere, just so long as it stayed in the College. We were just her *entrée* to Rhododendron, because she did a slide lecture here, ten years ago."

The office door opened, and Judith Brown put her head in quietly. "Mrs. Rose" (Amy had hired Judith before remarrying and thus hyphenating her own name, and Judith could never get used to it, and Amy didn't care) "two people to see you or somebody." There was a giggling outside, and a girl's voice said "Me first." Then she entering, suddenly demure, to Amy: "I didn't mean to interrupt. I'm Kazuko Kumagai, and my father asked me to meet him here."

"I'll be out in a minute," said Jiro Kumagai.

"I was waiting in the lobby," the girl continued, "when this person" (indicating Patrick Connolly) "got into a discussion with me."

"She followed me here," Patrick told Amy; "I understand you wanted to see me."

"Both of you wait outside, please," said Amy, and added to Judith, "Mind they behave." ("I will," said Judith Brown). Judith closed the door. Amy: "So here we are with a mystery piece. We're not sure what it is, we're not sure if it's old or new, Chinese or Japanese, real or fake. And its provenance is dubious. I have to admit that the problem intrigues me, like any mystery; you may not realize it, Dr. Kumagai, but all librarians are detectives at heart; I've read all the Sherlock Holmes stories, and I think Joy has too. Unfortunately we're quite out of our depth when it comes to Orientalia. Can you recommend someone to help us?"

"There is Toyoichiro Ueda. He is at Tumtulips University. If you like I will send you his phone number; I don't have it with me" (he patted his vest pockets).

"That's all right, whenever you can get to it," said Amy; "anyway, we have a directory of Tumtulips here. If you would be so kind as to write his name on this p-slip?" She hunted up one on her desk.

"Ueda Toyoichiro," said Professor Kumagai slowly, spelling it out. And for good measure he wrote the name in *kanji* .

Amy smiled when she read the slip. "Thank you very much, you've been very helpful."

"I am sorry I cannot make a definite statement," said Jiro Kumagai. "Good-bye, and do tell me what you are able to find out." Amy and Joy shook hands with him, very formally, and then he turned and escorted his daughter out of the office space. Amy could hear him saying something to her in Japanese.

"Now then," said Amy, beckoning Patrick inside. "Sit down." Then with a smile, "How is it that you know the daughter of Professor Kumagai, and what is going on?"

"I met her at the reference desk, last week," said the young man, turning red. "We got into conversation, and since then she's been teasing me."

"How perfectly dreadful," said Joy. "I can't imagine anyone teasing you. You are, after all, an extremely serious scholar."

The lad from the island of saints and scholars started to splutter something, when Amy said, "You must be very careful with undergraduates. You're not allowed to get close to them. Dr. Kumagai is incoming chair of the Faculty Library Committee. He could do us a lot of damage. So be careful with his daughter."

"She called me a long-nosed barbarian," said Patrick, sullenly.

"Sometimes you have to ignore people who say things to you that are unpleasant," said Amy.

"Even if they are true," added Joy.

Amy ignored her friend. "But this is what I wanted to talk to you about: You haven't, I hope, asked Professor Urbinese about the Clarendon-Bentley-microfilm?"

"No, but I was going to."

"Then don't. Professor Urbinese wants to buy everything. And a thousand pounds for a computerized polyglot concordance to the phallocentric poems of Aretino is not a suitable purchase for Rhododendron."

"It does seem a bit stiff," said the young librarian.

"It is," said Joy, "very stiff. Hard to beat, in fact." Patrick blushed, as Joy continued, "I wonder if the Bentley means that they're the same people who make the cars."

"I think you have to realize," said Amy seriously, "people sit around in board rooms trying to think up the next thing to produce in the hope that librarians will buy it. We have to resist that. You need to develop the wastebasket habit. Remember, publishers exist to make money, and they don't quite care how they get it."

"Aretino is an important poet," ventured Patrick.

"To the males of Arezzo," said Joy. "For Rhododendron College, perhaps not."

"The library budgets of private colleges and universities are even more constrained than those of public ones," said Amy; "our money comes entirely from student fees and endowments, and our faculty are forever threatening to leave for big schools if they don't get the pay they think they deserve. What I want you to do now, is take the cost figures for the most important journals in the fields you are responsible for, and compare them with the prices for five years back. You'll need the earlier issues of Ulrich's, and I'll leave it to you to find out which are the important journals—

you might try Katz and Katz. Here's a study I did some years ago"
(handing him a paper). "Now go; and let not your foot slide into
temptation."

"She means 'Hands Off,' " said Joy.

AMY COULD SEE PATRICK AND KAZUKO on a bench in
the library's garden court. The sun had come out; every iridescent
droplet promised a rainbow. Kazuko's long black hair, white shirt,
black skirt, small gold locket were dramatic because simple.
Patrick was explaining something to her; she was watching him
intently, without saying anything. He pleaded, hands out; her eyes
said "maybe."

Amy needed the report by the end of the day, and Patrick
Connolly was not getting it done.

"IT IS NOT A CALDRON," said Ueda Toyoichiro, ten days
later. "Whoever said it was a caldron? Caldrons are a meter across.
You cook ritual food in them. This is an incense burner. Possibly a
gui. But not a *hu*. Definitely not a *hu*." Professor Ueda was a tall
Japanese, thin, and his glasses kept slipping off his nose. He
seemed distressed that anyone would call this object a caldron.

"Mrs. Behaim left a note," said Amy, handing it to him.

Professor Ueda looked at it. "This note is worthless. The
inscription says it was made in the great Ming Dynasty of China,
but I cannot read the name of the maker."

"Then it's Chinese, after all," said Joy, "but what was it doing
in Mrs. Behaim's garden, under the topsoil? Unless it proves that
the Chinese got to Whidbey Island during the Ming Dynasty."

Professor Ueda settled his glasses again. "Unlikely. The Ming
voyages were all the other way, to the Indian Ocean. There are
those who believe in early Chinese voyages to Mexico, but I do
not believe."

"It certainly has been buried a long time," said Araminta
Vane, Associate College Librarian for Reader's Services, who was
sitting in a blue shirtwaist next to Professor Ueda. Amy noticed
how tired her colleague looked. Years of battling for every liberal

cause had taken much strength out of her; the nose was still more aquiline, the face more drawn, and gray was replacing red in her hair.

"In that you might be correct," said Professor Ueda. "But that does not prove early Chinese voyages. Could Mrs. Behaim have herself concealed it?"

"She was too gullible herself to do any faking," said Amy.

"I can think of a simpler explanation," said Joy.

"And that is...?" from Amy.

"Stolen," said Joy. "No, not by Mrs. Behaim, and probably not by her gardener. Some person or persons unknown, stole it from some collection, public or private; buried it, like a dog a bone; went off and left it; and then the gardener dug it up, and now we are in possession of stolen goods."

The other two women librarians looked at each other in bewilderment and distress. Professor Ueda sat, impassive, not even a blink. There was a long, long pause.

"Why choose Mrs. Behaim's garden?" Amy asked.

"Who knows?" said Joy. "A large estate, big overgrown garden, unlikely anyone would search there..."

"We will have to advertise," said Amy at last, "to see if someone is missing a caldron, I mean an incense burner, from the Ming, is it? Dynasty. Meanwhile, it, and its secret, stays in this room. Dr. Ueda, I trust your confidentiality."

"I will keep the secret," he said, smiling.

"Now I must talk with President Shepherd." (The former president of Rhododendron College, Mildred Collins, had died in office—literally; slumped in her chair, head fallen forward on her chest, her staff clenched in rigor mortis. Since no one had dared to claim that staff as an inheritance, the staff, with silver head and iron point, had been buried with her).

"Of course," Joy returned, "what I said is speculation. We have no proof that this thing was stolen. But it does explain the burial, and why Mrs. Behaim felt uneasy about it."

"And if nobody answers the advertisement," Araminta added, "then it's ours."

"And if it isn't genuine," said Amy, "then all this speculation is for nothing."

"But even a piece not genuine," said Dr. Ueda, "might belong to somebody."

"And that person might be dead," said Joy.

"And buried," said Araminta.

"With the thing on top of him," said Amy.

"Or her," said Joy.

"Did the gardener dig any further?" asked Araminta.

"I certainly hope not," said Amy.

NOVEMBER RETURNED IN FULL FORCE, blotting out the sun with clouds gray as a goose wing, with snow twirling, blurring the rhododendron bushes and scattering the juncos to reassemble under the eaves of Amy's office, and, at her home, to cluster around the feeding tray. The Steller's jays rode out the storm in the canoe cedars. On Saturday, when Amy came to the library to catch up on expenditures, she found the storm dwindling, and Patrick, in red ski pants and a Fair Isle sweater, getting into a Volkswagen bus. Skis and chains occupied the back seat.

"I thought you were on the reference desk today?" Amy asked.

"Tomorrow afternoon, Sunday," he answered with a big grin.

"Ah yes. You will be back on Sunday?

"Of course, Dr. Rose-Ogilvie."

"Where are you going, if I may ask?"

"Mount Baker Recreational Area."

"Quite a distance. You travel alone?"

"With four friends."

"Your roommates?"

(Blush; defiant stare). "With someone else's."

"Ah. Mind you're back, Sunday afternoon. People have got snowed in on Mount Baker."

"No such thing would happen in this car. It's air-cooled; air can't freeze."

"No doubt. Kindly return safely, and on time."

PRESIDENT LOUISA SHEPHERD held teas from two to four every Sunday, in all seasons. She had done this as dean and vice-president at Mount Holyoke; her mother had done the same, as teacher of English at Barnard, and her grandmother the same, as wife of the pastor at St. Edward the Confessor's Episcopal Church, Cambridge; and so why should not Louisa Shepherd do the regular tea-thing, as Amy called it, here at Rhododendron? Amy, who reported directly to President Shepherd (since the reorganization after Mildred Collins's demise), found it politic frequently to attend these teas, although she would rather have been gardening or writing poetry. "At least," she told Joy, "I don't have to wear long gloves."

"All I have," said Joy, as they entered what she liked to call "the Presidential palace," "are these fur-lined mittens from Norway."

"Then they're politically incorrect," said Amy. "They're undoubtedly whale fur."

"Rubbish," said Joy. "And here comes 'Miz Lou.' "

It took some time for Amy and Joy to advance and be recognized by Louisa Shepherd; there were so many people in the hall, getting their coats off; and while Mrs. Shepherd and two of her deans served tea, and a servant handed round plum cake, Amy, watching, thought nobody less than "Miz Lou" could possibly be imagined. President Shepherd was a stout, graying woman in her late fifties, with the benevolent smile of a grandmother all of whose grandchildren have won scholarships to Ivy schools. And such, in fact, was the case.

Amy finally took her turn to sit beside Louisa Shepherd at the tea-table (there was a table of precedence here, Amy knew, like the one in *Whitaker's Almanac*).

"I've been hearing about this Japanese caldron," said President Shepherd, with the smile of a grandmother who is eager for the confidences of her descendants.

"Professor Ueda, from Tumtulips, says it isn't a caldron. He thinks it's an incense burner, but not a *hu*."

"A *hu*? I thought that was a rock group."

Amy tried to keep the conversation from going off the rails. "The shape reminds him of a *gui*."

"*Gui!*"

"Or a *li*." Amy added, "He's a very good scholar. He wrote a note to us afterwards. But he has doubts about its authenticity. He can't read part of the inscription and thinks it's a modern fake."

"Then we can bury it in the basement," said President Shepherd, pleasantly, "and forget about it."

"It was originally buried," said Amy, "that's the point; and then the question is why. Is this some unknown person's practical joke, or is it genuine, and was it buried because it was stolen? That's what Joy thinks."

"All sorts of romantic possibilities come to mind, don't they?" said President Shepherd, whose business it was to bring the fantasies of her ambitious professors back to budgetary realities. "Swashbuckling Oriental pirates, and all that sort of thing."

"It really isn't that important," said Amy, "compared to book budgets; it's just a small mystery. Either we insure it for millions, or we use it for a cookie jar."

"I wouldn't worry about the insurance, if I were you," said President Shepherd; "Pacific Northwest Mutual has us safely stowed under hatches. And if it's stolen, then we contact the major collections and museums, and see if they're missing anything."

A maid came up to them, dressed in a frilly white uniform. "Mrs. Rose-Ogilvie? Your husband is on the telephone."

Amy was concerned. Sandy spent a lot of time in bed. Had he been unable to get up, after doing exercises?

His voice next: "I'm all right. There's a Mister Oyeyama trying to get hold of you. He's that bestirred about yon Chinese kailbucket."

"Are you sure the name isn't Kumagai? Or Ueda? And how did he get our phone at home? Judith never gives it out, and we're listed as 'A A R Ogilvie.'"

"Nay, it's Oyeyama. He had me copy it down letter by letter, as if I was a bairn at school. As for the telephone buik, he warkit it oot."

"But you got his number."

"Faith, I did. I tauld him the bucket wasna here in the hoose, and he would have to talk to you aboot it."

"And then?"

"I tauld him to mind his ain business, and hung up."

"You're a good watchdog, a valiant defender. Stay there and I'll be home in an hour to give you a medal and scratch you behind the ears."

Amy turned away from the phone, only to hear it ring again. Since it was not her house, she ignored the ring, and was half-way down the corridor to President Shepherd's floral-pattern parlor (Mrs. Shepherd was a devotee of the late Laura Ashley), when the maid came hurrying after her. "It's for you, again!"

It was Sherrianne Blake, head of Circulation, who had finally traced her to the Presidential tea. She reported that Patrick Connolly had never turned up at the reference desk.

Now at the Rhododendron College Library, the desk came first, whatever one's pleasures or preoccupations. Only catatonia or paralysis, Amy told her small staff, served as an excuse for absence without leave. Amy herself took her turn on weekends. Some manage by directives, others by objectives; Amy managed by example. As for Sherrianne, tall, ebony, upswept black hairdo, she had a proper pride. Librarians turned up on the job.

Amy was concerned for the young man's safety. "He's usually pretty reliable," she said, "and it's supposed to be snowing in the mountains all weekend."

"The storm has gone down, Amy" (Sherrianne called everybody by their first names), "and if you look out the window, you can see the mountains clear."

"Oh, dammit," said Amy, "then I or somebody will have to come in. It's already three...did he call in?"

"No, he didn't even do that."

"Probably he's far from a telephone...he should never have gone on that skiing trip on Saturday. I'll be there in a few minutes."

JOY VOLUNTEERED TO TAKE AMY'S PLACE, but Amy, who enjoyed reference work, told her, "Thank you, but it'll give me some leverage with him when he does get in. I trust it's for no worse reason than preoccupation with Kazuko Kumagai."

Amy left the President's tea with some regret, not because she liked official functions—although sometimes these were the only way she could meet the President and other important colleagues—but because she liked tea, and usually had a tea-break in her office for Joy and Araminta. Tea (iced) had served her well in summers long ago, when it was the only palatable drink she could share with visiting young people; now Okakura's *Book of Tea*, in its elegant slip case lay on her table. She would esteem its refined sentences at the reference desk, waiting for the next question. Here and now, however, she left the precious volume in the College Librarian's office, and before filling Patrick Connolly's space at the desk, found on the shelves and took down Michael Goodhuis's book on Chinese and Japanese bronzes.

Between answering reference questions, she pored over the plates, strove to understand the meanings of the Chinese words (which apparently referred to shapes and outlines, not decoration, as in Western porcelain), and compared her memory of the bronze in her office with the bronzes portrayed in the book.

She had to admit to herself, as she finally closed Goodhuis's tome to answer a flurry of students' questions, none compared favorably, in general appearance or workmanship, with the illustrations. It was certainly not as splendid as number 62, it lacked handles like the ones in no. 72, and while it had the mask designs of no. 65, they were not quite symmetrical, as she recalled the piece, and not cleanly, neatly done. Once again, Amy began to think the thing a clumsy forgery.

Amy set the mystery aside, as baffling as the *tao-tie*, the two-bodied monster on the bronze. It was now nearly five, and time to start calling around to locate Patrick Connolly. He wasn't at home; he had no answering machine, and no roommate was at home to leave a message with. Amy heard the phone ring in an empty apartment. Mount Baker, whither he had gone, was across Puget Sound and five counties away. With reluctance—she did not wish to be an alarmist, but as his supervisor, she had a responsibility to her staff, even when off duty—she called the Whatcom County sheriff's office.

It had begun snowing again. This aroused her apprehension; but then she felt less guilty about phoning the sheriff. What if his parents start phoning her?

Yes, it was snowing heavily up there, all the way to the interstate. Yes, there were lots of reports of cars off the road, but no loss of life. Being questioned, Amy suddenly realized that she couldn't recall Patrick's car; what it looked like, what the license number was. A call to the state Highway Patrol called forth a request for the same information; a search of their computer brought out a green Volkswagen van (now Amy remembered!) but there was no report of any trouble.

Amy hung up, and locked down the reference desk for the afternoon. She could waste time bothering the sheriffs of five counties, or she could wait until he got home, and call his number until he got there—a local number, without charge—until he answered. Meanwhile, the snow kept falling, and the bronze vessel stared at her from its box. She lifted it partway out. Yes, it's a *tao-tie* mask. The meaning of the monster, one head on two diverging bodies, is obscure.

MONDAY FOUND AMY back in her office, and on her desk, chrysanthemums in a silver vase with a relief figure of a mermaid looking over her left shoulder at Amy. It was Joy's gift, and Amy was pleased to note that the silversmith had only made the mermaid fish from the knees downward. The pelagic lady was thus enabled to be less legendary. Outside, the snowfall had diminished, but still no sign of Patrick Connolly. Amy would have him haled before her private court whenever he came in; and had told Joy, Araminta and Sherrianne to detain him—whichever one saw him first.

Came now into court, after Judith had admitted him, Aaron Dodder, head of Special Collections, and warder of such portions of the Behaim treasure as contained books. Mr. Dodder was an elderly, stooped gentleman with a low, husky voice, who declined retirement, although past seventy, because he had so little to retire on. He lived in an old country house, of which the cheap asbestos siding was falling off, with a great many books, including two encyclopaedias, and the latest in a dynasty of cats. Mr. Dodder had read all the books, and fed all the cats, in the past seventy years.

After the usual courtesies, Mr. Dodder sat down, crinkling his trouser knees. Amy watched him carefully. Then thus:

"I have been given to understand, Mrs. Rose-Ogilvie, that Mr. Connolly has unearthed another treasure from the Behaim archive. It is, I believe, a Ming dynasty vase. Now my uncle was a missionary in Sumatra seventy years ago, that will take us back to the nineteen-thirties, and though you may not believe it—he was the one who identified just before he died, ten years ago, aged ninety three, the wooden bark-book Mrs. Behaim gave us, and which I have in the Special Collections Department, I mean we have, as a Batak book, you know the Bataks are, or were, cannibals living near Lake Toba in Sumatra, and they had this alphabet, which Diringer thinks, I seem to recall, is derived from the Devangari, that's North India—my uncle, that is to say, if I may return to the point, digged or dug up on the coast of Sumatra, a bronze pot, or caldron, or whatever you call it, right there on the beach of the north coast of Sumatra, where it's very swampy, a bronze caldron, just like the one Patrick told me about, of course I haven't seen it, and the Chinese consul at Malacca, of course that's in Malaya, we call it Malaysia now, he had to take it across the straits in secret, that's a long story now, I won't tell you now, but at any rate he had to take it under his raincoat, and the Dutch authorities, of course it was the Dutch East Indies then, very nearly searched him, because there was a law against taking antiquities out of the Dutch territory, as there is in many countries, though of course the Dutch robbed Indonesia themselves, they didn't care about that, anyway, by the time he got it to Malacca, where you know a lot of elderly Chinese gentlemen once retired, the Chinese consul, at all events, said it was Ming, and was probably left there when the Chinese ships went through the straits to get to the Indian Ocean, of course you know about that" (Amy held up a warning pencil) "of course you know about Chinese history, I had forgotten, beg your pardon, Mrs. Rose-Ogilvie, you were in China in 1988, of course it's all different now. But, as I was saying, my uncle is dead now, but he brought the vase back to, I mean caldron, back to his church, the First Presbyterian Church of Drain, Oregon, that's where I grew up, and there in that church they used that Ming vase, I mean caldron, whatever, for a flower-vase on Sundays on the altar, and I used to go to that church, of course I couldn't avoid it, my uncle was the pastor, and he used to make me recite the Ten Commandments, and I've never broken one of them," (he probably never had a chance to break the Seventh, thought Amy, but I'm about to break the Sixth, if he doesn't shut up) "and so I remember that Ming article quite well, and here I'd like to interrupt myself" (no one else can, thought Amy) "and so I'd like a very kind favor, if you don't mind, Mrs. Rose-Ogilvie, I'd like to look at that vase, I mean whatever, and maybe it looks like the one my uncle dug up on the beach in Sumatra, and maybe not. I am sure my cat would like to look at it too, cats are so aesthetic, he inspects all the things in the house, prowls among the silver on the sideboard, so I'd like to bring him in tomorrow, if you don't mind; he's blue-eyed, white, and quite deaf." (Some cats are born deaf, and others have deafness thrust upon them, thought Amy). "I guess that about sums it up," ended Mr. Dodder.

I probably don't hold enough meetings with my department heads, Amy decided, and usually I do most of the talking. It's undemocratic and unprogressive, I know, but here's the reason why. She stood up, opened the door of a very large closet, and found the bronze treasure in the fireproof safe, which she had installed for microfilmed financial and personnel records; security had become a concern of her later years. She would be glad to have the bronze object out of there, whether fake or genuine, and whatever it was; it was taking up valuable space in the safe. The "caldron" was still in its hatbox, if you can call a square box a hatbox, when she lifted it out.

Mr. Dodder was safe enough. He had, after all, learned the

Eighth Commandment; and Amy knew him to be honorable.
She handed him the box; and waited for what would come next.

It came. "Why, I'm speechless," said Mr. Dodder; and Amy
thought, it isn't the Ninth Commandment, he isn't bearing false
witness, he just can't help himself. "It's the spittin' image of the
one my uncle digged up on the coast of Sumatra! Why..."

Amy had to shout to get his attention: "AARON! AARON
DODDER! Please, how could you remember that incense-burner—that's what Mr. Ueda called it,—from the days when you
were a small boy in Drain?"

"Talking of Drain," began Mr. Dodder, "when I was small, we
used to go to the beach at Reedsport, that's fifty miles away along
this narrow road, with lots of lumber trucks. And when we got to
the beach, I was always looking out for those glass floats, you know
the Japanese fishermen used to float their nets with, you see them
in seafood restaurants, the Japs use cork now, I guess the floats are
pretty expensive. Now here's this Chinese Ming vase, I wonder
how if, as Patrick says, it came here on a Chinese junk, were the
Chinese interested in exploring the Pacific too? I wonder ...."

Judith Brown stuck her head in the door. Behind her was
Patrick Connolly, wearing a Pendleton coat and shirt, and no tie.

Amy gently took the Chinese incense-burner out of Mr.
Dodder's hands, and set it on the coffee table. Then she raised
Mr. Dodder as you lift a baby, by his rib-cage, and turned him
round—he still talking—out the door. Mr. Dodder evidently saw
Patrick Connolly and grasped the situation, for he murmured
some husky apology, and passed out the door in front of Judith
Brown. "That's a remarkable piece Mrs. Rose-Ogilvie has there,"
he told her, and Amy, with relief, heard the door close behind
him. Patrick now stood in front of the door, next the tea-table.

Amy had read that the most intimidating examiner is the one
who asks the fewest questions and lets you invent your own
answers out of the silence. She folded her hands before her on the
desk and looked at him with confident tranquillity.

"I was unable to return to work on Sunday," he began, and
stopped.

Amy made the merest nod of assent. (Nods of this sort, she remembered, should be as mere as possible—just barely visible to the examinee—a one-centimeter nod is quite enough).

"The snow was terribly deep! We were forced off the road! Coming down from Mount Baker!"

Amy lifted her eyebrows, made another 1-cm. nod, this time inclined fifteen degrees from the vertical. A diagonal nod of fifteen degrees, she recalled from her reading, should be quite sufficient to interrogate the suspect, at a distance of two meters.

It worked. "With Kazuko Kumagai," said Patrick Connolly, "and two of her friends. We stayed overnight at her friend's lodge—we *had* to."

Amy spoke (wait to speak until the third statement, at least). "Professor Kumagai has doubtless heard all of this from his daughter."

Patrick turned red.

"It is inadvisable," Amy continued (in a level voice: always keep a level voice, it bewilders them) "for academic staff to date undergraduates. As long as they are still connected with the College. Also you have some time to make up. You had better arrange it with the Associate College Librarian for Public Services." (That's Joy).

"Don't think for a moment that I—" Patrick burst out; Amy folded her hands before her (she had been pretending to write something) and looked up at him with an almost gentle astonishment, the way cows do when you disturb their feeding. "Kazuko—is not pregnant. I didn't even sleep with her."

Amy blinked rapidly a few times. The books all said rapid blinking really throws them off. She let four seconds elapse.

"But of course not," said Amy, in a light tone, intended to be heavy with meaning. It was time to send this young man on his way; he was beet-red, drops of sweat formed on his brow; soon they would grow big and spurt off, like an embarrassed character in a comic book. His buttons might burst. Amy concealed a smile, then showed it.

"Who took my time at the desk?" asked Pat.

"I did. You may go now," Amy said, with as much charm as she could put into her voice. So charms the glistening berg the foolish captain...A second such event would appear on his evaluation. The rest was between him and Professor Kumagai. And his daughter.

TWO DAYS LATER, Amy was back to her writing. There was a tap at the door, then Judith Brown's voice, saying something indistinguishable, and Amy did not look up until she saw a Japanese face in the doorway. But it wasn't Professor Kumagai's. Nor Professor Ueda's. It was a roundish, darkish face, with the scowl of a mask in a No play (Amy guessed; she had seen only masks from a travelling exhibit); beetling, leonine, long in the tooth. The face surmounted, however, an impeccable Japanese dark business suit, and a hand offered a card. "I am Professor Hideki Oyeyama," said the visitor. "I was traveling in your country, when I stopped at Tumtulips. There," he added, "Professor Ueda told me about the incense burner."

Amy looked at him in astonishment. "We're not at all sure it is genuine," she said, "and I am very sorry that it has been brought to your attention." She did not like the appearance of this demon . from the No drama. Her hand reached out to Okakura's book: "The man has insufficient tea in him," she quoted to herself. Aloud: "Would you like some tea?" She moved the box with the incense-burner inside, putting it on the floor to her side of the tea-table. She carried the Japanese brass teapot to a private sink in the closet, emptied it out, put fresh water in it, and put the teapot on a two-coil heater to boil. There were two kinds of tea in her desk drawer. Selecting the Japanese blend, she asked (for there was time to interrogate Professor Oyeyama while the water boiled): "And how did you come to take an interest in this...object?"

Professor Oyeyama's English was accented, but not too Japanese. "I work at Keio University," he said, "and my specialty is archaeology." The heavy eyebrows contracted as he lowered his head for a moment. "I came to see the work of your Indians at the

University Museum; and then I visited Professor Ueda; and he told me about your *interesting* incense burner. So I came to see that, too."

Without a previous call, Amy reminded herself, and without any credentials other than a general degree in archaeology and mere curiosity. The water was boiling; she made the tea in the Japanese style, without lemon or sugar, and what Joy referred to as her "salty Japanese thingies" were in a square dish. Professor Oyeyama looked pleased.

"I understand that it was found buried in a garden," said Dr. Oyeyama, obviously looking around for the box which had been on the table only moments before; Amy had moved it while he was attracted by the bronze-colored chrysanthemums on her desk.

Amy found herself in no hurry to show off the "family treasure" to an uninvited stranger. She could always delay. "How did it happen," she asked (constructing her phrases carefully), "that you did not telephone before coming? Or Professor Ueda neglected to tell us."

Professor Oyeyama blushed with the required embarrassment. "Please excuse this rudeness," he said. "I neglected to tell Professor Ueda that I was coming here. I am indeed staying at his house, and only came over for the afternoon."

Amy did not know what to believe, and this made her uncomfortable. It was in her interest, she decided, to get him out of the library without letting him see the object of his desire. Right now he was looking around as if he expected to see a box, or the incense burner itself, on some one of Amy's shelves—up there with the little jade fish blowing bubbles, which she had picked up in China, or next to the bound issues of *College and Research Libraries News*.

The impudence of the man! thought Amy, and aloud she said, "I really don't think that I should be showing off this— object; it's not been authenticated, and its ultimate destiny is—in doubt." She sat down beside him, looked him in the eye, so that he might not turn around and see the green floral hatbox behind the door. "Also I will need to get back to work." She poured tea into her Minton tea set; "Is this strong enough for you? Please tell me about your work at Keio University."

It is never a mistake to ask a professor about his work; some signals are universal, and this is one of them. "I specialize in early Japanese history," he said, "the period before the arrival of Europeans. I am interested in early Japanese contacts with China and other parts of east Asia. Of course, when Ueda Toyoichiro told me about a bronze object found on Whidbey Island, I had to come immediately to see it."

"And are there similar discoveries recorded from our West Coast?" Amy asked, to keep the ball in motion.

"Ah, no, not as recorded...as authentic. We have to be very careful not to assign as genuine things which may only be rumor, you see." He was sipping tea; he was warming to his work. "Reports of early contacts across the Pacific are still unsettled. Chinese visits to Mexico—a Japanese cup found in South America—all must be treated with the utmost caution. But the rumors are interesting—very interesting. The Kuro Shiwo—the Black Current—boats could have come on it as far as the Aleutians, and objects from a lost expedition could have been traded among your Indians. Perhaps in some museum here in Washington...."

Amy found herself piqued with the idea in spite of herself, and she fought down an impulse to jump up from the tea-table and tell him everything, let him have the box, the incense burner—almost anything else. But tea-tables, she realized, usually react badly to someone jumping near them. Okakura would have advised against it. Professor Oyeyama hesitated before launching onto a discourse; Amy guessed he might not be up to delivering a lecture in English, on trans-Pacific archaeology.

Meanwhile, if she was to get back to work, and to not let him know that she had the incense burner, the only recourse she had left was to get him out of her office as soon as she could, without committing a rudeness like his own. She fell back on conversational cliches. "Is this your first visit to America?"

"Oh, no—I am sometimes here, for the past few years. I am also interested in buying material from American Indian cultures.

We have so little to study of that, in Japan."

Well, this isn't American Indian, whatever it is, thought Amy. The important thing is for him not to see it. "You should visit our Southwest," she said, aloud; "there are native American workers there, who would be interested in selling you something—baskets, pottery, whatever. And then there's Mexico," she went on hastily. "The charming black pottery of Tzintzuntzan."

"Ah, no. I am interested in older work," said Professor Oyeyama, teacup at lips.

Amy knew well enough that "older work" was a maze of complications. And she had heard of poachers and black marketeers. "Of course, we have nothing of the sort here," she said firmly. "Is that good tea?"

"Very good," said Professor Oyeyama. "Of course, nothing not legitimate," he added with a grin. Did he guess her mind? "I am not a *pocher!*" He giggled, sharp indrawn breaths; rhyming the word, Amy realized, with *gotch'er.*

Never trust a man who laughs backwards, thought Amy; it ought to be some ethnic proverb. Any minute now, he's going to turn around and see the hatbox; she watched him, as his eyes scanned the room. Better get it out of here: to Special Collections, for example, where it couldn't be viewed by every Tom, Dick and Harry who happened to drop in on the College Librarian. "We have so few treasures from antiquity, here in America," she said, "that we tend to be very tight-fisted about the ones we have." If that wasn't a hint, then World War Two was a backyard fist-fight.

"I know you are anxious about this piece," said Professor Oyeyama, setting down his teacup, "and perhaps I could help you identify it. I specialize in early Japanese history, you see."

It was time for Amy to be firm. "The vessel is secured," she said, almost as if it were a ship brought into port. She arose, rang for Judith, and when she appeared, Amy nodded silently, away from Professor Oyeyama, made a spiral wiggle with her forefinger; and Judith picked up the box, and withdrew. Amy knew that Judith would not let the box out of her sight until she had been relieved at her post by Amy herself. It's so good when people understand without missed signals and demands for explanation. Judith Brown, you're a nonpareil.

Amy noticed Professor Oyeyama catching sight of an object being carried away behind him. The No mask flinched. Amy went on: "You must please excuse this rudeness. The item which you inquire after" (she hoped she was being sufficiently curious to please what she imagined was the Japanese style) "has given rise to much talk. I am about to convene a panel of scholars" (she was making up this script as she went along) "to decide on this piece, its provenance and its authenticity" (she liked those long words, hoping that they would be more likely to impress a No demon than plain English) "and until then, the incense burner must be 'out of sight, out of mind.' Would you like some more tea?"

"No thank you," said Professor Oyeyama. "It is a pity that I cannot examine this piece in isolation, until, as you say, excitement has died down." (I said nothing of the sort, Amy thought confusedly—did I?) He produced a calling card, and added, "When the panel is summoned, I should be glad to join it; or if I will be back in Japan at the time, I should be greatly obliged to receive a copy of the report." He stood up. "I fear I too must commit a rudeness. It is time for me to return to Tumtulips, and later on, to Japan. I shall take the opportunity, someday, to visit your beautiful Southwest. Thank you for the tea. Thank you," he bowed, and Amy saw him out the door. The last she saw of him was the back of his head, swivelling about looking for the mysterious box. But Amy could see it was under Judith's desk, between her sensible brown oxfords.

Amy said "Good-bye," without any further speech, and closed the door behind him. It was suddenly warm in the room, although it was November outside, and she poured herself a glass of cold water from the closet. She sank back into her office chair. Where should the piece go? Special Collections, of course; there was a safe there too, and none of these outsiders knew where that was. But could Aaron Dodder be trusted not to tell?

Amy carried the tea-things to the sink in the closet and washed them up quickly. She telephoned for Aaron Dodder, who was not in, but was expected back shortly; retrieved the box with the incense burner from Judith Brown; and while waiting for Mr. Dodder, picked up Okakura Kakuzo's *Book of tea,* in order to calm herself from the tensions of abruptly dismissing Professor Oyeyama. Had that been wise? The serenity of Okakura's book might advise her. She opened the little volume at random, and found herself involved in calculations.

"The size of the orthodox tea-room, which is four mats and a half, or ten feet square" (she read), "is determined by a passage in the Sutra of Vikramadytia." Amy took out her pocket calculator: 100 square feet divided by 4.5 = 22.2; the square root of that is 4.7; assuming Japanese mats are square—a gratuitous and doubtless false assumption, she realized,—that means we have 4 mats, 4.7 on a side, or 88.4 square feet, plus another 11 square feet, that comes to 99.4 square feet or so—close enough. She looked around her office; this room was obviously too large for a genuine Japanese tea-room, or *sukiya.* She had been entertaining all these Japanese scholars in a room twenty by thirty feet, six times the area pre-scribed for a real Zen tea-room. She went on: "In that interesting work, Vikramdytia welcomes the Saint Manjushiri and eighty-four thousand disciples in a room of this size—an allegory based on the non-existence of space to the truly enlightened." Useless to reach for the calculator; the 84,001 Buddhists filled the room, ecto-plasms with a thousandth of a square foot between them, rustling sutras as softly as snnowflakes falling. "The non-existence of space to the truly enlightened"! To such as Professor Oyeyama, the authenticity and provenance, even perhaps the ownership, of someone else's property were non-existent, providing one was truly enlightened. What did it matter, whose incense burner it was, or even whether it was Chinese or Japanese or fake, providing it was placed in a suitable spot, where a reverent eye could view it in a room of four mats and a half? As for these other gentlemen, Professors Ueda and Kumagai, what did she know about them? After all, the non-existence of space implied the non-existence of objects within that space (wasn't that right?) and therefore, of the incense burner, and therefore, of Amy herself.

To those lacking enlightenment, the casual encounter with Buddhist thought is apt to induce confusion, even paranoia. Amy had never seriously sought enlightenment, but running an academic library is apt to induce its own kind of hallucinations; so she felt almost relieved when Aaron Dodder was admitted to her office.

"Aaron," she said sternly, rising from her chair and holding up the box with the incense burner in it, "this object—whatever it is—has already attracted too much attention. I had to chase a visiting Japanese scholar out of here, who dropped in unannounced, and without invitation, just to get a look at the thing. I want you to take this, and put it into the Special Collections safe. Not just the stacks, or your desk, the safe—do you understand?" (Aaron Dodder was somewhat deaf). "You're to put it in there with your own hands, and you're not to tell anybody where it is. Understand? And if anybody asks, you know nothing about it. Only you and I have the combination of that safe. Remember!" She added: "Come to think of it, you and I will put it there together. Then I'll sleep better tonight."

Amy closed the box, tucked it under her left arm—it was heavy—and ushered Aaron Dodder out the door, as he made his response. "I see what you mean about secrecy," he began. "One of my great-uncles came from England, and this was during the First World War, you know, the fourteen-eighteen, they call it, over there, and he had a job in British Intelligence, the MI5, they call it, and his job was to decipher the code of the Austro-Hungarian Navy, of course he found it out, but he couldn't tell us, and it took a long time, and he only figured it out by the end of the war, and by that time there wasn't an Austria-Hungary any more, and now that Austria and Hungary are all different, they don't have a seacoast, either of them, so they can't have a navy, what do you think of that, of course you know that...."

"THE WILHELMINA CATS COLLECTION IS IN DANGER!" cried Araminta Vane, standing, legs apart, in the doorway of Amy's office, her red and gray hair flaring behind her like some exotic flag. "One of the Trustees has found out that it's all about lesbians!"

Amy looked up from her desk. "Come in and sit down," said Amy. "There's always tea." ("Said Katsugen, 'The Sages move the world.'" That was from Okakura's *Book of tea*).

"There's no *time* for tea!" said Araminta, for whom, Amy realized, the Sages would be as irrelevant as the anecdotes of Aaron Dodder. "Richard Maule wants to get rid of lesbians!"

"Well, he can't," said Amy. "What's the status of the Cats collection now? I forget."

Araminta came in and sat down on the straight-backed chair near the tea-table, and stared at the chrysanthemums in the crystal vase on Amy's desk. "Wilhelmina Cats's son," she began, as if going over a lesson for a forgetful person, "you know even lesbians have children, sometimes" (by parthenogenesis? wondered Amy, but kept her thoughts to herself) "offered us his late mother's collection of lesbian fiction, poetry, history, sociology, *and* all the rest of it, *for*—" she paused for emphasis—"thirty thousand dollars, which is five dollars a volume, and a simply *incredible* bargain."

"Yes, but how far did we get with the negotiations? This was back in February, I think, and I recall we were going to see if anyone on the faculty would make use of it. You were going to report back to me."

"Well," Araminta admitted, "I haven't been able to stir up much interest. But…"

Amy cut her off. "That's what I feared. It's a huge amount to get through the budget of a small school like ours, even if it is a bargain, and wouldn't it be better off at the University? Rhododendron simply should not be buying large research collections. Remember what Mildred Collins used to say: 'Rhododendron College is not a university, and should not attempt university practices.'"

"But it's *lesbians!*" cried Araminta, sitting up straighter than ever. "And the collection is in danger!"

"How did it get into danger?"

"Someone heard about it," said Araminta, "and told *everyone.*"

"Who? How and where?"

"I don't know!"

"With whom did *you* talk about it?"

"With Joy. She'd understand; she's a lesbian too."

Amy knew that. "Was your conversation inside the library, or outside?"

"Inside...maybe; only once outside."

It was Amy's turn to get excited. "Outside! Where?"

Araminta brought it out with an effort: "The Tinglebell Tea Room," and sank back into her chair.

"The *Tinglebell!* My dear, I *never* go in there. There's this little bell which trips whenever anyone opens the door, and those little sandwiches, and everybody's spreading gossip about everyone else...it's the most *nauseous* little place north of Carmel. I'd rather tempt my luck at the Sockeye Saloon...nobody there knows *any* Trustee. So what happened?"

"You can get *raped* at the Sockeye!" cried Araminta, sitting up straight again.

"But you didn't," contiued Amy levelly, " 'cause you weren't there. Instead, you were at the Tinglebell, and..."

"We were discussing the Cats collection," continued Araminta, and then, defiantly, "I was telling Joy why you didn't want to buy it—"

"Thereby putting words in my mouth," said Amy sternly.

"I'm sorry—and—the *nicest*-looking lady, a little blonde person, came up to us, guess she had just finished her tea, and said, 'Isn't it nice you're going to buy this lesbian collection, I'm sure everyone will be so pleased,' and by the time I could get my wits about me, and ask who she was, she was out the door—tingaling-aling!"

"At the Tinglebell. She was probably the sister or daughter of one of the Trustees. *Nous sommes perdues.*"

"Exactly what I was going to say myself," said Joy, entering at that moment. "Except that it isn't necessarily true. This Maule person, who's on the Board, has been bugging Shepherd about the collection, and about my insignificant person. But dear Miz Lou isn't about to do anything, and in this case, it's just as well. You can't be fired, even here, for what you do at home." But she wrinkled her little nose, like a small predator sensing danger.

"Shut the door, one of you," said Amy. She picked up the phone and told Judith Brown, "no visitors, no calls forwarded." "Now look, this matter has gone far enough. By the way, was there anyone else you were talking to, at the Tinglebell?"

"Only me," said Joy, cutting Araminta off. "And I told her to keep her voice down."

"Then both of you have had something to do with the problem. The Faculty Club is the place to dine —they have conference rooms. But please God, never again the Tinglebell; you can hear everything in the room when it's quiet. Now, have you any idea who this blonde person was?"

"No," said Joy, "I'd never seen her before; and she wasn't blonde any more, she was—getting older, like the rest of us."

"Now—Richard Maule—what do we know about him—and what does he know about us?"

"He's new—on the Board," said Joy, who had taken command of the answers, Amy noticed; Araminta was slumped down in her seat, like a student who knows she has already failed in the orals, and is relieved to be replaced by a pupil better prepared; "but not new to Rhododendron—class of '54, I believe. Rich— airlines and lager beer. Conservative? American Family Association. Church—Episcopal; politics—Republican. Looked him up in *Who's Who*."

"Person or persons unknown, therefore, brought the whole thing to his attention, one of them being a blondish person—"

"*D'un certain âge*," Joy said. "But it really doesn't matter, because the Trustees aren't concerned with the daily running of the library—surely?"

"In this college, the Trustees can do anything they really want," Amy pointed out. "At bottom, this is a mom-and-pop operation, and they can, if they really want, fire you for the color of your eyes. That's not the point. What I was going to say, is—"

Judith Brown poked her head inside the door. "Professor Kumagai."

"Please, tell him—"

"He won't wait. Very urgent."

"Excuse me." Amy got up, went to the door, shut it behind her. Jiro Kumagai was blinking rapidly, he was rather red in the face; there were snowflakes on his overcoat, and the wart on his nose flared dully. He had obviously walked rapidly here through the snow. "You must ask Mr. Connolly to stop telephoning my daughter," he began, without preamble or apology.

"Dr. Kumagai," said Amy, "I have already told him that it is inadvisable for members of the academic staff to date undergraduates." Why did everything in her professional life begin with, or end up with, sex?

"Date? He wants to sleep with her!"

The lad is normal, if not wise, Amy thought. "I cannot control him, I can only warn him."

"He must not sleep with my daughter! He must not phone her any more!"

"To stop that, is quite beyond me, I'm afraid. I've told him not to date undergraduates."

Professor Kumagai blinked rapidly. Amy went on: "I'll remind him again, but in the long run, it's between your daughter and Patrick Connolly. She has to tell him to stop, and he has to understand. There's a College regulation against harassment," she added, and then: "We're in the midst of a crisis meeting. Could you—?" She hoped that he would finish her thought for her. But instead, Professor Kumagai backed away, almost bowing. "I understand, I understand," he said, and she thought she heard menace in the phrase. "Good-bye, Mrs. Rose," leaving out the "Dr." and "Ogilvie"; not everyone remembered or could be expected to, but this time it made Amy feel uneasy. "Good-bye, Mrs. Rose." And he disappeared.

Amy re-entered her office with nothing like relief. "Where were we?" brushing her hand over her forehead. It had been her mother's gesture, which she had always resented, but now she was using it. Well, these things come around in time.

"You were about to say something you were about to say," said Joy, accurately enough.

"About the Cats collection," said Araminta.

"Of course, about the Cats collection." She resumed her seat at the desk. It was safer there, now that she remembered what message she had to deliver. "I just don't think Rhododendron should be buying this collection. Araminta hasn't been able to stir up much interest among the faculty, and this is a huge collection for a small college like ours. Indeed, our collection is too large for a school of less than a thousand students; we've accumulated three hundred thousand volumes, placed many in storage, but still large amounts of the collection are seventy years out of date and don't belong here at all."

"But we can't get rid of it," said Joy, "because Miss Willow Goldfinch went around and solicited gifts and bequests from the county's *haute bourgeoisie.*"

"And she put bookplates with their names in them," said Araminta. "I know. But surely those people are dead. Can't we have a grand clearance sale, after removing the College book-plate?"

"You can't, in a place like this," Amy said wearily. "People find, and discover, and come, and accuse. At the Tinglebell," she said, with a sidelong glance at Araminta. Araminta kept silence and stared at the chrysanthemums on Amy's desk. "No, the Cats collection has nothing to do with what we're trying to do, here at Rhododendron, and certainly not with a library which needs to have every extraneous non-gift title weeded clean out of the building."

"But if you *don't* acquire it," said Araminta, sitting erect again, "you've capitulated to Richard Maule!"

"And if we do get it," Joy said, placidly, "we've wasted the Trustees' money."

"Quite right," said Amy, "which is why I vote no."

"But you're forgetting Joy," said Araminta. "Evidently Richard Maule knows that Joy is a lesbian. And you just got through saying that they could fire us for the color of our eyes."

"Not quite that," said Amy, "and anyway, how do they know?"

"Let me speak for myself, please," Joy cut in. "We don't have any evidence except the oral. Something Prescott's wife said at one of Shepherd's teas. She knows two or three wives of people on the Board. All very ladylike and quite vicious. But no proof of anything."

"We can't ignore it, for all that," said Amy. "The important thing, however, is to do the right thing; and the right thing is to turn down the Cats collection and start weeding back issues of the *Zeitschrift für erlöschene Zentralasiatische Sprache*. Now that Professor Popov has died, we no longer need to retain them."

"But it's a *lesbian* collection!"

"Araminta, *please…*"

"And this is an *intellectual freedom* issue!"

"Only if we decide it is," Amy told both her colleagues. "It would be different, if the collection were already here, and Richard Maule wanted us to get rid of it. Even so, we'd still have to ask ourselves how and why we got a research collection of that size in the first place, with no faculty activity to justify it. We can say no, and let Maule think what he pleases."

"You're forgetting the L-word," said Araminta. "Lesbians and gay men will be watching this."

"'This is a watchbird watching a College Librarian,'" quoted Joy. "'This is a watchbird watching *you*.'" But she was smiling; and Araminta was not.

"My dear Araminta, dear both of you. If I did things because people were watching, I'd go paranoid. I remember one time at PNLA, some progressive librarians—they called themselves that—wanted us to endorse the cultural aspirations of the Armenian people by recognizing the republic of Armenia in its 'historic territory'—whatever that means; what Armenia was somewhere back in the second century. When I asked what this had to do with library concerns, I was told that it was a cultural matter, and finally that some people were watching us. I didn't notice any Armenians with binoculars at the conference, but the resolution failed anyway. The time comes when we have to stand up and say no, whether to Armenians, lesbians, or librarians." Amy leaned back in her chair as she finished. *I'm now in my* fifties, she thought; I'm getting too old for this.

"Then I'm to tell the Cats family we don't want the collection," said Araminta.

"Yes, but don't feel too badly about it," Amy said. "The Cats collection is not a cat, at the pound. If you don't save a cat at the pound it will be put to sleep—"

"Gassed," said Araminta, "within forty-eight hours."

"—but the Cats collection will not. They'll offer it to Wyoming, or UC Santa Cruz, or New York Public, and it'll be off our desks."

"And Richard Maule will triumph," said Araminta.

Amy was quiet for a moment. "I think that we better get back to our work." She stood up, to indicate that the meeting was over. "Joy, I want to see you in the Library courtyard, if you don't mind a walk in the snow."

IN THE COURTYARD OF THE LIBRARY, the walkways were newly shovelled clean of snow. The snow was banked on either side, and the meltwater made the paths black as midnight. Overhead the skies had been cleared by last night's sharp wind. The aspens in the courtyard were bare; their winter buds were tight as secrets. Only the witch hazel offered small shy November blooms.

Amy was dressed in a lamb's-wool overcoat and cap to match. Joy had on her camel's-hair coat and a green muff to warm her hands in. The outside thermometer said: minus five degrees Celsius.

Amy looked at her friend's outfit. "You look like a Kate Greenaway lady," said Amy.

"Do I? Aren't they all little girls of no more than twelve? But you're a Russian princess."

"Perhaps I should go back and claim a throne," said Amy, "or at least an estate. But I'm just a College Librarian." How much she and Joy had been through together: early loves, travels, administrative crises, a second marriage for Amy, a lover for Joy.

"You know," Joy began as they paced the walkways, their

breaths a pair of clouds before them, "sometimes you have to get away from this sort of trouble. You should take a vacation—go back to the Spokane family. You can take Sandy easily if you go by train; it won't tire him."

"I might go at Christmas," said Amy; "I haven't been for three years. But people keep manufacturing crises behind your back. And there aren't enough of us to go round; I can't shovel these problems at some assistant underling."

"You don't treat us as underlings anyway, which leaves only the Tingalings."

"If you mean the people who go to the Tinglebell Tea Room, I can't get rid of Araminta, and I *won't* get rid of you. President Shepherd may not be strong enough to shout down the Trustees, but she's too lazy to order me to fire you. Anyway, we all have contracts."

"They say something about 'moral turpitude.' And that's been upheld in the courts, against a gay man."

"That was a school district, as I recall," said Amy. "This is an academic library. Joy, if the Trustees try anything: resignations, resolutions at PNLA, feature articles in the *Chronicle of Higher Education*—they'd never hear the end of it. No, they'll sit on this problem and let this fundamentalist go off the Board at the end of three years. Next question."

"Our colleague."

"As I say, similarly protected. I inherited her from Miss Goldfinch, and she's too old to change. Let's face it, she runs a good reference desk. She's totally forthright about controversial questions, and she knows everything. She knows the states by their dates of joining the Union, she knows the distance to Mars, and yesterday I heard her carefully distinguish the flag of Latvia from that of Belorus, and both from that of Austria,—all without consulting the *World Almanac*."

"But she could forget. She *ought* to look it all up in the *World Almanac*. One day she'll start getting Alzheimer's, and get Arkansas mixed up with Michigan."

"We can't prevent that," said Amy. She was silent a moment.

"Do you know that the proper size for a Japanese tea room is a hundred square feet, that is, ten feet on a side, which is four Japanese mats and a half? I've been serving tea to those scholars in a room six times too big. The Japanese mat could be four point seven feet—a square; or four by five and a half feet; or nearly seven and a half feet by three feet. But I don't have a proper tea room."

"Then call it an audience hall," said Joy, "like the one in Nijo Castle. Have Professor Kumagai knock his head on the floor several times when he dares—*dares!*—to interrupt you."

"An audience hall! With nightingale floors!"

"And Patrick Connolly as Lord High Executioner!"

"Ah, no, he is to be executed. Miserable creature—in only a T-shirt and loincloth, kneeling, head on block—I'm afraid he's a source of trouble."

"You must, you absolutely must, send him a written notice regarding his conduct. Professor Kumagai is perfectly capable of going to the Student Affairs Council. At that point you should have a file copy of a letter of warning."

"You're right. But I hate doing it to people. The boy is just too full of hormones. And too empty of judgment."

"You have no time to lose, then. Draw up a paper, call a meeting, and he will have to sign it, in our presence."

"Within the hour. Then can I take the vacation you're urging me to take?"

"No, sorry, you'll still have to lecture Araminta. You say she's too old to change. She's totally competent, true, but still she butts into areas not her concern. After that, you'll have to persuade Aaron Dodder to retire, and then defend the latest round of merit salary increases, and then—I'll let you go to Spokane for a week. Detours to Sun Valley prohibited. You're right, we're both getting too old for this."

"Aaron Dodder is getting too old for this, too," said Amy, as she watched him limping up the wet-slippery path. His large nose was red and his sunken cheeks glowed faintly. Was it the cold, or was it excitement?

"Mrs. Rose-Ogilvie," he began, stammering, "Professor

Oyeyama was here, he wanted to see the bronze object which you had entrusted to my care, and I let him look at it when he was in my office, and when I was called away to greet another scholar in the front reading room of the department, Professor Oyeyama and the caldron—I mean the incense burner—"

"Oh, no," said Amy and Joy together.

"—were gone."

Amy looked at the ground, and then raised her face to Aaron Dodder's. He looked as if he had been stricken with a terrible fever. His eyes were bright, his nose dripped, his aged frame shook like a cottonwood leaf. There was a long silence. The three looked at each other.

Amy never felt in herself such mastery as when she did not call Aaron Dodder a fool to his face. He was not supposed to have to let any visitor know he had the treasure.

"He had a confederate. Or he was supremely lucky. Joy, please go call the campus police." Joy left immediately. "Aaron," with a sigh, "was that other person a real visitor?"

"A real visitor? It was Dr. Brady, from the university. He wanted to look at our sixteenth-century Bibles. We have several of them, as you know, the Fleming bequest, and—"

"I know. Where were your staff?"

"Gudule" (Meeus, second in charge of the department), "was helping Larry and Cory unpack and sort the SRRT correspondence. They were in the back, and—"

"So Oyeyama got out the door with the incense burner in a box, past you, past Circulation, all the while you were talking with Dr. Brady. He must have walked right under your nose! There aren't two public exits from your department."

The nose dripped with a tiny, clouded opal. "I fear I became engrossed in discussing the typographical oddities in early Bibles. Therewas the 'Breeches Bible', and the 'Printers' Bible', and the 'Adulterers' Bible', and—"

"Follow me, please." Amy led the way to her office. In the few minutes before the campus police arrived, she managed to reach Professor Ueda at Tumtulips, who gave her to understand that

Professor Oyeyama's return flight to Tokyo's Haneda Airport was expected to depart Seattle sometime late that afternoon.

Chief Mulvaney's interrogation of the four librarians—Patrick Connolly had been summoned at the Chief's request—was long and arduous. When Amy pointed out that Oyeyama had quite possibly already left the country, Chief Mulvaney, a big, smiling man, placidly assured her that Japanese customs officials would be informed long before Oyeyama's flight reached Japan. Then all four librarians were taken down to the campus police office to be fingerprinted, and released without charges, until further notice. Their departure, through the back door of the library, did not pass unnoticed by the mail room staff—a cornucopia of rumor and misinformation.

THE POET VERGIL tells us that Fame is a monster. She has so many eyes, so many sounding tongues; she goes upon the ground, yet flies above the clouds; and she terrorizes great cities. Who, then, launched this creature on evil wings? Was it Aaron Dodder, who noticed the safe open? Was it Gudule Meeus, the gentle Belgian girl, who thought no ill of her supervisor, but knew him to be overage for his job? Was it slender Larry and lovely blonde Cory, who came out to Aaron's cry of dismay? At all events, when Amy, Joy, Aaron and Patrick had returned from their visit to the campus police station, some sort of tale had spread beyond Special Collections and the Administrative Office, and connected with another from the Mail Room. Then who, in the name of Erinnye and all the Furies, brought the news to the ears of Dr. Kumagai?

Professor Kumagai was everywhere, like heat lightning: telephoning the Student Affairs Council about Patrick Connolly, telephoning the police and his lawyer, until Mrs. Kumagai, a plump Japanese woman who rarely commented on anything but the weather and family affairs, suggested that such activity would not be good for the reputation of the house; and his daughter, in tears, begged him to stop. But Professor Kumagai was in the grip of a conspiracy theory, and conspiracy theorists do not know

when to stop. He left messages for Amy, who was in council.
Amy did not answer them. She was herself pressed for time.

First of all, she had all the players, including Araminta, in, to
impose absolute silence on the matter. (She did not know that
Rumor, with feathers, tongues, eyes, etc. had already lifted off and
was in full flight). Araminta, for once, did not talk back, perhaps
because she resented being fingerprinted; for her, all contact with
the "pigs" was the prelude to unwarranted arrest and brutal,
unprovoked assault. Afterwards Amy dismissed all but Joy.

"We've never faced anything like this," Amy said, chin in
hand.

"If we could get hold of the box—and its contents—before he
left for Japan—?"

"Impossible. We shall have to wait until the Japanese return it
to us."

"If he could be detained in Seattle…"

"If we knew his flight."

"Once back in Japan, he's free for further depredations."

"If Chief Mulvaney were to call the airlines, and ask if there is
a Professor Oyeyama on any passenger manifest…?"

"Then Chief Mulvaney has to arrest a distinguished foreign
scholar."

"If we were to place the call instead…?"

"The police don't like interference with their activities."

"No matter how well-intentioned."

"True. So now we have to sit and wait."

"Hoping that no one has said anything."

"You must induce Aaron Dodder to retire."

"Before he drops dead."

"Before he does. Indeed."

"Indeedydead," Amy said.

INDEED HE DID. Aaron Dodder went upstairs, slowly, to his
Special Collections Department, went into his office, placed his
elbow on his desk and his chin in hand, and presently elbow, chin
and head were slumped on his desk. This was no foul and most

unnatural murder; Providence, merciful Providence, had taken
Aaron Dodder to its—bosom? The poets are not as explicit about
the anatomy of Providence, as they are about the monstrous con-
stitution of Fame.

Gudule Meeus, having observed her supervisor's quiet, and
later his collapse, went to his office, knocked gently; and then,
seeing no change in his position, touched him oh so delicately
behind the ear, and finding him cold, found herself *de facto*, if not
yet *de jure*, Acting Head of the Special Collections Department,
Willow Goldfinch Library, Rhododendron College, Rosetree,
Washington. It greatly explains her elevation to permanency in
that headship, that she first closed his office blinds, next dismissed
Larry and Cory for the day, closed the department and secured
the doors, and then, without many words, calmly informed (by
telephone) Amy of Aaron Dodder's decease. Then Gudule sat
down in the outer office, and with hands folded, and curly head
bowed, she recited ten Hail Mary's and ten Lord's Prayers. By the
time she had finished, Captain Mulvaney had arrived.

Captain Mulvaney was rather surprised at having to be called
twice to the Goldfinch Library,—first for a case of theft, second
for a dead body on the second floor. He summoned a doctor from
the student clinic, and the county coroner. The coroner himself
looked like a case for the coroner: long wrinkled face, and nico-
tine-stained teeth. The doctor and the coroner pronounced Aaron
Dodder dead, after the doctor, a plump, elderly man with a gold
watch chain, had endeavored to revive him. The department
remained closed; the body would be removed to the morgue, after
the building was closed, by way of the back door. Judith Brown
was sent to look up the next of kin, who was David Dodder, his
younger brother in Florida,—at the extreme opposite corner of
the Republic.

"Have Aaron mummified," said Joy, looking drawn and tired.
"They'll never know the difference."

Amy was about to reply, when the phone rang. It was the
press; another phone ten minutes later, then another, until Amy
decided to hang up, go home, eat a decent meal (with wine), and

ignore the answering machine. Thereby she avoided calls from the press ("Dr. Rose-Ogilvie could not be reached for comment,") but also one from the excitable Professor Kumagai.

PROFESSOR KUMAGAI WENT BALLISTIC. Against the advice of his attorney, Mr. O'Malley, he telephoned the press, suggesting that the incense burner, of whose provenance he had been not at all sure ten days ago, was (whether Chinese or Japanese, Han, Ming, or Kamakura) surely (whatever that means, or meant) a valuable artifact; that Amy had sold it to Professor Oyeyama, a notorious dealer in stolen Orientalia; and had wrongly blamed Aaron Dodder, who had stabbed his life out in despair.

Readers of the histrionic press (Left or Right) will recognize the methods by which the formerly cautious Professor Kumagai, roused to fury by the suggestion of a *gaijin* that his daughter yield her maidenhead, constructed a dubious possibility, two outright fabrications, and a fabrication based on a half-truth (Aaron Dodder was dead, yes, but not a suicide) into a full-fledged conspiracy theory. When next you read an item, findable in the tabloids at the grocery counter, about JFK, Marilyn Monroe, or Elvis—think: you may buy your tale too dear: Remember Dr. Kumagai.

The next seventy-two hours were difficult. Amy was obliged to meet the press. But she had to change her tale as time went on, because Patrick Connolly, heedless of Amy's reminder that the police like to solve their own cases, jumped into his VW bus and went into pursuit of Dr. Oyeyama. He decided not to check first at the airport at Port Angeles; instead he drove all the way to Kingston, took the auto ferry to Edmonds, and then straight through Seattle on Interstate 5 to the international airport, in the surely hopeless task and impossible chance of finding Dr. Oyeyama about to board a plane.

And he did find him. Standing in line before the Northwest Airlines counter, Dr. Oyeyama heard a young voice call out: "WHERE IS THE INCENSE BURNER?"

Everybody turned round; so did Dr. Oyeyama.

"The incense burner? I have not got it. See, I have just these two bags."

"You checked it through!"

"No, I have not even come to the counter yet!"

"You shipped it air freight!"

Dr. Oyeyama looked around him. "I am at the end of this line. No one is behind us. Therefore, I just arrived."

"From the air freight place, wherever that is."

"You do not believe me. Go and ask them. I did not steal the College Library's property. I merely wanted to examine it. I would not have taken it back without permission. Dr. Rose was suspicious, but I am not a 'pocher.'"

Patrick, red hair unkempt, stared at Dr. Oyeyama wildly. The man certainly had a sinister, even ugly, mug; but "go and ask," was either the sheerest bravado, or the simplest truth from a man who did look unpleasant and had pushy manners. Patrick, who had no more tendency to think in stereotypes than most youths, was discovering that unpleasant people can be honest.

(Later, on the way home, he realized that the reverse was true about himself).

The two bags were obviously the wrong size and shape for concealing a bulky cubical box like the one that the incense burner had been in; and even without the box, it could not have slipped inside an attache case or a folding garment bag. Patrick turned away with a four-letter word which was clearly audible within a radius of two meters.

"And even if you had gone to the air freight center, would they have told you who had shipped what freight where?" Joy asked Patrick when he got back that evening. "And if they had, how would you have laid claim to it? If he got it out of the library and as far as the airport, it's as good as in Japan already. Then it's up to the Japanese to take care of it."

"Then maybe he didn't steal it after all?"

"Maybe he buried it, somewhere in the College gardens," said Joy, contemptuously. "Now get back to the reference desk; I see you have students waiting."

FLOODS IN TEXAS AND CHINA took up the attention of
the press within a few days, and only a local paper informed its
readers that Dr. Kumagai had been admitted to the observation
ward of the University Hospital. The campus police, too, filed a
case in which there were (for the present) no clues, and merely
sent a descriptive letter, through the proper channels, to Japan.
Amy and her colleagues were left to pursue the mystery alone; or
to bury it, as it had once been buried, as probably not worth further time and effort.

Remained, however, Aaron Dodder. Several people, fur-coat-
ed, emerging from his memorial service, were heard to breathe
sadly, that poor Aaron had died after having been falsely accused
of collusion in theft (nobody in the library had suggested such a
thing—but see above under "Rumor.") Though without a clue,
Amy, Joy and Araminta were somehow expected to come up with
the incense burner, and thereby clear poor Aaron Dodder's name.

Some days, however, passed before there was even time to
discuss the matter.

"Possession, *Aimée chérie*," said Joy, "does not prove theft. Even
if we went to his house and found it in his bathroom, that merely
tells us that he was going to use it for some unspeakable purpose,
not that he was stealing it; it would merely be in the wrong place.
On the other hand, if we found a bill of sale to Sotheby's..."

"If Sotheby's took it, it would be the worst mistake in their
two hundred fifty years," said Amy. "We must hunt up every clue.
We must question his staff, we must have the garden beds examined, we must look in basements—before Dr. Kumagai gets out of
the observation ward."

"Amy, Amy, you'll end up there yourself if you don't let this
thing go."

Aaron Dodder's office was locked, but Amy used her master
key; it was obvious that the bronze vessel was not in there. Amy
examined the safe; Aaron's desk was locked and no one knew
where the key was, but the drawers looked too small to hold the
vessel, the way the librarians remembered it. No accurate mea-
surements had ever been taken, since there had been no need for

them while the "caldron" was still in the library's keeping; once it
was gone, it seemed to grow bigger every time they thought of it.
In Amy's dreams it became a ritual bathtub, it widened to oceanic
dimensions; in it floated the planet Saturn.

Amy had the staff questioned, the department searched; the
library was discreetly examined from top to bottom, with the aid
of Amy's master key to the building. A man was brought in from
Buildings and Grounds with a mine detector from Fort Lewis.
He went over the tulip beds, his boots destroying, as Amy noted,
any footprints in the rain-soft earth. A metal object was brought
with much careful digging to the surface; it proved to be an old
plowshare.

"Amy, Amy, the thing is *absolument disparu.*"

The official inquiry went farther; to the air freight counter at
Northwest Airlines; no, they had no record of any Oyeyama, nor
any shipment by anyone of that name; to Professor Ueda, at
Tumtulips, who had no recollection of Professor Oyeyama's having brought the incense burner, and who was indignant at the idea
that the incense burner was either in his house, in his office, or in
his possession; to Dr. Kumagai, now out of the University
Hospital, who was at home but wouldn't come to the phone.

"Amy, Amy, *cela n'ira pas.* You're driving the whole staff crazy,
we're behind on the budget process, and you have three new gray
hairs in your raven coiffure."

"But what was it Sherlock Holmes said? 'When you have elim-
inated all the obvious explanations, what remains, however improbable, must be the truth.' Things don't look well for Mr. Dodder."

"You sound more like your Nancy Drew."

"We haven't searched his house yet."

"You get the warrant, Amy," said Joy, and left Amy's office:
turned on her heel and walked out.

Within the hour Judith Brown announced Daniel Dodder,
who marched in briskly. He extended his hand to Amy, and he
shook it hard. "I am Aaron Dodder's younger brother and his
executor. Where is his desk key?"

A man less like Aaron Dodder, Amy could not imagine.

Instead of the lank, stooping, large-nosed Aaron, here was a man of broad shoulders, middle height, black brows, hair cut short, bronze skin and high cheekbones. Amy thought of gunmetal; harsh orders.

"You've lost the key. Never mind, I have a duplicate. Aaron was always losing things. You wouldn't have an inventory? No. Please open his office and have the goodness to remain while I gather up his papers."

Amy took Daniel to Aaron's office. The department staff hovered at the door.

Daniel Dodder unlocked the middle drawer of his late brother's desk, sorted through it hastily, handed Amy whatever papers bore the College letterhead, while Amy tossed into the wastebasket whatever was no longer relevant. Some letters bore a date ten years earlier.

The middle drawer, the top left, the bottom left, files: it took some time to go through those. The top right: more junk. The bottom drawer, large. The key opened the lock with difficulty. The drawer slid open.

There was the incense burner, in its box, and the box on top of its lid. It was smaller than Amy remembered, and yet it was the same: Amy saw that. Gudule, at the door, saw it; so did Larry and Cory; Joy, coming upstairs to find Amy, saw it too. Araminta was looking through the glass partition that separated Aaron's office from the rest of the department.

Amy lowered her eyes; closed them. There was a long, long pause.

"This isn't mine," said Daniel Dodder.

Amy opened her eyes, made herself lean forward, take the bronze vessel in its box, place the lid on top of it, and carry it outside Aaron Dodder's office. She heard Joy tell Gudule to let Daniel Dodder out of the office when he had finished; she had no time, herself, for explanations or excuses. Amy carried the box down to her office, followed by her senior colleagues. No one spoke a word.

Amy set the box on her desk, sat down in her big chair and

covered her face with her hands. Her hands were presently wet. Araminta slipped discreetly away, no doubt to spread the news. Joy sat down at the tea-table, where lay Okakura's little book, ready for consultation.

"Now I see what must have happened," Amy said at last. "Aaron let Oyeyama look at the thing, but instead of putting it back in the safe, he put it back in his desk drawer, and locked it. Then after he had finished talking to Dr. Brady, he came back to his office, and saw the safe open and the thing missing. He forgot that he had simply locked it in his desk drawer, and came down to report it lost. Then he went upstairs and died, with his desk still locked."

"It wasn't Sherlock Holmes you should have been reading," Joy answered, "but Poe—his Charles-Auguste Dupin. 'The purloined letter.' The thing sought in the most out-of-the-way places turns up in the obvious place."

Another contemplative pause. Amy picked up the box and placed it in her own safe, where it originally been stored. "But what about his desk key?"

"Whoever emptied his pockets, assumed it was just a household key."

TWO WEEKS, and the administration and staff of the Goldfinch Library had begun to forget the events of late November. Christmas was coming, and it was time to think of the tree in the lobby and the holiday party. The incense burner was back in Amy's office safe, and Joy had discreetly searched for, and found, a Japanese metallurgist with a knowledge of ancient bronzes, who was expected to come from Michigan Technical University, where he was a visiting professor. The search had been long and arduous, and Amy was obliged to pay his airfare out of her own pocket. Her husband decried the expense.

"A' that for a phony kail-bucket," Sandy said. "Amy, ye could ha' sent it to him parcel post, return postage prepaid."

"I can't let it out of my sight again," Amy replied.

Aaron Dodder having been buried, Gudule Meeus was run-

ning the department with quiet efficiency. The only addition to
the library was the assignment of a security officer, Lieutenant
Dirk Van Wirth, who was expected to roam the stacks and check
in at the administration office and Special Collections once a day.
Amy had objected to this addition, but President Shepherd insist-
ed on it. Besides, two women students had reported a flasher.

So great was Amy's surprise when Richard Maule was
announced, and stood in her doorway. Amy had never seen him
before, nor had she bothered to look up his picture in the *Annual
report* of the College. With a name like Maule, she assumed he
would be a thickset man, or even a sinister fellow, rather like a
hammerhead shark. Instead, she saw a small man in his seventies,
with a white beard and goatee: imagine Colonel Sanders, but
shrunken and shrivelled, in a white suit half a size too big for him,
with a pink carnation in his buttonhole. Amy thought irrelevant-
ly of the old pun: if everybody in the United States drove a pink
car, we'd have a pink car nation.

Richard Maule did not wait for an invitation, any more than
he had requested an appointment. Instead he introduced himself,
and took a chair, while Amy stood frowning at him, in spite of her
efforts to remain "unflappable." That reputation had become
shaky of late.

"I have come," he said, in a reedy voice, "to ask about the
Wilhelmina Cats collection."

Amy cut him off at once: "The Cats collection has been sold
to the University of Arizona—where it is doubtless known as the
Wild-cats collection."

Richard Maule looked puzzled. The U of A Wildcats had
played the U of W Huskies, and lost to them, 10-14, only last
week. Amy normally had no interest in football, but a pool was
going round the library, and although not betting, she remembered the names. By the relevant pun, she had gained a momentary advantage: her visitor paused.

"I am glad to hear it," said Richard Maule at last. "I am still
concerned about our library's collection. I am a member of the
Eagle Forum."

The worst censors in America, Amy thought. Well, maybe not the worst, but a bunch of self-righteous fire-eaters, anyhow. "I have with me a list," he continued, producing a rolled-up paper, "of titles which do not, in our opinion, contribute to the stability of family values and community service."

To Amy's astonishment, the paper which he thrust at her unrolled toward her like the tongue of a monstrous chameleon. Amy thought of Senator Joseph McCarthy's list of homosexuals in the State Department; of Leporello's list of his boss's female victims.

"Ugh!" said Amy.

"I beg your pardon?" said Richard Maule, in his thin voice. "This is a serious list of undesirable titles."

Amy glanced over the list, in spite of herself. There were the works of Gide, and the periodical *Calyx*; these every college library would have, and so, no doubt, did Rhododendron. She was fairly sure that the library did not subscribe to *Fag rag*, or *Zap comix*, or hold *Fuzz against junk* by the notorious "Akbar del Piombo". Such titles were best left to be acquired by the Bancroft.

Amy came out of her dreamy scrutiny to realize that acceptance of the list might imply doing something with it. She thought a moment.

"If you want to know if we have any of these titles, you're welcome to use the online catalog. Of course, I suspect that you'll be disappointed; some of these books are highly specialized."

"I was expecting that you would have your staff do the searching. My time is valuable."

"So is theirs."

"Mrs. Rose, I fear that you do not realize the earnestness of this request. I and some of the other Trustees of Rhododendron College have been for some time concerned ourselves with the presence of sexual deviants on this campus. Some of them may have infiltrated the library and ordered books. We need to weed the collection, and perhaps select the staff more carefully, too." His voice rustled like paper. "I realize that it is probably impossible to discuss all this with you on a busy morning. Perhaps if we could visit you, two or three of us, in your home."

Amy's home was a house with a great shingled roof and a wide prospect of the Strait to the north. Over the fireplace was the portrait of her naval ancestor; the missionary organ stood in the corner; and now a telescope with a four-inch lens, of Japanese manufacture, fitted with an erecting prism, stood in the living room to allow guests to view and to try to identify passing ships. There was a wonderful Hawaiian couch for Sandy to lie on. The idea...!

"My husband is an invalid," she said coldly. "We do very little entertaining." How the hell do I get him out of here?

"I am disappointed," said Richard Maule, rolling the tongue of paper back again. "We shall mention this disappointment to President Shepherd."

"This library," said Amy hoarsely, "subscribes to the Library Bill of Rights."

"A liberals' document without the force of law."

It was true. The effectiveness of a code such as the Library Bill of Rights depends on large measure upon the complainant's willingness to agree with its basic principles. Anyone sufficiently ruthless can brush it aside.

"Nevertheless," said Amy, "I must resist any attempt to purge the Goldfinch Library's collections. Whatever weeding we do, we will do without regard to ideology. And now, if you will excuse me"—she touched a button under her desk, and Judith Brown stuck her head in the doorway—"Colonel Mustard is here in the library to see me about a large donation."

This was Amy's own device, invented after the Oyeyama incident, to get rid of a real, unwanted visitor, by imagining an unreal, much desired one. This signal, known to Judith, was intended to summon Prescott Friend, the head of the Catalog Department, an enormous military-looking man with the mustaches of a grenadier. His appearance had been, and would be in future, enough to deter the most importunate visitor. Thank God Richard Maule took the hint, thus unknowingly preventing the appearance of the gigantic Friend. She did not want to summon Prescott, still less Lieutenant Van Wirth, who possessed an authority that a catalog librarian

noticed, as if they were Lewis Carroll characters; she noticed, also, that their remarks consisted of accusations in the language of cliches). Like Alice, confronted with one and one and one and one and one and one and one and one and one and one—she lost count. She was beginning to doze with her eyes open when a staff person peeked in and spoke to Louisa Shepherd.

Araminta, noticing this, leaned over and whispered to Amy, "He's coming."

Amy [*sotto voce*] "Who?"

[*s. v.*] "The man I told you about. The man from FTRF."

[*s. v.*] "What's his *name*, for heaven's sake?"

[*mezzo voce*] "I can't remember! But he says he remembers you!"

[*m. v.*] "Who???"

[*pieno voce*] "I've stupidly forgotten his NAME! He remembers you from way back when! His plane from Spokane was delayed an hour! She" (nodding toward Louisa Shepherd) "told me as we came in!"

Both Richard Maule and William Feigenblatt ceased their reading, and turned around to stare at the chattering women. There was a full-dress pause, the kind that is designated in music by a dot under a half-circle, or the letters. "L. P." = Long Pause. Then entered, slender, beginning to bald, in an ash-black suit, a small portfolio in hand, a thirty-fivish man, still to Amy's eyes, and forever, a young one, confident, gentle, firm—however one remarries, Love never forgets its own, never, like poor dumb Araminta, forgets his name:

Will Newcastle. Amy all but dissolved. Her arms hung at her sides; she stared at him, as he advanced to the table, close to President Louisa Shepherd, and took in everyone: a single lingering tender glance at Amy. And a longer questioning one for Araminta, and a smile for Joy. He settled himself, placed the portfolio on the table, and waited until Messrs. Maule and Feigenblatt had finished their reading. Then he took a copy of their paper from the table and scanned it.

Will's counter-arguments were long and persuasive. His gen-

eral line of approach was that as long as the conservative point of
view was well represented in the library, the two Trustees were not
being ignored; that an academic library was not a public library,
and that even for purposes of study, the scholars needed to have
material available that might not be considered for purchase elsewhere. In addition, there were no obviously silly purchases. *College
and Research Libraries News* had reported the sale of the Cats collection to the University of Arizona. Much of the Trustees' list
was devoted to titles that various conservative groups had condemned; but Rhododendron did not have them. Those that they
did have, like *Calyx*, were defensible on literary grounds.

Amy heard, half-heard him. Her champion, her lover, from
the long-lost past, was all she saw and heard. The debate went on
for two hours and a half; all were tired. The two Trustees seemed
to be appeased; said they would report; picked up their attache
cases; left. Louisa Shepherd showed them out the door. "They
seemed reasonably satisfied," said she.

"They never once got around to personnel," Araminta said.

"And that was the whole point," said Louisa Shepherd. "I have
an appointment at three. Let's reconvene two days from now. I'll
call you." And she swept out, billowing in the gray woollen dress.

Together at last. Amy and Will fell into each other's arms.

"*Mes enfants!*" cried Joy, tenderly, her own white arms spread
wide.

"WHERE ARE YOU STAYING?" asked Amy at last, while
Joy fairly danced around them. "And why didn't you tell me you
were coming?"

"Your Araminta Vane summoned me, and I naturally
assumed that you knew," said Will, looking tenderly down at her.
"I have to be back to Bettina and the children tonight."

"There's got to be a later flight: later tonight or early tomorrow. We must phone. I have a Japanese metallurgist staying in the
guest bedroom, but we can put up a folding bed in the study. And
we have to go shopping, for we have to get a party under way!"

"A party?" said Araminta. "A party?" asked Will. "A party!"

cried Joy: all together.

"You simply can't imagine what's been going on here at Rhododendron in the past few weeks. Not only censorship, but accusations of theft, unearthed bronze treasures, jilted hearts, and even a dead body in the library. Leave your car here, Will, we'll pick it up in the morning. Come along with me, I'll tell you everything. Joy, you have to come to this thing too, and bring Laura, and Araminta, you want to come? We'll do a stir-fry, Napa Valley wine. Do you think Dr. Hasegawa will approve?"

Everyone Amy had invited was there. Laura in light blue wool, Araminta in a red pantsuit, and Joy in a silver dinner dress she had rushed home to change into. Sandy was there in a rumpled Einstein-sweater and chinos. Only Dr. Hasegawa was still dressed in coat and tie, and Amy made him throw on an apron and had persuaded him to assist in the making of an Oriental stir-fry, or as close as the Pacific Northwest ever gets to that delicacy.

The most disparate people, from all parts of Amy's life, had come together in Amy's kitchen; and they managed to warm up, then rejoice together with Amy's rejoicing. The party, in short, took off, with songs and anecdotes. It was Amy, who was at the center: the clouds in her life had begun to lift.

From Sandy's chair, the old voice began, a little reedier than in times past:

"Gie us a sang, Montgomery cried,
And lay your disputes a' aside;"

and stopped, the singer reddening. But Amy had heard it so often that she took it up:

"What signifies 't for folks to chide
For what was done before them?"

Then both together, helping each other, while the others listened, smiling:

"Let Whig and Tory a' agree,
Whig and Tory, Whig and Tory,
Let Whig and Tory a' agree
To drop their whigmagorum;
Let Whig and Tory a' agree

> To spend this night wi' mirth and glee,
> And cheerfu' sing, alang wi' me,
> The Reel o' Tullochgorum."

They went through all the dancing, reeling twelve-line stan-
zas:

> "Let warldly worms their minds oppress
> Wi' fears of want and double cess,
> And sullen sots themselves distress
> Wi' keeping up decorum.
> Shall we sae sour and sulky sit,
> Sour and sulky, sour and sulky,
> Sour and sulky shall we sit,
> Like auld philosophorum?
> Shall we sae sour and sulky sit,
> Wi' neither sense, nor mirth, nor wit,
> Nor ever rise to shake a fit
> To the Reel o' Tullochgorum?"

Amy saw that her man was tired. She helped him to a glass of
water. Will said, "I don't think your censors would rise to the Reel
o' Tullochgorum."

"They're too sour and sulky. But we must get you on the last
flight. Bettina might just be jealous."

TOKIO HASEGAWA'S LAB REPORT was two days in coming.
Amy was back in her office, her staff around her. Professor
Hasegawa, a pleasant smiling man, always addressed her with the
doctorate she had been so hard at work earning so many years ago.
She didn't mind that many of her staff called her "Mrs. Rose," but
she had expected more of the other three Japanese scholars.

The incense burner sat in its open box on Amy's desk. Amy
had moved a Japanese celadon vase with chrysanthemums in it,
out of the way, to make room for Mrs. Behaim's treasure. "Would
you like some tea, before we get started?" asked Amy. "I'm afraid
this office is far too large for a proper tea room; it extends beyond
four mats and a half."

"No thank you, Dr. Rose-Ogilvie," said Dr. Hasegawa; "and

don't worry, I did not expect to find myself in a tea room. Let us proceed to business. This incense burner—for that is what we have been calling it—is not properly an incense burner at all."

"My husband thinks it's a kail-bucket," said Amy.

"I had it tested by laser borings and by small scrapings," said Dr. Hasegawa, "and the tiny cores and samples examined with the spectroscope. It is indeed made of copper and tin, about seventy-five percent copper and twenty-five percent tin, but there are impurities. Very unlikely impurities, in fact. You would not expect to find them in a Chinese or Japanese bronze of this period—the ones it's supposed to come from."

"Such as?"

"Aluminum, and nickel, plus traces of gold and silver. As you know, smelting the first two metals was not known until centuries later. Aluminum, not until the nineteenth century."

Amy raised her eyebrows and nodded, pretending to be sagacious. The others stood around her desk, waiting.

"In addition," said Dr. Hasegawa, "I believe it has a false bottom, but I dared not open it without your permission."

Amy peered at the inside bottom rim, and thought she could detect a hairline crack. All her lately-frustrated Sherlock Holmes instincts were roused at once. Joy stood behind her chair, as Amy opened her purse, took out a metal nail-file, and with the file began to wiggle the bottom loose.

"Careful! Let me help you," said Dr. Hasegawa, and taking the incense burner gently from Amy's hands, he started to work on the other side of the rim, with a tiny screwdriver. Both scholars, American and Japanese, were now prying, prying up the lid—as it appeared—of the chamber which lay at the bottom of the bronze vessel; it seemed to be held in place by something in the center of its circumference. Suddenly the center post, or whatever it was, gave way with a pop.

"Oh-oh," said Amy and Tokio together.

The lid of the hidden chamber they removed easily. Inside was nothing but a round piece of wood, glued to the center bottom, with signs of the dried glue which had held the lid in place before the two detectives had popped it off. The dimensions of the disk, were roughly a centimeter in diameter and two millimeters in thickness. In the middle of the wooden disk, blurred by damp and obscured by dried glue, was the inscription:

$$\text{``5¢''}$$

"I suggest that this is not an article from the Heian or Ming periods," announced Dr. Hasegawa, "particularly as the inscription is unclear and the spectrographic tests reveal unwarranted impurities of aluminum, and also, nickel."

Sherlock Holmes could not have put it better himself, thought Amy, if we had been observing him in his London laboratory. But then, ol' Sherlock was never the victim of a delayed practical joke, especially one intended for somebody else.

"Poor Mrs. Behaim!" she said after a moment; "what a cruel trick to pull on her! Faking this—thing—and then burying it in her garden, so that she could find it, and report it as a treasure! Why, it's worse than the Piltdown skull, and that plate of brass down in California! Lucky that she never investigated it all the way!"

"Worse than that," said Dr. Hasegawa, "one man was accused of stealing it, and another man died of shock because he thought he had lost it."

"What are we to do with it?" Amy wondered aloud. "Melt it down, what?"

"Put it in storage, carefully labelled," said Joy, after she had got over her giggling, "so that no one can believe in it again. After a while you can take it out, and use it as a flower pot."

"If it doesn't leak," said Dr. Hasegawa.

"In that case, you can fill it with pebbles and earth, and use it to raise hyacinths in. You put the bulbs in now, and you will have a lovely pillar of white flowers at Easter," Joy instructed her.

And Amy did.

AND SO THAT WAS THE END, Amy remembered, of the Adventure of the Four Japanese Scholars. She had a fine bill to pay, for Dr. Hasegawa's work at the metallurgical lab; Dr. Ueda and Dr. Kumagai had to be appeased with apologies, and she had been obliged to find Dr. Oyeyama and mail him the whole story, with further apologies. Of the four of them, only Dr. Hasegawa remained her friend, and they exchanged greeting cards at Christmas. Dr. Kumagai retired three years later; she never really was sure he had forgiven her. Meanwhile, and very fortunately, Patrick Connolly's attention had been attracted by a plump blonde senior named Connie Beach—and she's Connie B. Connolly today. As for Richard Maule and William Feigenblatt, they subsided after a long talk with President Shepherd and her attorney, Walter Threatt.

NOW HANDEL'S GREAT MUSIC was drawing to an end. "Worthy is the Lamb," the chorus told her, fortissimo, "to receive power, and riches, and wisdom, and strength, and honour, and glory, and blessing." These things, Amy knew, came to those who trusted true friends, who took the initiative with courage but were not afraid to seek help, who accepted defeat and found ways of working around it, who hoped all things, believed all things, yet refused to take wooden disks of slightly greater than one centimeter in diameter as lawful coinage of the United States—no, nor even of the great Ming Dynasty of China.

The conductor brought the glorious music to a stop. The chamber rocked with applause. Amy made her way out of the hall, chatted briefly with some professors' wives, and returned to her car. It was a bitterly cold night: snowflakes had begun twirling down from the black sky.

She drove home, to find Sandy dozing in his big chair. It was past nine o'clock, not quite time for bed.

"Would you like some tea, dearest?" Amy said.

"Only if you put some rum in it," said Sandy. "Or substitute a nichtcap of whisky. I think we've had eneugh tay for the present."

THE END